Praise for

"*Seeds* is a wake-up call from the future – to make the choices today that will defend our freedoms tomorrow."
—Dr. Vandana Shiva, physicist, environmental activist and author of *Earth Democracy; Justice, Sustainability, and Peace* and *Manifestos on the Future of Food and Seed.*

"With an ominous echo of Orwell's *1984*, Hugo Bonjean's provocative novel exposes the 'terminator' values beneath today's complex global crises, challenging us to live with courage and compassion to create a more just and sustainable world."
—Diane Dreher, professor of English, Santa Clara University and bestselling author of *The Tao of Inner Peace* and *Your Personal Renaissance.*

"*Seeds* is a heart-stopping story of one woman's courage in the face of evil. Set in the near future, the seed industry is controlled by one corporation with the power of life and death over an entire planet. If anyone thinks this is far-fetched, ask the small farmers and peasants in India or Brazil who controls their lives and crops today. *Seeds* is prescient and moving. A great story!"
—Maude Barlow, chair of the Council of Canadians, activist and bestselling author of *Blue Gold: The Battle Against Corporate Theft of the World's Water* and *Blue Covenant: The Global Water Crisis and the Fight for the Right to Water.*

"A plot to rule the world by the most evil of corporations sets the stage for encounters with a fascinating variety of experimental communities. Demonstrates the range of human possibility and stirs the imagination."
—David Korten, bestselling author of *When Corporations Rule the World* and *The Great Turning: From Empire to Earth Community.*

To my dear Brother-In-Law
Piul ... because you
grow precious seeds that germinate
Love Irene

"Although set in the year 2084, *Seeds* is a tight, well-written suspense novel that is as poignant and as relevant today as it will continue to be for many years to come … reading it will leave you both shaken and stirred."
—Synchronicity Magazine.

"Never before have I read a book so inspirational and, at the same time, so entertaining I couldn't put it down. Bonjean paints a compelling picture of the different worlds humans can still choose between, and how, as we say at Sustainable Harvest International, we can still plant the seeds for a better tomorrow."
—Florence Reed, founder, Sustainable Harvest International.

"*Seeds* is a fascinating read nearly too late in coming as the focus on corporate profit has stripped humanity of its conscience. A Tribal Prophesy warns that the White brother will find the blueprint of life itself and will turn loose on The Nature something that will seem to be harmless but will bring great harm on the Grandchildren. *Seeds* alerts us to how close we are to the fulfillment of this prophecy and delivers a call to return to the Teachings of the Sacredness of ALL Things."
—Woodrow Morrison, Haida elder.

"*Seeds* is a lesson in responsibility, leadership, and relationships, bringing with it wisdoms of the earth. The storytelling of this adventure captivates, moves and amuses. A great read for anyone interested in sustainability and the present and future state of the world's natural food supply."
—Eve Zarifa, activist, producer.

"*Seeds* is in one word - fantastic. This book will create a lot of stir!! It is a difficult task to write about the possible truths of our future from a position of commitment but still sound human and honest, and Hugo Bonjean does this again. Bonjean writes with such passion and relevancy you cannot help but get caught up in the urgency of the consequences of our choices. *Seeds* is a journey through a future that feels not only real, but reachable. Bonjean challenges us to be the change for the Earth our children will inherit. We are left with hope and the challenge of change."
—Robin Grimstead, development advisor/aid worker.

"*Seeds* illustrates the diversity of human values alongside the striking reality that, despite our differences, we all depend on the earth and the food it provides. It is an exciting read that will cause timely reflections about culture, big business and the future of life on our planet."
—Kathryn Kuchapski, biologist.

"Hugo's captive storytelling again lures in my imagination leaving me to ponder the power of little actions against the big picture. Is it fiction or future reality? It is so bad, yet so hopeful. The hope is in me... to stand up against the seemingly impossible. I feel like David with my slingshot loaded. *Seeds*, like *In The Eyes of Anahita*, helped me believe the power is within to be the change."
—Daren McClean, designer for sustainability.

"*Seeds* touches upon a critical issue for all of us who want to continue eating food and are concerned about the fate of farmers worldwide. If anything, the issues facing Terminator Technology are even more dangerous as the world's biggest corporations move to develop Zombie seeds that can only be brought back to life by buying the companies' chemicals."
—Pat Mooney, executive director, ETC Group.

"*Seeds* is an astonishing book. A very well written, clever story of many important issues that need to be addressed, spirituality, women's rights, the environment and most importantly the development of 'terminator seeds.' A great book that draws out emotions in the reader; sorrow, humor, compassion, frustration, love, all of which are encompassed in *Seeds*. This is an extremely eye-opening, soul-searching read suitable for any audience. Highly recommended! Congratulations Hugo on another amazing book!"
—Curtis Shannon, fan of *In the Eyes of Anahita*.

"I found *Seeds* to be both thought-provoking and difficult to put down. With a handful of corporations controlling much of the world's agriculture and food supply the premise put forward by Hugo is not beyond the realm of possibility. We must remain vigilant and remember that we are all neighbors, and what affects one affects us all. A must read for anyone in agriculture."
—Tony Campbell, rancher.

"Hugo, I finished reading *Seeds* almost two weeks ago now. I found it a difficult book to put down, as you have managed to combine a gripping storyline with strong themes of morality, spirituality, and the human condition. Although the act of reading it is now over for me, thoughts of the intriguing ideas that you have presented in *Seeds* remain. *Seeds* will awaken many to the issues of where our world is, where it could be headed, and what some of the better alternatives might look like. To continue the theme of *Seeds*...when people read this, seeds of thought will be planted...and in some, those seeds will flower into an idea or action that will make the world a better place with a brighter future! Kudos!"
—Ryan Phillips, world traveler.

"Socially: a wake-up call; philosophically: valuable questioning of the paradigms surrounding us; politically: thought-provoking, controversial; in social psychology: examples of a self-fulfilling prophecy, you get what you strive for, as individual and as community. *Seeds* encompasses all that, it graciously makes one think, question, challenge the level of comfort one is willing to give up to come to terms with nature, while relying more on one's self, one's talents, one's spirit."
—Sara Pelizer, financial trader.

"*Seeds* is a thought-provoking and thoroughly enthralling story that underscores the connection between ethical behavior and environmental consciousness."
—Tom Pitoulis, teacher.

"I finished reading *Seeds* last week and have been thinking and absorbing the content since. I enjoyed it and read it as the adventure it was firstly. The message I have been absorbing quietly since. At no time in history has it become more imperative for all of us to pay attention to how we live our lives. The choices we make today, the dreams we hold dear and what environmental footprints we leave behind will surely impact the world. What impact will we make? To quote one of my favorite historical leaders, Gandhi, 'we must be the change we want to see in the world.' Perhaps never before has that statement been so profound as today"
—Seija Webb, book club member.

SEEDS

...of germination
...or termination

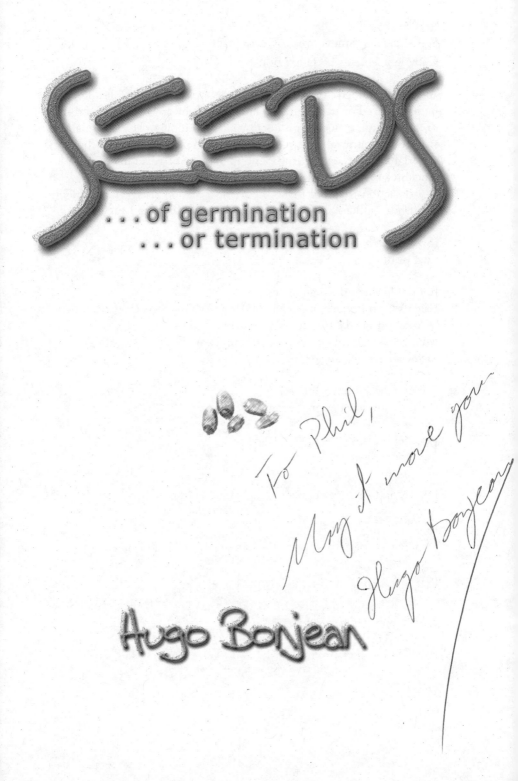

To Phil,

May it move you

Hugo Bonjean

Hugo Bonjean

Published in October 2008 by Eagle Vision Publishing Ltd, Calgary,
Alberta.
ISBN: 978-0-9737542-2-3
First printing.

For publishing information contact:
Eagle Vision Publishing A128-1600 90th Avenue S.W. Calgary, Alberta,
T2V 5A8, Canada. Phone (403) 933 3913
www.seedsofgerminationortermination.com
eaglevisionpublishing@gmail.com

Editor: Elizabeth Zack
Cover & interior design: Suzanne Oel

ISBN: 978-0-9737542-2-3

Library and Archives Canada Cataloguing in Publication

Bonjean, Hugo, 1965-
    Seeds --of germination --or termination / Hugo Bonjean.

ISBN 978-0-9737542-2-3 (pbk.)

    I. Title.

PS8603.O557S44 2008   C813'.6   C2008-903834-7

Our Commitment to a Sustainable World

This book is printed on Rolland Enviro 100 paper, made with 100% post consumer waste, processed chlorine free. For each 1,000 books of this title printed on this environmentally friendly paper, the following resources are saved:

- 11 fully grown trees
- 6,622 gallons of water
- 1,606 cubic feet of natural gas
- 702 pounds of solid waste
- 1,541 pounds of greenhouse gases

These numbers were determined using the eco-calculator of the Cascades Fine Paper Group (www.environmentalbychoice.com).

Traditionally the paper industry has been structured around wood as the source of fiber. According to the Worldwatch Institute, over 40% of the world's industrial wood harvest is used for the manufacture of paper. This has resulted in the decimation of our old growth forests, which continue to be clear-cut to make paper.

We honor paper and printing companies that are committed to introducing environmentally friendly paper at competitive prices to the book printing industry, while at the same time diverting waste from landfills and addressing pollution issues. May many follow this responsible path!

For information on Houghton Boston Printers
(an environmentally friendly printer) visit:
www.houghtonboston.com

Acknowledgements

Throughout my life I've been blessed with people and experiences that encouraged me to follow my dreams and allow them to germinate. I'm grateful to all of them as this book is the fruit of their support and the insights I discovered along the way. A number of individuals deserve special thanks for their help and contribution to the creation of *Seeds*.

First of all, Elizabeth Zack, my editor who has her way of polishing my language without putting words into my mouth, or should I say writing. It's a joy to see how through her craft she lets my words shine while respecting my simple writing style.

Next there is Suzanne Oel, an amazing artist who through her creative talents manages to let the story reach out to the readers via her captivating cover design.

Then there's Paula Kroeker whose detail-oriented eye and keen sense of observation made sure to perfect the spelling and grammar. I also thank the volunteers who proofread the book and helped with that task: Kathryn Kuchapski, Meghan Lyons, Seema Dhawan, Garry Hoffart and John Robertson.

While the man probably has no idea of the impact he has made in my life, I would like to thank Paulo Coelho for his inspiring writing. His books are not only a wonderful gift to the world, but reading them over and over helped me to hone my own writing skills.

And last but not least, I thank my wonderful wife, Ilse and my precious children, Bjorn, Fabian and Amber for putting up with me during the months when I wrote until late into the night and had little or no time for any family events.

Thank you all for allowing me to germinate my dreams.

For the dreamers,
for the creators,
for the pacifists,
for the activists,
for the spiritualists,
for the scientists,
for the peacekeepers,
for the rebels,
and
for the parents,
...
but most of all
for the children
of this world.

I don't believe that

A dream is a seed. What we do with that seed is a choice—a choice of germination or termination—a choice we make that is reflected in our every action, every second, every breath. Are we following our dream, are we giving it life and letting it bloom, or are we stifled by fear, hiding it in the shadows of convention and rational thought? The dream is our soul talking, or it might be the soul of the world. Possibly it's the guidance of divine Creation Herself.

I'm not sure whose voice it is, nor do I think it's important—let's leave that to mystery. What I do know is that it guides us on our journey called life. Follow it! Listen to it! Drink it! Let it consume you, delivering to you both ecstasy and deep wounds along the way, because the dream is the path of your divine expression, the journey of a life in grace.

Life is not rational, nor is it secure or conventional. It's always in motion. It never stops, always flows, and continuously transforms, even in silence and in death. It's an exhilarating journey of discovery and transformation, an adventurous cycle of death and rebirth guided by our dream, which serves as a torch lighting the path for us to follow. Let's allow our seeds to germinate!

–Hugo Bonjean

"We do not err because truth is difficult to see. It is visible at a glance. We err because this is more comfortable."

–Aleksandr Solzhenitsyn

I dream of a delightfully diverse, safe, healthy and just world, with clean air, clean water, clean soil and clean power—economically, equitably, ecologically and elegantly enjoyed by all children of all species of all times.

–William McDonough

We are what we dream, as individuals, institutions, societies and cultures. The world is a dream realized through the sum of our actions, actions that follow from the choices we make. We are what we dream. Which dream lights your path?

Dallas, capital of the American Confederacy
March 21, 2084

The heart in her chest was pounding, her mouth was dry and her lungs were gasping for oxygen as the damp evening air rushed by her face. Nayla was running, running for her life! If she could just get to those trees in the distance she would be safe, or at least have a chance to escape, for on the other side of them was the main road.

Without slowing her pace she looked over her shoulder at the tall silver building. It was being wrapped in the night's shade; the last light of the sun had set behind the horizon. Its sirens were squealing uninterrupted, which meant there had been a major security breach. The building would now be in the process of a full lockdown, and soon the entire country would be brought to the highest state of alert. How many times had she participated in such security drills?

The brightly lit red letters on top of the imposing tower read: Carsanto. For years this building had been her second home, her lifeline to what was called the American Dream, that elusive dream which years ago had pulled her parents from their motherland, the United States of Bolivar, to the American Confederacy.

It was the dream to which Nayla had dedicated her life. She had been living it! She had fulfilled the dream of her parents and so many others, people who had risked everything to establish a life in the American Confederacy, the country of liberty and riches. But now she had destroyed that life forever. She had burned all bridges. There was no way back; she would be lucky if she could even make it out of this country alive.

How could the man she loved, the man in charge of this governing corporation, be so cruel? And how could she love someone with no conscience? Could he have lied so blatantly to her, using her while expressing so much love to her? Had it all been an act? Why couldn't he see the consequences of his actions? She knew he would do what was expected of him if they caught her, and a shiver of fear ran through her body.

Her fingers tightened around the cotton bag in which she'd wrapped her precious parcel. As she focused her mind on the seeds inside—seeds of germination, seeds of life—her resolve strengthened. Her fear slipped away, and she focused her mind. Every fiber in her body charged and she was ready to do what had to be done.

She reached the tree line. Twigs snapped under her speeding feet. She felt something cutting into her leg, and some branches scratched her face, but she would not slow down. She *could not*. The life of her child depended on the successful delivery of this package. The life of all children of all species depended on it!

She sprinted, and made it through the trees. She waved down the first taxi, jumped in and gasped out in an exhausted but determined voice, "Just drive!"

For a number of years she had known deep down inside that something about the company and the work she had been doing wasn't all that ethical. When some of her relatives who still lived on the Latin continent questioned her about the company's activities, she would brush it off, saying things like, "It's just a job," or, "People here have hearts too. They don't intend for things to turn out badly for anyone; they just have a different dream for the world. They achieve things, and have large beautiful houses and anything they wish for."

However, when she offered these platitudes, her voice had never sounded really convincing, not even to herself. Deep inside she knew there was a truth to their questions, a truth she was just not ready to face. So she always quickly changed the subject.

This had left her for years in the comfortable position of doing nothing. As a scientist she focused instead on her enjoyment of achieving innovative breakthroughs, and did not occupy herself with how the new technology was being applied. She spent the money from her high-paying job on whatever she could think of. As long as it kept her distracted from delving inside herself to question the consequences of Carsanto's actions and her role in them, life was good, life was easy.

Lately Carsanto's executives had become impatient with the stubborn position of the United States of Bolivar; the country had kept refusing to buy their seeds and agro-chemicals. And Nayla knew the company's goal was to control the world through its seed trade.

The power Carsanto could unleash was formidable. It was a power she had created: the famous mutating terminator seed! Not only did the genetically modified seed render the seeds that grew from its plant sterile, it was also prone to cause the terminator gene mutation in other plants. As a result, once the seed was unleashed in a certain region, all the farmers in the region became dependent on buying new seeds each year from Carsanto, since the seeds they normally saved for replanting were now rendered sterile. Control of the seed industry, and in essence the world's food supply, had given Carsanto control of the entire world, with the exception of the United States of Bolivar. Nayla knew how deadly and devastating the introduction of mutating terminator seeds would be to the country where she had her roots— the country that now spread out over the entire Central and South American continent.

The events had forced her to consciously examine what she had been doing with her life. How was she impacting this world? What was the real value of all her money and possessions? Was she creating the world she dreamed of? The American Dream was certainly making her rich, but how happy did it make her? What would happen to her five-year-old daughter, Gaya, who lived with her Mayan father, Julian, in the jungle of Central America, if she didn't act?

3

For months she'd been tormented by such questions. But today's board decision to spray unwanted mutating terminator seeds across the continent from high altitude planes had put her in a situation where she could no longer postpone action. She'd stayed at the office until late in the evening—which wasn't unusual for her to do. When it looked like everyone was gone, she'd walked to the lab just like she had done so many times late at night before she left. This time, though, while her walk and composure had appeared as calm and collected as ever, her heart had almost pounded out of her chest.

She had greeted the security guard on his round through the building with a friendly smile, just like she always did. The door had slid open after the security camera at the entrance had scanned her eye. Inside the room she'd wasted no time, and had collected all recently developed mutating germinator seeds from each crop species into small, aluminum-coated envelopes. She'd carefully labeled each pouch, and then sealed the seeds into waterproof bags, which she had wrapped in the cotton cloth.

Chances were good that nobody would even notice their disappearance. After all, she'd been the company's only scientist who worked on the germinator seeds; all other researchers concentrated on terminator technology. The mutating germinator seeds were unique not only because they were immune to terminator cells but also because they could pass this defense on to other plant organisms. But to the company there was no commercial value in seeds that could mature and develop their own fertile seeds again. In fact, she'd only received permission to develop a mutating germinator seed after her persistent pressure to create a backup plan in the event the terminator technology got out of hand.

She'd planned to call in sick the following morning, and that would have given her at least a few days before they would come looking for her. This should have been a walk in the park—no problem at all—if it hadn't been for a new security guard who had insisted on doing everything according to the book. He had totally ignored her executive position, and had insisted upon searching her bag. Security could have done this any other day for the last fifteen years without finding anything, but not tonight.

Sure, she'd tried to charm her way out of it. When that had failed, she'd explained to him that she was the head of the genetically modified seeds division; a well-respected member of the company's board of directors; and that she'd always worked late for the last fifteen years and had never had a security guard search her personal belongings. She had even threatened to take his actions up with his supervisor the following morning.

But the guard had been undisturbed by her threats, politely responding, "Ma'am, I understand what you're saying, but I'm merely following the instructions I received during training. They hired me because of my track record. It wouldn't have been that good if I hadn't always followed the procedures to the letter. I'm afraid that tonight I'm going to have to search your bag. Maybe tomorrow you can take it up with my boss and ask for a search exemption, which I'll then gladly adhere to."

She'd handed over her bag in the hope that he wouldn't look inside the cotton wrap, and had walked through the metal detector. But when the guard had put the precious package on the table between them and was about to unwrap it, she'd had no other choice. In an impulsive move she'd grabbed the parcel and sprinted for the front doors.

"Hey, wait!" she'd heard behind her. "Lady, what're you doing?" the bewildered voice of the guard had shouted.

It had taken the poor man a few moments to recover from the shock. After all, Nayla was a board member! Board members don't hide things in bags and most certainly don't run. So by the time he'd pressed the alarm, Nayla was already out of the door. She'd heard the building lock down behind her. She had headed for the trees and the road beyond, realizing there wouldn't be enough time to get her beloved sports car out of the parking lot.

While the taxi cruised down the multilane boulevard Nayla tried to calm down and digest what had just happened. A mere five minutes ago she was a board member and Senior Vice President at the mighty Carsanto. Now she was a fugitive on the run! She had destroyed a lifetime of work in one impulsive move. The penalty for stealing the state secrets of the nation would be death!

"No time to reflect on this now; I have to stay focused," she thought. "My life is in the balance now!" It wouldn't take too long for the powers-that-be to be informed. She estimated that by the following morning the entire country would be in a state of alert. She had no time to waste. She had to think quickly and couldn't afford any mistakes. The cargo in her hands could save the planet!

"Right!" she directed, as the taxi approached the first junction.

George entered his living room, and threw his briefcase and jacket on the bench next to the entrance. As he passed the mirror, he straightened his shirt over his slightly extended belly, ran his fingers through his graying hair and headed straight for the bar. He poured himself a glass of Scotch, contemplated the sweet aroma of his favorite drink, and raised it in the direction of the cross on the wall.

"Thank you, Jesus!" he saluted, and emptied his glass in one gulp. The warm glow of Scotch flowed from his throat into every cell of his body. He filled up his glass again and dropped into the couch while swinging his feet up onto the living room table.

"Music!" he commanded as he loosened his tie.

The voice-activated computer system responded, and the room filled with the silky voice of his favorite singer, Kelly Clarkson—an old-timer, but without a doubt the greatest American Idol ever.

"Isn't it great to live the American Dream?" he thought as he reflected over the events of the day. Damn, he was good!

World control was within his reach! His father and grand-father would have been proud of him. For three generations now, the Shapura family had been in control of the mighty Carsanto Corporation. Carefully they had executed a strategy that had led the company to its current position on top of the world.

It all started in 2016, when his grandfather, Roberto Shapura, orchestrated the biggest merger in history between some of the then

7

most powerful companies, creating a conglomerate that touched every aspect of life, from oil and gas, to cars, bio-chemicals, agriculture, banking, computers, software, entertainment, weapon manufacturing and food production. It didn't happen all in one step. Over a four-year period, major leading corporations in America were merged into the all-powerful Carsanto. Most were absorbed on friendly terms, but in some cases Carsanto simply used its economic muscle to take over the target company.

After four years there was no doubt that Carsanto was the most powerful entity on the planet, with an economic value that dwarfed even that of the richest countries on earth. Initially, Carsanto's mergers and acquisitions were all approved on the basis that none of them were within one industry. It was argued that within each industry, there was still ample competition. However, soon thereafter the powerful conglomerate started to use its power to squeeze its competitors out of business. As more and more of them closed their doors, Carsanto expanded its market reach, and effectively became the controlling power of all economic life on earth.

While Carsanto's reach was global, the company's power was concentrated in Europe, North America and Australia due to the sophisticated economic nature of those regions. The lack of a strong centralized corporate economy in Asia, Africa and South America, and the vast scale of small entrepreneurs in those areas, made it more difficult to control those regions by economic means alone.

As time passed, governments started to recognize the threat of Carsanto's effective governing power. China was the first to respond by nationalizing all the company's assets in a move to develop its own internal economy and escape the dominant power of the conglomerate.

George's grandfather recognized the possibility of a future government ruling to break up the company and its assets. So in 2021, he acquired Whitefog, the largest private military force in the world. It had handled all of Carsanto's security needs over the last decade. In return the Duke family, which owned Whitefog, received a large stake in Carsanto, and control of the company's security forces.

8

When the governing authorities questioned Roberto about acquiring an army, he called it a "private security force." He defended the company's rights to provide for its own security by comparing it to the right of each man to be armed and able to defend his private property. Whitefog had already been providing such protection for Carsanto for a decade, he argued. This was simply an economic decision. It made more financial sense for Carsanto to acquire the company than to keep contracting for its services. Furthermore, in light of the increase in looting and systemic sabotage of the economic infrastructure by anti-civilization rebels, Roberto's argument sounded reasonable. Soon, Carsanto's army became more powerful than the United States military; after all, the company was simply much richer, and could easily accumulate weapons and pay handsome salaries to its security force.

Now with an army in place, the company could advance its quest for power more aggressively. Roberto's credo was: "Carsanto brings liberty and riches through market efficiency and creativity. Carsanto *is* the American Dream!"

When in 2022 anti-civilization rebels not only killed the American President but blew up the White House, the Senate and one-third of the Pentagon, it was only natural that Carsanto offered its army in protection of liberty and the American Dream. Most Americans wanted to maintain their lifestyle and were more than prepared to offer their allegiance to Carsanto and its leader, Roberto Shapura, in return for their physical safety and access to the goods and services the company provided.

The rebel activity had commenced around the same time Roberto had acquired Whitefog. At first there had been sporadic, uncoordinated attacks at some small river dams. While no one had foreseen where this insurgency would lead, it had been necessary for the company to protect not only its assets, but also its executives during those years. This task had given Whitefog many headaches. The rebels were not organized, so it made it impossible for Whitefog's counter-intelligence to anticipate the next target. As a result, the insurgents' attacks were often successful.

By the time of the Presidential assassination, the rebels—influenced by a vision of a culturally diverse and sustainable agricultural society—had such a following along the West Coast, most of the Northern States and Canada that the country had entered into a full-fledged civil war. The lines of this were almost identical to those in America's first civil war.

The rebels' strategy had proven to be very effective. By attacking the electrical and transportation infrastructure of the country, they paralyzed the economy and made life in the large cities impossible. It took only a few years for American icons like New York, San Francisco and Chicago to be turned into ghost cities controlled by urban gangs who grew their food in the city's parks and green spaces.

Rather than trying to subdue these people with their different ideologies, Carsanto used its media arm to rally people in the Southern States behind the great American Dream, and concentrated its armed forces on the protection of the borders of those states. In a surprise move it sent part of its army south, into what was then Mexico.

The problem, as Roberto saw it at the time, was border control. For the American Dream to stay in existence while the world around it was developing different ways of living—ways that were called "sustainable"—Carsanto had to be able to control its borders. But with the Northern states in turmoil and a huge border running coast to coast across the North American continent, they couldn't afford the threat of Mexico possibly joining up with the United States of Bolivar, which now had extended its borders as far north as southern Mexico.

Therefore, in order to stabilize the lines of power and bring peace to the world, Carsanto's air force launched one strategic attack that destroyed Mexico City with its entire population of more than thirty million people. At the same time, the company set up a major communications campaign that promised Carsanto would bring liberty and the American Dream to the remainder of the Mexican people.

The media, which by now was controlled by the company, hailed Carsanto as the savior of Mexico. They claimed Carsanto had saved the country from its own leaders, who were about to betray their citizens by joining the socialist United States of Bolivar. It was said repeatedly that such a move would have brought the Mexican people even greater poverty, and prevented them from ever realizing the great American Dream. Mexicans could now keep on living in liberty.

The media strategy worked, and most of the rest of Mexico was taken without too much trouble. There were some areas of fierce resistance, but any insurgency was always met with unrivaled brutality. Such a response caused those who were considering fighting to rethink their plans and embrace the American Dream and the liberty that Carsanto promised. After all, for years Mexicans had tried to get across the border into the United States in search of this elusive dream. Now it was being delivered to them on their very doorstep!

Carsanto also negotiated a deal with the rebels in the Northern and Western states. It then dubbed the new country the "American Confederacy." Its southern border was just south of the city of Oaxaca, Mexico where the company built a wall that extended from coast to coast at the very point where the distance between the Gulf of Mexico and the Pacific Ocean was the smallest. A vast army was stationed there, with the instructions of killing anyone who tried to enter the country illegally.

The northern border now ran almost in a straight line across the continent. It started in the East, south of Virginia, and ran north of Tennessee, Arkansas, Oklahoma, New Mexico, and Arizona. It then cut what was formerly California in half, to end on the coast halfway between Los Angeles and the now-ghost city of San Francisco. Within this newly created country, Carsanto was the government, the law, the army and the economy. Carsanto provided liberty and the American Dream to its citizens. It ensured unlimited consumption for its residents, and protected them from foreign invasion, terrorism, and socialist or sustainable living ideas.

By 2029 peace had returned to the world, and Carsanto could again shift its focus towards conquering the rest of the planet through its trading power and providing the American people with the almighty consumer goods that were central to the way of life they fought for. Although tightly controlled, both the northern and southern borders reopened to traders and travelers.

George's thoughts returned to the present when the enchanting voice of the singer was suddenly interrupted by a ringing tone.

"Aaah, not now," George hissed in irritation.

"Caller: Head office. Importance: Urgent," droned the monotone computer-generated voice.

"Answer!" George commanded the system.

"George, there has been a security breach at the head office!"

The cold voice of Dick Duke, alias "the General," echoed through the living room.

Dick was Carsanto's stocky, bald-headed chief of security and the armed forces—and a direct descendent of Whitefog's founder. Dick never panicked, and kept his cool when most other people would crumble under pressure.

He was always direct and to the point. Things were simply black or white for Dick: You obeyed the rules, or you didn't. And if you didn't obey, he would make sure you would reconsider or suffer the consequences.

Even to George, it sometimes seemed like Dick had no heart. But that was exactly why George liked him in his position: Dick simply was the law in the American Confederacy!

"A woman ran out of the head-office building after refusing to let the guard check her bag. The guard's description seems to indicate it was Nayla. She told him she was a member of the board and head of the genetically modified seeds division. Were you expecting her tonight?" Dick's voice said crisply.

"She's coming over later, yes. She said she had to finish some research first. Did you check her office and the lab?" George responded casually. "Now, why do you think it's Nayla? She would never do such a thing. Did you check the surveillance cameras?" he added. George was positive it wasn't Nayla who had bolted out of the building.

"No, not yet. I first wanted to find out if she was with you."

"I'll let you know when she arrives. Now, Dick," George said, slightly irritated, "don't ruin my perfect day simply because the security guard gave a description that's similar to Nayla's. Nayla has everything she could ever want. She has absolutely no reason to steal anything from the building. Just check the surveillance system and identify the woman first!" he lectured the security general. "When you do so, find her and deal with it as you usually do."

"I'll do that," Dick responded, sounding slightly embarrassed before he ended the conversation.

"Music!" George commanded again, and his favorite singer continued.

He got up from the sofa and checked the bedroom. He was pleased. His servant had done a good job in setting the atmosphere for a romantic night. Beautiful red flowers were casually spread across the bed. The candles were lit.

He thought of Nayla's Latin passion, the grace with which she moved and her stubborn sense of independence. That last trait made her unpredictable, an aspect he appreciated in her as a lover. Now, where was she? It was getting late. Surely there must be a reason. "Nayla always has an explanation," he smiled in thought. No doubt it would be one she would fiercely defend to him.

Besides being a sensual lover, Nayla also made a great executive for the company. How could Dick even think of Nayla as a thief? George knew Dick didn't like her. But accusing her of theft based on a security guard's description only? Ridiculous!

He thought about how he and Nayla would laugh later on when he shared the story with her. It would give her months of ammunition for pushing Dick's buttons.

He returned to the living room couch, and one of his favorite Kelly Clarkson songs took him to dreamland. Some forty-five minutes later the awful ring of the computer phone shocked George out of his sleep.

"Answer," he snapped.

"George, it *was* Nayla!" Dick said triumphantly. "I saw it personally on the surveillance video. Nayla has run!"

"I 've got to get home first and grab stuff for my escape," Nayla's thoughts raced. She knew George was expecting her tonight, and that the security cameras had registered her escape. Once they confirmed that it was she who had run from the building, they would certainly pay a visit to her home to question her.

The General must be drooling at the vision of getting her into the interrogation room! It was a pleasure she was not planning on granting him. She had to act quickly.

But where would she go? How could she stay a step ahead of her pursuers? Once they realized that she had stolen all the new mutating germinator seeds, they would know she would try to deliver them to the United States of Bolivar. She now was glad her parents had returned to their home country just a few years ago, so she didn't have to worry about leaving any family behind here in the Confederacy.

"Darling," her father had said while he'd stroked her long, shiny black hair, "we are proud of you! You are living the American Dream."

His gaze had dropped to the floor while he searched for the right words to continue. Then he'd looked her in the eyes, and she had seen not only his love but also a deep sadness.

"I am now not so sure anymore if the American Dream really is the best way of life, at least for us," he had continued hesitantly. "We are comfortable and have things in this country, but each time when we visit our brothers and sisters in the United States of Bolivar, they share a happiness and a sense of community which we have never found here. Your mother and I are getting older. While you are our only child, you're working very hard and have little time to spend with your family. We understand this. But your child—our granddaughter—lives in our home country, close to the rest of our relatives."

He had paused, lowering his eyes again in an effort to gain courage. He had then taken Nayla in his arms and said, "We're going home. We long for our family and for being part of a community. I am tired of just fending for myself. There's no joy that flows from this."

Nayla could see how difficult this decision had been for her parents. Her mother's blue eyes, inherited from her grandmother's Northern family, had embraced Nayla's soul with the pain of letting go, as well as a love that stays forever.

When she hugged her mother, Nayla felt a connection like she'd never felt before. It was like the merging light of two souls. Souls that understood each other, knew each other, and would always be there for each other. Souls that could never be separated, neither by space nor time.

"We'll come and visit," her mother had consoled her, knowing well that years would pass between those visits. The journey took so very long, both by boat or road, for commercial air travel had ceased to exist when she was still a child.

The General knew Nayla's daughter and family all lived in the United States of Bolivar. It was the only logical place for her to go and be safe.

But if she headed to the United States of Bolivar, he would lock the southern border down before she would be able to get there and put a high price on her head to motivate citizens to turn her in. No, she had no real chance to make it there safely. She couldn't join her family just yet.

The shortest distance to safety, or at least relative safety, was to go north and cross the border into the United Canadian Communities. The border there wasn't as well guarded ever since the country had become dependent on Carsanto's terminator seeds, which assured peace and trading between the two nations. Yes, she would go north—and Carsanto would bring her there!

There was a seed train ready to leave some time after midnight, she knew. She would hide on the train and travel north! A faint smile appeared on Nayla's lips as she thought about the irony in this, and how the General would rave if he found out that Carsanto's train had been her means of escape from the country.

When fifteen minutes later the taxi stopped in front of the luxurious downtown apartment complex where she owned the penthouse suite, she asked the driver to wait. She didn't want to lose any time in trying to find another ride. As an avid hiker, she had just the things for this crazy cross-country journey.

She quickly changed her office dress for her favorite hiking clothes: army-green heavy cotton pants, a tight tank top, a light sweater and a black hoody. Her small hiking pack she stuffed with two warm fleece sweaters, a pair of fleece pants, some extra warm socks, a loaf of bread, four large water bottles, some beef jerky, raisins, nuts and chocolate bars. In the pack's side pockets she put a lighter, compass, headlight and pepper-spray.

She then took the precious cotton package, and held it tightly to her heart while taking a deep breath with her eyes closed. Life! The world's life depended on her!

She put it in the top of her pack before closing it, tightened the laces of her light hiking shoes, and was ready to go back out of the door when she suddenly had a marvelous idea that could buy her some more escape time.

She would leave George a note. Yes, that's what she would do. She would leave a note apologizing for the security breach!

While she grabbed a pen from her desk, she noticed the old leather-bound diary from her grandmother. Her parents had given it to her when they had returned to the United States of Bolivar in the hope that she would read it. She never had.

Her grandmother had been an anti-civilization rebel during the first uprising shortly after the Carsanto conglomerate had been formed. As a board member, and thus one of Carsanto's leaders, Nayla wasn't exactly proud of her grandmother's history as a rebel. But in her current situation as a fugitive with a cause, the diary held a surprisingly mysterious attraction. Who was her grandmother, and why had she put her life on the line to destroy the American way of life?

Nayla grabbed the diary and put it in her backpack. Then she scribbled the note:

My dearest George,

I know you must be worried by my reckless and crazy behavior. But then again, you would not love me if I weren't reckless and crazy. I apologize for the security breach. The guard had simply no business in my personal belongings and he did not want to listen to any reason. I just need to take care of something personal. I'll be back in a few days and will explain everything. Don't be worried. I love you.

Your love,

Nayla.

P.S. Please forgive me for using Carsanto's security service as mail deliverers.

She put the note in a little envelope on which she wrote, in large letters, *For George Shapura.* She placed it on her living room table and smiled when she walked out of the door. The General was going to be furious when he found a note that wasn't his to open, and George was going to be amused by how she used Dick as mail boy. If her plan worked, it might take days before they would find out that the seeds were gone. By then she would be somewhere north in the United Canadian Communities.

She asked the cab driver to bring her to a fast food restaurant some two miles from Carsanto's train depot. She told him a phony story about how she was meeting up with a friend there, and that the two of them were taking off to the mountains near El Paso that were marked on this old treasure map she had found.

The driver had been very interested in the map. She told him she'd accidentally discovered it, and had already gotten into trouble with the country's security forces because of it. That would be enough to really confuse the General and put him onto a wrong lead once they found and interrogated this driver.

When she got to the restaurant, she made sure the taxi had left before she reached the diner's entrance. After all she wasn't planning to enter it.

Once the vehicle was out of sight she started, unnoticed, the two-mile hike to Carsanto's train depot. Her black hoody blended into the darkness of the night and concealed her face. The streets in the warehouse district around the depot were empty. She kept a brisk pace, looking over her shoulder every few steps. This was not a neighborhood for a woman to be alone at this time of the night. She felt her heart pounding heavily, and her breath became short.

A car suddenly appeared from around a corner. It was still a few blocks away from her. Frantically she looked around for cover, and quickly hid among some broken down old cars next to one of the warehouses.

The car slowly made its way down the streets—way too slow for someone driving home from work. Whoever was in there was up to no good. It stopped a little distance past her and kept idling. By now Nayla's heart was racing. After a few minutes though, the vehicle continued at its suspicious pace. Nayla stayed in her hiding spot until the car turned right some six blocks further.

She waited for a while until she was convinced that the street was totally empty again. Her yoga deep-breathing techniques were proving to be really helpful in collecting her composure. The depot was just a little further away.

A few minutes later she was sitting between some shrubs along the open area that gave out to the fenced-off train depot. For over an hour she sat there carefully observing the single Carsanto security guard she'd spotted. He kept patrolling up and down the side of the train. As soon as he had reached the end, he would turn around and start walking the other way.

She did, however, notice that during the entire time he'd never once looked behind him. She decided to run towards the train once the guard had passed the few warehouses that were built right up to the fence. They were located only a short distance from the rails, and the tree next to the buildings could be of help with crossing the fence. This meant she would be in full sight however, so she hoped the guard would not hear her or accidentally look over his shoulder. Otherwise she had plenty of time, since it would take the guard a full ten minutes to reach the point where he would turn around.

Minutes later she reached the sighted location, and to her relief noticed someone had cut an opening in the fence right by the tree. At least there would be no need for aerial acrobatics to cross the fence. She knelt alongside the building, and waited for the guard to pass. She was focused now, and the anxiety she had felt earlier when she crossed this warehouse area had faded away.

When the guard was far enough beyond the building, Nayla slid quickly through the opening. Then she sprinted, silently as a leopard, over the grassy field towards the railroad tracks. All the while she kept a worried eye on the security guard who continued walking away from her. At the tracks she slowed down her pace, and tiptoed quietly over the loose gravel.

She reached the train unseen and immediately took cover between two cars. The guard still had a distance to cover before turning her way again, giving her another few minutes to find better shelter. She peered out from between the train cars on the other side, and when she couldn't detect any security patrols there, started making her way along the train towards the grain silos. A few minutes later, after she had verified the train was destined for Canada, she climbed one of the cars that had already passed under the grain silo and been filled with oats. Before she climbed to its very top, she checked if any guards were in sight.

When she couldn't detect any, she opened the lid of the grain car and carefully lowered herself into it. Her feet sank a few inches into the seeds, and some kernels made it into her shoes. Carefully she sat down. The grain formed a natural seat around her body.

"This might make for a comfortable ride," she thought, although she recognized if she wanted to stand, she would have to open the lid.

For a while she just sat there in the dark. Her body pumped with adrenaline, her mind wired; now she had to calm down! There simply was no way she could sleep, even though she had found safety in this metal cocoon. She remembered her grandmother's diary.

"I might as well read a bit," she thought. "It will distract my mind from this eventful evening."

She turned on her headlight, made herself comfortable, and opened the diary.

February 8, 2021.

If the Universe had a message today on my 26th birthday, it came through loud and clear: Everything happens for a reason! This morning, the radio news sounded almost like any other day: an ultra-severe storm hit Florida; after a warm and brown Christmas, Chicago finally saw its first snow this winter—six feet of the white stuff was dumped on the city; in Europe winter temperatures were so high that they now had eliminated the possibility for any snowfall at all this winter—an act of nature that was bankrupting most of the region's winter tourism industry; another monsoon with some severe flooding hit somewhere in Asia; and millions of people were on the brink of starvation in Africa due to severe drought. All of this, courtesy of global warming and climate change. What really gets me is that instead of taking harsher action to combat greenhouse gases, politicians are still debating the cost to industry and the economy. Does anyone in the administration ever factor in the cost of all these natural disasters?

The reconstruction of course drives economic activity, but surely this isn't what we are after. I'm puzzled why we don't charge those large corporate polluters with the cost of all these catastrophes? It's kind of like what happened years ago with the tobacco industry. Eventually the tobacco corporations were held responsible for the cancers they'd caused. We have known for decades now that CO_2 is severely damaging the atmosphere and causing our weather to change with all its devastating consequences to both the environment and our economic infrastructure. Governments should simply hold polluters responsible! That's when the true cost of products would be accounted for in the corporation, and then at least we, as taxpayers, wouldn't be paying for such corporate complacency. Or is it greed? I guess it must be since the executives know their companies are polluting—without having to pay for it. Doing so makes money for their shareholders, which in turn is good for their personal bank accounts.

Why do we allow some people to get filthy rich by destroying our environment and making all of our lives miserable while we, the taxpayers, clean the mess up behind them? Instead, we should present them with the true bill of their actions! But anyway I'm deviating.

What really got me this morning was that on top of all the typical daily news, Carsanto announced that it would start with the commercialization of its genetically modified terminator seeds. Twenty-one years ago the CEO of the bio-chemical corporation that got absorbed by this powerful conglomerate wrote in an open letter that the company wasn't planning to commercialize its terminator seeds. But then again, we all should have known that no corporation would ever spend money researching something it wasn't planning to make money from at some point in time. With the removal of the moratorium on field trials in 2016, I guess we knew this was coming. The Carsanto company argues that all public issues have been addressed; that the genetically engineered terminator seeds are both safe for consumption and no threat to the environment.

A terminator seed contains a cell with a dioxin—one of the most poisonous substances on the planet—and another cell that acts as an activator of the dioxin cell. The activator cell can be turned on or off through external stimuli like heat or a certain chemical. When activated, the dioxin is released in the late embryonic stage of the seed's development and renders the seed sterile. This practice allows seed farms to produce seeds with the dioxin gene. The activator is only added upon sale of the seed to the farmer. This typically happens by coating the seeds with tetracycline—putting more antibiotics into our food systems. Ultimately the produce that we will get to eat is from a sterile plant. Sterilized by releasing a dioxin—a really bad poison—during its germination. And of course, this would do no harm to us.

How many times do we need to be confronted with the same story before we learn from it? DDT wasn't supposed to harm us either, nor were any of the other chemicals we have sprayed on our land and food over the last seventy years. That is why the majority of all women feed breast milk with dioxin to their babies now! We didn't ask for this! Actually, we were told it was safe! How on earth did we ever buy into the story that chemicals, produced by corporations during World War I and II, would improve our food production if we sprayed them onto our soil and vegetables?

Anyway, I'll stop ranting... as you can see, this really gets to me, and I could go on for hours about our cultural stupidity. But again that's not what I was going to write down here. It was the synchronicity of events today that really made me think about my life and the world that I'm creating. Tonight my girlfriend took me out for my birthday to see a speaker. The topic was "Be the Change!" When we arrived, the auditorium was almost full, and in big bold letters the screen up front read: "What kind of world are you creating now?"

The question startled me. It was suggesting I was creating the world around me! I thought about Carsanto's terminator seeds, and feelings of anger boiled up inside of me. How could someone ask a question like this and therefore be suggesting I could do anything about this corporate criminality?! Of course I want to create a different world, but what power do I have?

On the way over, my girlfriend had told me the presenter was a corporate executive who had changed his life, and now focused his time and skills to create a more socially just and environmentally sustainable planet. Of course such a question could only be asked by a "corporate executive," someone with money, someone who didn't have to be concerned about making it to the next paycheck! I didn't want to disappoint my friend, so I politely stayed, but in reality, I just wanted to bolt. Some five minutes later when the auditorium was filled with more people than seats, the speaker walked in. There was no introduction, so I assumed most people knew this man.

"I'm going to start with asking all of you to close your eyes," was the first thing he said with a slightly charming accent. I wasn't planning to follow his request, but when I looked around and everyone had their eyes closed, I decided to follow suit.

"Now think about the time when you were sixteen, seventeen or eighteen years old," he continued. "What dreams did you have? What kind of a world did you dream of?"

Silence engulfed the room, and eventually the question made me float back to my teenage years. I had so wanted to change the world. I had wanted to make a difference—to create a world that was more peaceful, where people cared for each other and respected each other's differences. A world with clean air, clean water and clean soil. A world with lots of love and laughter! I sure was planning to change the world!

His voice brought me back with the question that cut straight into my soul: "And what kind of dream are you living today? What kind of world are you creating today?"

The stark contrast between the two pictures made me choke. While he had asked in essence the same question that had just minutes before made me really angry, I now felt rather puzzled. What had happened? I did have great plans and worthwhile dreams, so how did I end up working in a cubicle for a large corporate insurance company, and only seeing the sunlight when I went for lunch?

I ended up barely noticing the rest of the man's presentation, for the question had shaken the entire foundation of my life. What dream was I following? What world was I creating? What had happened with my own dream? When did I lose it …or more accurately, forget about it? For I still had it. It still was my dream! But I wasn't living it, nor was I making any efforts to make it happen. Life had become something that happened to me. So I would complain, blame, get angry, feel frustrated, protest, and then make my contribution to a system that was nothing like the world I had dreamed of. How did I get here? When did I stop believing in <u>my</u> dream?

The presentation ended. The presenter took some questions from an audience that clearly struggled with accepting the fact that they had been accused of

24

creating the world they lived in. I was glad that at least I wasn't the only one who had been shaken to the core.

Upon leaving the auditorium there was the opportunity to purchase the author's book, which he was signing. That's when the day's coincidences came to a peak. The book was titled, <u>Seeds ...of Germination ...or Termination.</u> Carsanto's terminator seed announcement came immediately back to mind, as did some new questions: "What did I allow to germinate in my life? What did I terminate? And why?"

Nayla scooped up a handful of the seeds in which she was sitting. Terminator seeds! Life that could only germinate once! Life poised to terminate! They were seeds that would germinate only to grow a sterile plant—one poisoned and reduced to a shadow of its true life-giving potential. It was all like a dream that takes root, but becomes corrupted and turns into an impotent mirror of its pure creative power.

Nayla wiggled herself into a comfortable position while the seeds embraced her like the kernels of a beanbag. She then drifted off to sleep with her mind occupied by questions: "What kind of world do I dream of? What kind of world am I creating?"

"Why did she run?" Dick Duke questioned the guard in his coarse, interrogating manner. He decided he liked this new recruit. Most people who worked for him were more or less trembling when he asked them something, but this guy stayed collected and calm. Good thing this man had been on duty tonight. Nayla would have been able to bluff her way past any other guard, but not by this good man.

"I don't know, sir! But it must have had something to do with the cotton wrap which I was about to unfold. She grabbed it and ran before I could see what was concealed in it."

Together the two men traced Nayla's steps over the past day via her security access card and the various surveillance cameras in the building. She'd spent most of the evening in her office and some time in the lab. Nothing unusual for Nayla; that's where they would expect to find her. It made Dick realize that it could be a long time before they might find even a clue about what had been so important to George's lover—important enough to run from the building, terminate an exemplary career and put her life on the line.

A faint smile appeared on his normally grim face as he thought about the idea of getting this Latin cat in his hands for interrogation. She had such a gorgeous, athletic body with sensual curves and well-toned muscles. And that passion! Oh, she would fight him. It was going to be a real treat. And George wouldn't be able to do anything for her without compromising his leadership authority in the country. Something he simply couldn't afford to do—even if he claimed to be in love with her. After all, what man would put world control on the line for a woman?

Yes, finally he, the General, would get his turn with Nayla. He had thought the day would never come when his nightly fantasies would come true. "But let's not make the same mistake as earlier tonight, when I disturbed George before having all the facts. Let's be thorough and follow due process. It is the patient and well-timed, calculated action of the hunter that will bring her into my hands," Dick told himself as he banned the more pleasant thoughts of the events to come from his mind and concentrated on the problem at hand.

"Let's go and see if we can find her at home," he said to the guard. "I'll have someone else cover for you here tonight. You might be of more use to me in questioning her, or at least searching her apartment for clues."

Dick noticed how quick and eager the guard was to join him. This would be a good opportunity to see if this man had any other security skills. If the guard performed well tracking Nayla down, he would consider bringing him into his inner circle.

As Dick had somehow expected, Nayla wasn't home. Soon after they forced the door and started to search the penthouse, he found an envelope on the living room table. He fumbled it between his fingers, frustrated. What game was this woman playing? The envelope was sealed. The big, clearly rushed, handwritten print read: "For George Shapura." What was she up to?

The General badly needed to know what was written on this note, but couldn't open a letter addressed personally to his boss.

"Let's go and get this letter to George," he grumbled to the guard.

He had to hand it to Nayla: She was smart. She was buying time. And there was nothing he could do about it. He shrugged his shoulders while collecting his thoughts. It would only be a matter of time, but eventually his pit bull tenacity would bring her into his interrogation room.

The thundering, squeaking noise of the train as it struggled to come to life had woken Nayla a few hours ago. While she was relieved that her escape was going according to plan and the immediate threat to her life had somewhat diminished, her mind had been racing back and forth between the events to come and the events behind her.

She had to concentrate on what her next move would be. How was she going to get off this train? Where was she going to go? Who would she be able to trust? She didn't know anyone in the United Canadian Communities.

Yet the more she questioned the days ahead, the more she realized her precarious position. How had she gotten herself into this situation? This wasn't what she had been working for all her life. She had thrown everything away in one impulsive move! Her whole life, gone, in just one night!

She grabbed her precious parcel in a protective embrace as she reminded herself that life, and not just her life, but the life of all living things on the planet, was at stake. After all, no scientist had ever researched how the terminator cells affected the animals and people who consumed the sterile plants that carried their own poison.

In her arms she held the only cure against the terrible terminator mutation campaign Carsanto was about to launch: Mutating germinator seeds! Seeds of life! Seeds that could save the planet!

As Nayla thought about her ultimate destination, her mind drifted back to the research time she had spent in the United States of Bolivar some seven years ago, in an area which used to be called "Guatemala."

Carsanto had assigned her to a joint research team of American and Bolivarian scientists who studied vegetation suitable for poor soil parcels, typically land deforested through slash-and-burn farming practices. After losing the protective shelter of the tree canopy and root system, such land would be stripped of its topsoil by wind and rain in just a few years' time.

One hot afternoon she was sitting in the shade of some trees, writing down her notes on the growth progress of a new seed Carsanto had developed in the hope of entering into the seed trade with its southern neighbor. It was then that she saw him for the first time. He passed her on a nearby trail, machete in hand and obviously returning from harvesting some sugar cane for their research project. His bronzed, naked torso with its well-toned muscles gave away his athletic abilities. He wasn't very tall, and the features of his face left no doubt about his Mayan heritage.

Just when she realized she'd been staring obviously at this attractive young man who moved so gracefully through the jungle, he offered her the most brilliant smile. Later that evening when she joined the other researchers for dinner, he showed up again.

"Hi, my name is Julian."

He smiled at her again with sparkling eyes full of energy and with a mysterious twinkle lurking underneath.

"What's your name?" he inquired.

And so their conversation started. That first night they talked over dinner, and chatted some more while they went for a walk. Then, they lit a fire and conversed until deep into the night attracted by an unknown mystery, in eager discovery unveiling layers of each other's being.

Nayla learned about Julian's deep respect for all living things, his awe for Creation and his ambition to pursue dreams that serve the common good. When he modestly pointed to his cultural heritage as the foundation for such noble traits, she only admired his humbleness.

Julian intrigued her. His self-confidence, comfort in the jungle, rooted wisdom and balance had almost a hypnotic effect on her. She noticed that at times she asked new questions not out of curiosity for the answer, but because she was afraid their conversation would end. She didn't want him to leave. But in the early morning hours he did. Gracefully, politely, he had embraced her and kissed her good night on her cheek.

The second night, they talked again. This time he shared with her stories about life in the United States of Bolivar and the sustainable technologies that had been developed in his country. As a scientist he was proud of the leading edge innovations, like the air car—first invented in Europe, but perfected and embraced as the travel vehicle of choice on the Latin continent.

On the third night, Nayla and Julian sat together in silence, neither of them sure how to share their feelings and simply taking comfort in each other's presence. She laid her head on his shoulder. He wrapped his arm around her and softly caressed her hair.

"Nayla," he started uncomfortably some time around midnight.

But afraid that he would leave again, she held her finger in a silencing motion in front of his mouth and whispered, "Sssshhhh." Next, she embraced him and tenderly kissed him. This time she wasn't planning to let him go.

That night they made love. It was a passion-filled night she would never forget. Two hearts, in ecstatic flow, were dancing, loving and uniting their very souls.

The following six months were the most beautiful and memorable of her life. The tropical jungle with its hidden waterfalls, river swimming holes and brightly colored flowers was a paradise to be discovered and explored by her and Julian. Nayla had always enjoyed fieldwork, but sharing it with this man elevated that joy to a new level.

Now she wondered why she'd ever returned to Carsanto. She could have stayed there in paradise. As a top scientist with roots in the country, she would have had no problem finding another job. But she didn't stay.

For her this was adventure. And adventure was not real life ...or was it? It was something she certainly didn't know at the time. She enjoyed the jungle, but could never connect with it like Julian did. It was like he was an integral part of it. He was in perfect harmony with it. He could feel the forest breathe, and was connected to this paradise with his heart. She was only able to relate to it with her mind.

For her, the plants, seeds and jungle were an object of study, beautiful and to be respected, but also to be understood and controlled through bio-technology. It was like looking into a theater and studying all the actors in a play. In contrast, Julian wasn't a spectator in the theater, he was an actor in the play, he *was* the play, or at least part of it. It was exactly this deep-rooted oneness with nature, that mysterious energy—balanced, calm like a kitten at rest, and at the same time all-powerful and wild like the jaguar—which attracted her so much to this Mayan man.

In the end that same attraction drove them apart. She convinced Julian to come with her to the American Confederacy to experience the American Dream. Soon after they were back she got pregnant and they decided to marry. But Julian was never able to settle in the Confederacy. To him the American Dream proved to be an insult to his paradise. It wounded his heart deeply and daily.

In this new country, there was no respect for nature, and only a fake expression of community. People didn't really care for each other; they only pretended to do so. Relationships with others were always second priority; the first priority was their wealth. He was neither impressed by Nayla's exquisite rooftop penthouse nor able to find any friends that could even vaguely understand his deep connection with all living things. All this was amplified by the fact that the American Confederacy had developed into a racial state with white people as the ruling aristocracy and those of color in servant roles. While Nayla had Latin roots, her blue eyes and somewhat lighter skin—both traits she had inherited from her Caucasian grandmother—had allowed her to move into one of the top research positions in the country. However, Julian's strong Mayan features were not accepted. While at home he was regarded as an important organic farming scientist, the best job he could find in the American Confederacy was as a gardener.

And then, their precious daughter Gaya was born. Gaya was a gift from God. She was simply adorable, and had clearly inherited Julian's beautiful smile. She brought peace to Julian's heart. For the next two years he became a caring, nurturing housefather, focusing all he had to give to his child, this new life that loved unconditionally and touched hearts with a simple smile. Gaya was a soul straight from paradise.

But paradise …wasn't that the world they had left after the first six months of their relationship? While for Nayla, the American Dream was still the ultimate ambition to be pursued, she couldn't deny she had experienced a glimpse of something more powerful and beautiful in the Bolivarian jungle when together with Julian. Her heart had sensed its magnificence but she had been unable to surrender to it, to let go of her need to control, to abandon fear and dance in unison with Creation. But Julian knew paradise intimately. He had not only observed it and tasted it, he could feel it, and allowed himself to be fully immersed in it. He had been part of it for most of his life until he chose to follow Nayla, his love, to this new world of the American Dream.

They say love conquers all. But the loss of a caring and respectful community was slowly killing the passion in Julian's eyes. Nayla had noticed how the mysterious twinkle in his eyes had made way for a melancholic gaze. She'd seen the struggle in his heart, and knew he was wrestling to hold on to his love for her while the flame in his own heart was slowly dying out.

One evening after putting Gaya to bed, Julian took her to the patio deck overlooking the city and poured her a glass of wine. "See how everything around us is made from concrete and stone," he said. "Everything is hard. That's how I feel my heart is becoming: like a stone! Gaya has made it soft again, but I wonder how long that will last, and more importantly, I wonder how long it will take before her tender soul will be suffocated and becomes as hard as all this concrete."

Nayla sat silently after hearing these words. She thought about the jungle, the soft waving palms, the breeze that brought the sweet aroma of colorful flowers, the early morning sounds as the jungle came to life, the chirping of the crickets on a hot afternoon. But that was not what life was, was it? Here there was progress and science and research and innovation. Here there was power and money and control; the opportunity to buy silk from China, eat fruits from far continents and live in large comfortable mansions. Here, there was the American Dream!

For a moment she considered explaining that Dream to Julian, but she didn't; he wouldn't understand. In her heart she wanted to hold him, tell him how much she loved him, pour her soul out and share with him how much she missed the jungle, how she had never again—or ever before—felt such joy as during those six months. She wanted to ask him to take her back to that place, to help her leave the American Dream and find a way to live in paradise. But just when her heart was gathering the courage to share all this with him, her mind won the battle.

"Julian, I'm sorry you feel that way," she said carefully. "But many children are born in this country, and they all grow up to be perfectly healthy and caring adults. You'll see Gaya will be just fine. We can take her to the park more often if you like."

Her words sounded hollow, even to herself. She knew she was merely attempting to provide a rational answer—something that justified their current lifestyle. She saw how he lowered his eyes in defeat, attempting to hide his sadness and disappointment from her.

"I'm making great progress with this new mutating germinator seed," she said, changing the subject in the hope of soothing his feelings and cheering up the somber mood. She added, "In a few months it will all be ready and done. Maybe we should take Gaya on a vacation, and show her where her mother and father first met?"

"Sure, that would be great." Julian answered unconvincingly. He took her head in his hands and tenderly kissed her forehead, but his eyes were unable to hide his deep sadness.

The following evening when Nayla returned home from work, she found a note.

My dearest love,

Please try to understand. My heart is dying. When it becomes like the stone of this city, it's not able to love. You only deserve to receive the highest love, but how do I honor you with that, when the light in me is dying out? For two years I've tried to find beauty and happiness in the American Dream, but I've found none. I only see the destruction of nature, the disrespectful treatment of fellow human beings, the abuse of animals and the total disconnect with nature itself—like man controls it, stands above it, and can use and abuse it. It pains my heart, and more importantly, it frightens me when I think about how it will impact Gaya's pure soul, to grow up in a society that has forgotten the meaning of community.

How will she learn to care and to discover the wonders of creation if she doesn't see others care and is surrounded by a noisy jungle of stone, steel and machines? Our daughter deserves to grow up in an environment that nurtures the pureness of her soul and appreciates the love of her heart. I'm taking her home to the United States of Bolivar, and I beg you to join us so we can start a new life as a family in maybe a less luxurious but most caring community.

For always,
    Your love.

Julian.

All night she cried. She cried for the loss of Gaya and her dearest husband, her soul mate. She cried because deep down she knew Julian was right. And she cried even more because she simply wasn't able—or brave enough—to give up what she had. It wasn't just the expensive penthouse suite, but the position and recognition within Carsanto. She had made it to the top. She was *someone* in this country, in this powerful corporation. How could he ask her to give all that up for a life in the bush? He was confusing vacation and a sense of adventure with reality!

By morning, her heart had hardened till it had the firmness of concrete. She went to work and for the next few months buried herself in her work. She poured all her passion into developing the first mutating germinator seed which could function as an antidote if ever anything went wrong with the mutating terminator seed she had created a few years earlier.

During that period when she kept her mind occupied to shield herself from feeling the loss in her heart, she found solace in the arms of George Shapura. At first it was purely sexual; they had a strong physical connection. The sex allowed her to release tension and stress. Mentally they shared a fascination with the Carsanto Company, and its progress and growth. They both knew how to live and enjoy the American Dream. They each loved their work, the long hours, the innovation, the power and the money.

From time to time during this period her mind wandered off to Gaya, Julian and the paradise she'd experienced during her six months in the United States of Bolivar. When that happened she quickly focused on something else, afraid of the attraction and potent pull of such a life. It held a power that could shake the very foundation of her belief in the American Dream—a power that frightened her. It was much more comfortable to ignore it and take solace in some regular internet video calls with her adored Gaya. She longed to hold her precious daughter in her arms, but had decided to leave her with Julian since it would have been difficult for her to take care of Gaya due to her work obligations. She hadn't even paid her beloved child a personal visit, fearing that if she did so she would lack the strength to return to her life in the American Confederacy, and therefore derail her successful career. Thank God for the sophisticated fiber network that connected the two countries and allowed her to maintain at least a long-distance relationship with her Gaya.

As Nayla's relationship with George developed she found him to be a great listener. While she had always admired his decisiveness and leadership, she now also got to know his tender side. He started to share his uncertainties and doubts with her. It was a side of the company's leader—and the country's ruler—that others never got to see. She got to know the human, very ordinary man behind the all-powerful leader. A man with his own pitfalls, failures, internal struggles and doubts—not that he would ever admit to any of that. He was a man isolated and very lonely, unable to share his doubts and grievances with his employees or the country's citizens, as they would interpret them as weaknesses, and behavior unworthy of a leader! It would negatively impact their respect and ultimately dilute his power.

In this way Nayla got to understand how lonely it could be at the top. And so her maternal instincts focused on nurturing and caring for this great leader by being his passionate lover, supportive friend and energetic business partner.

A shrill ringing tone shook George from a deep sleep. It took him a few seconds to come to his senses and realize that the phone was ringing.

It was a wonder he'd dozed off at all after Dick's last message. Once it had been confirmed the runner had been Nayla, he'd tried to contact her by phone while pacing up and down the living room wracking his brain over different scenarios of what might have transpired. It wasn't in his nature to panic or think the worst, so he'd been pretty sure there would be a logical explanation for everything. Still, the absence of any word from Nayla had bothered him. Eventually he'd turned the television on as distraction, and must have fallen asleep.

While collecting his thoughts, he instructed the computer to answer.

"George, apologies for the third call tonight, but I've an urgent message from Nayla that you should read," said Dick in his usual direct manner.

As George glanced at the clock, he realized he had slept for several hours.

"Just give me the message, Dick," he said shortly. "It's well after midnight, so this had better be good!"

"I don't know what the message says, George!"

"What? Why not?"

"Well, I found a sealed envelope with your name on it in Nayla's apartment," Dick responded in agitation. "I didn't want to open something that was personally addressed to you, so I'm on my way over. I'll be at your place in ten minutes."

"All right! Come on over."

As George lay down on the couch again waiting for the General to arrive, his mind wandered off to Nayla. Where would she be now, in the middle of the night? Why had she not called him, but rather left a note for him at her home?

When Dick arrived at George's mansion, he ordered the guard to stay in the car. The disappointed look on the man's face didn't escape his honed observation skills. However, he didn't want to run the risk of having a third party present in what could become a very personal conversation between him and George.

Besides, who knew what the envelope contained? It would be much easier for George to share the contents without anyone else present.

Dick waited impatiently to be allowed admittance into George's high security mansion. His anxiety rose when George started opening the envelope. Hopefully, the note would provide a helpful lead. His over-zealousness in accusing Nayla of a security breach had made him look like a rookie once already during tonight's events; Nayla had better not cause this to happen a second time!

His heart sunk in his chest when he saw a smile flash across George's face as he was reading the note.

"What does it say?" Dick asked impatiently.

George handed him the note. Then he walked away while Dick was reading it and asked casually: "Anything else tonight, Dick, or are you finally going to allow me my sleep? I suggest you get some yourself."

Dick was careful to maintain his cool. At this dismissal, he politely said goodnight.

But beneath his collected appearance he was fuming. Who did this woman think she was, just totally trashing all respect for the rules and security procedures of the company? Causing a lockdown because the guard had "no business in her personal belongings!" This was simply unacceptable behavior for a board member. She was going to pay for this! One way or another, one day he would make her pay for this!

And then it occurred to him …what if she was shrewdly playing them? What if she did steal something and was simply buying time with this note? George could go to sleep, but on second thought, Dick wasn't planning to quite yet.

"Let's find out how she got home," he suggested to the guard with renewed vigor when he arrived back at the car.

The General could tell the guard could barely control his curiosity about what had been written in the note. However, Dick didn't intend on sharing it, and he knew the guard wouldn't have the nerve to ask, for fear he might tarnish his current good standing.

Now it was simply time for some diligent security work. Nayla was up to something. She could have phoned George to give him this message. So Dick was almost certain she organized it this way to gain time. But, time for what?

When Nayla woke up she had no idea how long she had slept, nor if it was day or night. Was she still on the soil of the American Confederacy, or had she passed the border already? Afraid to make a mistake and give away her hiding place, she decided not to open the lid above her.

Instead, she drank some water and nibbled a bit from her food ration. To kill some time and distract her mind from the precarious situation in which her impulsive actions had put her, she turned on her headlight to read some more in her grandmother's diary.

April 21st, 2021

This journaling thing isn't really for me. Life is so busy, I just never seem to find the time to write on these pages …and whom am I writing for? Well, whatever, it might be a good thing to read when I'm old. But I think I'm going to limit it to really important events in my life. Doing this daily just doesn't work for me.

Anyway, I'm ranting again. Might do this more. It's difficult to keep my mind—or my writing—focused.

Not sure if this is a really important thing in my life; after all, it's just about a book. Or really, one in a series of books that have lately come to me. See, first I read Seeds, which I picked up at that presentation in February. It had lots of great ideas about the type of world we could create. It made me think; helped me to build a vision. It gave me hope—the hope that things could be changed as long as we all started to walk towards the dream we have, one step at the time. I realized that as long as we keep our eye on the dream and align our actions with it, we will make progress.

But things might not always go easy or fast. And not all action might be within the law—look at the great leaders of social progress in the past! Gandhi violated the law by making salt, Rosa Parks broke the law by taking a seat on the first row in a bus during a time Black people didn't have such a right, Martin Luther King was arrested and jailed multiple times for protesting without a permit, Thomas Jefferson, George Washington, James Madison, Benjamin Franklin and other founding fathers refused to obey the rules of the English King and took up arms against the British, Nelson Mandela spearheaded the armed struggle against apartheid and was imprisoned for 27 years, and Che Guevara and Fidel Castro broke the law of a corrupt government in a country of haves and have-nots when they took up arms against a dictator. The lesson is clear: For humanity to progress we have to focus on what is right, rather than on what is law. In the end those who persevere in the struggle for righteousness prevail!

I got pumped when I realized the power I had. My first step towards my dream was to grow my own rooftop organic garden. There are so many things within my reach to progress, step by step, towards a better world! But it was up to me to start and keep on walking towards that dream. To never abandon it! I was so glad that I'd finally found my stride. I was on my path, a path to a sustainable world.

That was until three weeks ago, when my girlfriend and I went to 'Socrates'—our favorite bar which attracts all those idealistic souls in New York who are going to make this world a better place. Not sure who brought him in our group, but in the middle of all the solutions we were sharing, he got my attention with his somewhat arrogant question: "And you guys really think this is going to make a difference? Sure it feels good, but get real! These are all drops on a hot plate. How many acres of ancient forest are disappearing each day because of the brutal deforestation practices of some powerful corporations …and you think your organic garden makes a difference?"

His dark eyes flaming, his Latin accent charming, and his Brazilian passion seducing, his arrogant stance captured the attention of us all. He was athletic, handsome, well-spoken and unapologetic in his presentation and observations. His flamboyant gestures gave life to his words, while his arguments were well-calculated and cut straight to the essence. When he looked me in the eyes,

I melted. Was this love at first sight? Or was it simply carnal attraction? After making passionate love with him that night, I still was not sure, but it was well worth it.

Since that night we've spent almost every evening together. Alejandro is supportive of my organic garden and the ideas and visions I've developed to build a better world. However, he keeps warning me that those in power will not go down without a fight. He has been reciting Latin American history for me, and given that context it's understandable why he thinks that way. But this is America, the country of liberty and democracy. Where people elect their leaders. Where freedom of speech exists, and where I can set up my own organic rooftop garden if I decide to do so.

Last week Alejandro gave me a book, which I just started reading tonight. What I read prompted me to pick up my journal and write all this. The book is titled, <u>Endgame.</u> There are two huge volumes—not sure how long it is going to take me to read all 900-something pages—but I'm determined to read through them all after what I read on the first few.

The author starts off with some premises, the first of which is that civilization is not sustainable, most particularly industrial civilization—not sure I agree with that. With the rest of the premises and the first chapter of his book he justifies the reasoning of that statement—and he builds up a compelling case for his perspective. But the book goes further and examines a question that shook me to the core: If civilization, as we know it today, is not sustainable—and therefore amoral, is it morally justifiable to <u>not</u> take it down?

At first I was quite outraged by the attack on my culture. But then I placed the question in a somewhat different perspective; I looked at it on a smaller scale. Where do I draw the line when I see lawful injustice, and what do I do about it? Surely we have to take steps in the direction of our dreams like suggested in <u>Seeds.</u> However, if someone else has a dream that is mutually exclusive from yours and they fight for that dream, shouldn't you fight for yours? Am I prepared to fight for my dream? What am I prepared to fight for?

Synchronicity as usual was also at work today. This morning I watched a short video on the internet. In the clip, Julia Butterfly Hill—an environmental activist who lived 738 days in a 600-year-old California Redwood tree to prevent

loggers from cutting it down—asked the following question: "What is your tree?"
Meaning: "What is it you will stand up for?"

As I'm writing this, I realize that while the question in Endgame is shocking in itself, it isn't why I'm writing now. The reason why I'm writing this is my answer: "I don't want to fight! I'm not ready to fight! I want to work towards creating my dream, but I don't want to fight!" Shame engulfs me as I realize that I simply don't have the guts to put my comfortable life on the line for my dream. Is that how I lost it in the first place? Did I trade my dream for the convenience and comforts of this culture?

I think I'm going to stop writing now. This diary stuff becomes unsettling. The more I write, the deeper I dig and the more disconcerting the questions become. Not sure I want to look any longer into this mirror. Maybe another day. Tomorrow I am going to tend to the seedlings that are growing in my garden. So long as no one is whacking those down, I might not have to think about my tree.

Would I fight for my garden?

"You wrote it for me," Nayla thought as she realized how much comfort the diary was offering her. Her grandmother was talking to her through time at a moment when she was struggling and in need of a lighthouse to help her on this new course.

While over the last few months Nayla had asked herself some questions about the ethics of Carsanto and the dream she had been pursuing, she'd never allowed herself much time for the answers. It was much easier to push the questions aside and concentrate on the work she had in front of her. But now she had acted. Impulsively, recklessly, but with determination, because too much was at stake. And she was not going to sit by and let things happen without a fight.

Would she have done it, if her little girl Gaya and the rest of her family were not living south of the border in the country that was targeted by Carsanto's campaign? Nayla wasn't sure. Who was she fighting for? Was she fighting for the future of this planet, or simply for that of her child? Since both coincided, it had made her action a lot easier.

"But isn't the future of our children not always directly linked with the future of our planet?" she pondered until she finally concluded, "I'm fighting for the children. The children of all species and of all times!"

Four days had gone by now, and no word from Nayla. George was getting concerned.

Dick reportedly had traced the taxi driver who'd driven Nayla home and subsequently had dropped her off at a fast-food restaurant. She'd mentioned something to him about a treasure hunt she was undertaking together with a friend. And something about a map, too. Had that piece of paper been what she was trying to conceal from the guard? Dick had finally conceded that Nayla might have run for reasons of a private nature, and he'd decided to back off.

But what bothered George was that Nayla hadn't told him what she was up to. Nayla was unpredictable, impulsive and passionate in all she did. But she trusted him, just as he trusted her. They shared their experiences, pains, concerns and joys with each other. Why had she not let him in on her plans? What if something serious had happened to her on this crazy treasure hunt? She could be dying from thirst somewhere in the desert!

With Nayla gone, George made a profound realization: It is often only in the absence of our loved ones that we realize and appreciate their love. He resolved to tell Nayla upon her return how much he loved her. God, did he miss her!

But did she miss him? Could she be with another man?

There had been no signs of anything being wrong with their relationship. Or had there been? He'd noticed Nayla had been more quiet over the last few weeks. But this had happened before! She seemed to have these periods when she was simply more introverted.

He always assumed that during those times she was missing her daughter. He'd respected that private silence, and thus had never questioned it. He'd just made sure he was always there to comfort her.

A knock on his office door brought his mind back to the business at hand.

"Come in," he called out.

"George, bad news! Nayla ran because she stole top-secret materials from Carsanto!" Dick blurted out as he marched resolutely into the office.

"What are you talking about, Dick?" George responded in disbelief. "I thought the note made it clear that she was taking care of a private matter. The treasure hunt, right?"

"Well, we've just found out that she stole all the mutating germinator seeds!"

"What? Are you sure?" George questioned again as his mind refused to accept the implications of Dick's words.

"Yes! And it's not just a few of them, George, it's all of them! I had my guys check every single species before coming over here. They're all gone! I would love to tell you that my research uncovered this theft, however we had stalled our investigation once we learned Nayla had taken off on this treasure hunt. No one really noticed that the germinator seeds were missing earlier because she was the only one working with them. Discovering the theft was simply a fluke: A junior assistant was looking for terminator seeds in the wrong cabinet, and questioned why there weren't any seeds in there."

George stared in silence at the picture on his desk. It was that of the attractive, passionate, but most stubborn woman. What a fool he had been! He should have seen this coming. He should have known Nayla wasn't going to sit idly on the sidelines while they sprayed terminator seeds—the very seeds she had created—over the country where her family and her daughter lived.

He reflected back on the board meeting where the fateful decision had been made. She'd avoided eye contact with him after that meeting, but what had surprised him the most at the time was that she hadn't put up a fight during the meeting. She had been quiet, looking defeated and taken by surprise.

But he should have remembered that Nayla didn't know defeat. It simply wasn't part of her vocabulary. It was exactly that tenacity which made her such a good researcher …and executive. The woman just never gave up. How could he have thought that she would bend over that easily? He'd made a crucial mistake in withholding this plan from her until that board meeting. He had done so because he'd been afraid of how she would react. Well, clearly he should have been. Now not only their relationship, but the entire mission was at risk! And because of her impulsive determination, she could even pose a risk to Carsanto's ability to secure world domination.

While George pondered all this, his only words for the General were, "You know what to do."

But his mind was wondering how he could manage this situation without throwing Nayla into the hands of this uncompromising man. He had seen the lust in Dick's eyes when he looked at Nayla. George knew the General desired his lover, and that he would use his position of power to quench his carnal appetite once she was in his hands. But for now George couldn't do anything else but send the General after her. The man was most valuable to the security of the country, and George needed Dick to execute his family's vision to gain world control.

The new implications of the situation rocked George's comfortable life. Nayla had been the first lover whom he'd been able to trust, and life had been so much nicer with her by his side. Sharing things with her not only made life at the top less lonely, it also helped him to get clarity in his decision making. He didn't want to give up either one of his valuable companions, but he had just been presented with a serious challenge to amicably resolving this situation.

Why hadn't he prepared her with news of Carsanto's latest strategy in advance? Last week they had taken a break and gone horseback riding along the coast. After walking their horses for a few miles, Nayla had challenged him to a race. They had flown over the beach on their steeds, the wind rushing through their hair, and the sand flying high in the air as the pounding hooves of their animals propelled them forward. Then they had lain down under some palm trees. The setting was stunningly romantic, as tender and fragile as a butterfly's wing.

Nayla had obviously been relaxed, and was clearly enjoying their time off.

"Let's just listen to the sounds here," she'd suggested while putting her head on his chest.

They had. And the symphony of rustling leaves, soft blowing wind and endlessly breaking ocean waves had touched their souls.

Nayla had jumped up and danced barefooted in the sand like a child, unconcerned with who could be watching or the impression she was making. When she was done, she'd sat before him, embraced him and passionately kissed him. When their eyes had locked, he'd seen love in hers, as well as deep mystery.

"Nayla," he'd started. He'd planned to tell her now, get her prepared.

But how would she react? Yes, he could have simply told her the plan. He could have invited her input and engaged her in exploring how they could make the Latin continent dependent on their seeds. He could have asked how she envisioned Carsanto getting world control. But he was afraid. Afraid of spoiling this perfect day, and so instead he had continued, "It feels so good to see you so happy. We should spend more time like this. Travel and enjoy each other's company."

She had taken his head in her hands and softly kissed his forehead.

"I would love that!" she'd gently smiled.

He should have told her too, during the following days they'd spent in the office. After all, business was business. She had known the company's strategy of world control for some time, and she was a good strategist. She might have understood. But he'd failed to do so. Instead, he now found himself in this mess.

He liked challenges, but this one could have been avoided had he been open and honest with Nayla. He was normally so good at banning fear from any of his actions. But this time the action—or in effect, inaction—had been driven by his anxiety about alienating or even losing the woman he loved and cared for most. His failure of dealing proactively with his fear could now lead to exactly the results that frightened him so much: losing his partner, his love!

Oh, why were women so complicated?! The United States of Bolivar was the last country that needed to be brought under the economic rule of Carsanto. Spreading the seeds by plane would just accelerate the inevitable! And it wasn't like they were going to bomb them. They weren't going to kill anyone. Besides, making the world dependent on their seeds had brought order to the world. It had secured the resource flow for everything people wanted in the American way of life. Order and security was a good thing! Control resulted in predictable events and that led to security—even for those on the lower steps of the ladder. After all, was that not what all people wanted? His plan, though, included Nayla being by his side. Together they could have ruled the world!

George leaned back in his black leather chair and closed his eyes. His mind drifted off to the smiling face with fine Latin features, her long black silky hair, and those determined blue eyes which always held something back—something unpredictable, something to be discovered. It was that hidden part of her that fascinated him. Her impulsiveness brought him ever-new surprises—like this one. And although he hated the situation she had put him in now, deep inside he admired the strength of her spirit, and the pureness of her heart. In fact, that was why he loved her!

"Mmmmh, interesting," his wandering mind suddenly observed, "I love her *because of* her unpredictable behavior! It's what keeps our relationship exciting. So is it accurate to assume that people really want security?"

The question was both surprising and intriguing to him. However, he decided to explore it further at some other time. Now he had to take care of the business at hand: spreading mutating terminator seeds across the huge land mass of their neighboring country to the south. However, it made no sense to execute this plan as long as they hadn't recovered the mutating germinator seeds. And that meant he had to find Nayla.

Determined, he picked up the phone.

"Dick, did you close the southern border? Nayla is going home. She's going to get those seeds to the United States of Bolivar!"

"Already did that four days ago," came the matter-of-fact response. Yet its very tone betrayed Dick's pride at being ahead of the game again. "I closed all borders the very evening she ran. Commercial and tourist traffic is still going across, but everyone is being checked and all border agents have her picture. There's no way she's going to get past the southern wall!"

"Good thinking!" George complimented him, and he felt his mind adjusting to the cat-and-mouse game with which Nayla had presented him. "Let's get the taxi driver back for interrogation, and see if you can find any more clues. You know she's smart; she planned this well by buying valuable time with her note. She's not going to make it easy to catch her; she never does," he mused, smiling about that particular trait of hers.

The man left his rustic log cabin nestled in the foothills of the Rockies on this chilly morning sometime before sunrise. He was dressed in pelts and skins, materials that were local and kept him warm on even the coldest winter hikes. He would blend well into the forest he would be visiting on today's hunt.

His supply of dried meat was getting critically low; it was time to remedy that. He prayed in his medicine wheel like he always did before the sacred hunt, and asked the deer people for an offer of life, an offer that in turn would provide life to him. Then he set out at a strong pace for his hunting grounds.

He reached the top of his favorite ridge, which faced east, by the time the sun was about to come up. The spot allowed him to gaze over the valley of pasture land that was dotted with small groups of trees. Wildlife was always on the move at this time of the day, and it was a good location to spot deer on their way from the fields to the trees, where they would bed down. If he could locate where they were going to rest for the day, he could stalk them later on. Of course, there was always the chance one of them would walk along the trail up to the ridge within the range of his bow. He shouldn't be spotted, because he had good cover with nice, clear, shooting lanes that would allow his arrow to reach the target without being deflected by any branches or shrubs.

He was gazing in the distance through a pair of binoculars— his treasured object from the days when the world was entranced by the American Dream. The thundering noise of a train heading north across the valley broke the silence.

The man was always in awe of the locomotive's power to pull such a long load of cars. This morning, though, the train's sound was an intrusion at a time when all his senses were heightened due to the hunt—an event when man, nature, animals and the elements were all connecting into one sacred dance: the dance of life and death. The sharing of life. The experience of flow, of being one.

The sudden squealing sound of metal-on-metal broke his concentration. He focused on the train, and noticed it was making an unusual stop.

"Probably some fallen trees across the track in that far patch of bush," he thought.

Once the train came to a complete stop, two men got out and walked ahead of the long iron horse. He heard the sound of a chainsaw, and smiled contentedly due to the accuracy of his guess.

Movement at the other end further down the train drew his attention.

Someone was climbing out of one of the grain cars. By the way this person carefully observed the men in front of the train, the hunter concluded the individual was a stowaway. This person didn't want to be seen by the men ahead.

As he focused better, he noticed the long black hair and elegant female features. It was a woman. She'd managed to climb down the train car and was making her way through the field, heading in his direction to the hills. But she had no cover. At first she was walking carefully, so as not to make any noise while moving on the dry grass of the brown winter pastures. Obviously she was hoping the men up front would not notice her, consumed as they were by their task. When she must have thought she was far enough away not to be heard, she started running. It looked like she was going to reach a small group of trees just below the hill when the noise of the chainsaw stopped. The men started yelling, and came running out of the trees. One of them headed after the woman; the other returned to the locomotive.

By now the woman had run through the trees and was climbing the trail up the hill. He could now discern her fine facial lines more clearly. "She must be around her thirties, and from somewhere south, based on her somewhat darker skin and exotic features. Where is she going?" he pondered.

If he didn't move, she would soon run right past him without ever knowing he was there. She had a good chance of getting away, he thought; the man chasing her hadn't been able to close the distance. It seemed she was in good shape, and was able to outrun him. But the second man had now reappeared from the locomotive, and was also sprinting in the direction of the hills.

The hunter had just decided to stay as an observer to the unfolding scene and let the woman run past him when, "Bang!", the thundering sound of a high-powered rifle ruined the magical silence in the valley and the play that was unfolding before him. "Bang, bang," went two more shots.

The woman was approaching the ridge now. He could hear her heavy breathing as her heart pumped furiously to maintain the brutal pace up the hill.

"Bang!" went yet another shot. The second man intermittently paused in his run to take shots at the escaping woman.

The hunter knew that once the stowaway crossed the ridge, she would be out of reach of the rifle. But not for long: Once the men climbed the hill and gained the high ground, she would be a sitting duck while she tried to cross the next valley. If she stayed in the open, she wouldn't have a chance. Only some skilled knowledge of the terrain and the area could get her to safety.

The woman reached the ridge, and stopped for a brief moment to look behind her. Another missed bullet soared by her.

Just when she was about to run again, the hunter moved and shouted: "This way!" His hand motioned her in his direction. How could he leave a woman in need to the mercy of two men with a gun?

The sudden movement in the high grass in front of the rocks scared Nayla. It took her a moment to realize it was a man. Judging by his dress, it was a local. He was offering help—something she couldn't refuse in this critical moment. She changed direction and ran towards him.

The man led her quickly past some large rocks into a soft gulley that ran along the ridge. His knowledge of the landscape allowed him to use this lower-lying terrain to get them out of sight of the two men that were following her.

They soon reached a small creek. Through years of erosion this little stream had cut out a wide creek bed that now provided cover for their descent. Its banks were decorated with some hardy shrubs, and Nayla and her angel rescuer made their way down the west side of the hill as fast as possible. Once in a while the man looked over his shoulder to the ridge.

They were only a short distance away from reaching a small group of trees when the first guard reached the top of the hill. The man in front of her stopped immediately and pulled her down to the ground. They crouched behind some leafless bushes.

"Don't move!" he whispered while he kept his eyes focused on the guard. "The eye catches movement. Even with our little cover it will be very difficult for him to see us as long as we sit still. Just become a shrub."

Nayla was glad the man spoke her language. She'd heard that the United Canadian Communities were a hodgepodge of multi-cultural independently governed villages with their own customs and culture; some even had different languages. The man's accent was slightly different than what she was accustomed to, but she had no problem understanding him. He was a primitive-looking man who wore skins and fur that made him blend perfectly into the terrain. She also noted that he carried a bow and arrows, plus a knife.

"A primitive hunter," she concluded.

The man was tall, muscular and clearly in good shape. She estimated him to be in his early forties. His blue eyes sparkled, and inspired confidence and determination.

"See those trees ahead of us?" he pointed. "We should carefully move over there before the guy with the rifle gets to the ridge. They'll provide us with better cover and allow us to continue our escape."

Nayla nodded in agreement.

"Follow me. Do as I do. Move when I move. And hold still when I freeze!"

His piercing eyes sized her up to make sure she understood and would follow his instructions.

Carefully he started to crawl in between the shrubs through the creek bed in the direction of the trees. First he would inch forward, then immediately stop to observe the guard. He did this a few times before he moved on for longer distances. At each stop he kept a close eye on their pursuer.

After a few minutes they reached the tree line. They kept low as they made their way through some leafless poplars until they reached a group of evergreen trees. Once surrounded by spruce they stood up. Just at that time the man with the rifle made it to the top of the ridge.

Nayla watched the guards peer over the valley in a desperate attempt to spot the woman they had been chasing. They had an agitated conversation before finally, in defeat, they turned around and headed back east, down the hill in the direction of the train.

A relieved Nayla faced her rescuer. "Thank you. Thank you for saving me. My name is Nayla!"

"I'm Rowan," he replied, then suggested, "Let's keep moving. We can talk later."

They walked through the forest at a more relaxed pace. Nayla noticed how graceful and silent Rowan was as he moved through the trees. She found herself to be clumsy and noisy. She felt bad each time when a branch broke under her feet and Rowan threw her a disapproving look.

Before they got out of the trees to cross the rest of the valley, Rowan stopped her while he carefully examined the ridge again. There was no sign anymore of their pursuers, but to be on the safe side, he kept using the low-lying terrain and any shrubs or trees to maintain cover. They didn't speak during this time.

A few hours later, after crossing the valley and a few more hills, Nayla heard the deep growl of a dog. She knew they were approaching a homestead. A majestic, almost pitch-black creature ran like the wind towards them. It was only when it stopped a short distance away from them that Nayla realized it was a wolf—a creature of the forest she'd only seen in movies and pictures!

The animal was massive, with paws the size of a man's hand. Its lowered head, threatening growl and uncovered teeth made the hairs on the back of her neck stand up. Nayla glanced at Rowan who stayed completely relaxed and, based on the soft smile she observed on his lips, even thought it was funny.

"Odin, calm down! She's good company."

The wolf's posture changed as soon as Rowan spoke and the animal became more inquisitive than threatening.

"Don't worry. He's not going to hurt you," the trapper comforted Nayla. "He's just not used to company here. Let him sniff you so he can get to know you."

"You have a wolf as a pet?" Nayla asked with a soft, nervous tremble in her voice as the wolf approached her.

"Odin is a half-breed—half wolf, half dog. He has the body and look of a wolf, but inherited his social traits from the dog side of his parents. He loves to be scratched behind his ears."

Odin almost reached to Nayla's waist, and he was making himself thoroughly acquainted with the new visitor, sniffing at her feet, legs, and hands. As the wolf's body posture got more relaxed, Nayla stroked his silky, glistening flank, only to discover the coarse texture of the animal's warm coat. She then scratched him behind the ears.

Odin pushed his head against her hip in delight, so as to encourage her to continue. His tail began spinning in circles.

"He likes you," Rowan laughed, "Things definitely would have been more complicated if he hadn't."

A short distance from where she had met Odin, they reached a large clearing in the mature forest. A sparkling freshwater creek ran alongside a small log cabin. The chimney was breathing out smoke, betraying the cozy warmth inside the homestead.

Most of the rest of the clearing was fenced off with log poles; from behind them, two horses alertly observed their approach. Nayla noticed a smaller pen next to the cabin with some goats and free-range chickens scratching the soil near the creek. She didn't see any other houses, or people.

As Rowan pushed the heavy wooden door of the trapper's cabin open, she felt a new fear creeping upon her. Here she was in a strange land, with a strange man, and with no other living soul around. Had she gotten herself into more trouble?

"But he wouldn't have saved me if he wanted to harm me," she thought.

"Maybe he did it to get you for his own entertainment," another voice inside of her warned.

As Nayla was having this disturbing internal conversation with herself, Rowan took off his warm pelts. Long blond hair fell to his shoulders when he removed the fur coyote hat. He then turned towards her with friendly, inquisitive eyes, seemingly grounded and unmoved by their harrowing escape.

His presence silenced her internal voice of fear. This was a good man, a godsend. The universe was helping her.

"Let's sit down and talk," Rowan said with a warm voice while offering her a cup of steaming soup. "I guess I don't have to tell you that I have a whole lot of questions. So why don't you share your story as to how you came here and what plans you have?"

Nayla stared at the polished wooden floor. She felt hesitant to tell him the whole story. Was it all that smart to share with this man the power of the secret package she carried with her? What if he would return it—together with her—to Carsanto for a ransom? But how could she change the story if she didn't tell him the truth? What reason could she give to be there? And what, in fact, was her plan? She had given it some thought over the last few days while lying in the dark enclosed space of the train car, but hadn't been able to come up with a specific strategy. After all, she was traveling through a part of the world she knew very little about.

While the border between the American Confederacy and the United Canadian Communities was officially open, very few people ventured across it because the lifestyle in the United Canadian Communities was very primitive, and its citizens didn't make efforts to cater to the travel needs of Americans. As a result, very few Americans had explored the country since it didn't offer the luxuries they were used to. Those who did go north mostly traveled there for professional reasons, like the seed train's operators and guards, and the military that guarded the important oil sands industry far north—the lifeblood for the American Confederacy's lifestyle.

George had told Nayla the story of how his grandfather had conquered the rich energy sources there in a time when oil supplies in the world were dwindling. Carsanto had obtained control of the region with its military barely releasing a shot. As it happened, the force had encountered great support from a large number of locals who all favored the American way of life. Those Canadians who didn't approve of the American presence had hardly any weapons to use for resistance. Some guerrilla groups organized isolated attacks in the years after, but ever since the company had started selling the residents terminator seeds and the farmers had become dependent on Carsanto's seed supply, the region had been at peace.

As it turned out, there were very few Canadians who visited the American Confederacy as it was far too expensive for them. The few who came to the country failed to appreciate the unlimited availability of goods and services; rather, they were appalled by the noise, fumes and American lifestyle, and left quickly.

Now, as Nayla looked into the friendly eyes of Rowan, all her concerns faded away. She felt intuitively she was looking into the eyes of a good man, someone she could trust. Besides she had to rely on him as there was no way she was going to be able to reach her destination by herself. She needed help.

And so she told the whole story of why she stole the seeds and her journey north. Rowan listened intently, without interrupting.

"Thank you for saving me, and I apologize for getting you involved in this," she finished while taking the cotton wrap with the seeds from her backpack. "Thank you for saving these seeds. These are seeds that can save the planet and restore diversity to this world. I will continue on my journey to bring these seeds to safety, and I will have to move quickly. The guards will inform the head office there was a stowaway, and it will not take long before they figure out my identity. Carsanto's air force will start dropping in soldiers, and use its helicopters and planes to search this region.

"This package is considered a state secret. I'm sure they have figured out the seeds are missing, and are now considering me an enemy of the state. The man in charge of the security forces is smart, and he'll do anything to get this package back. The guards didn't see you aiding me, so you should be fine, but I have to move on before they get here."

The peaceful silence that fell over the cabin was only accentuated by the crackling of the fire. Nayla observed Rowan carefully to gauge his reaction.

"Why don't you get some sleep," he said calmly while petting Odin, who was spread out on the floor. "I need to think about what we should do next."

Her fear had been that he would send her immediately back out into the forest, to avoid getting further involved. While she had quietly hoped for a more engaged response, she did notice the 'we' in his words. It provided a glimmer of hope that gave her great comfort. She knew Dick would soon know where to look for her, but she considered her situation greatly improved.

Rowan showed her a bed with some warm hides in a small bedroom in the back of the cabin.

"Take some rest," he instructed. "I have to do some chores and take care of the animals before it gets dark."

Before he walked out of the room, a faithful Odin by his side, he turned around and said, "You're a brave woman. What you did was a good thing!"

Nayla smiled. It was good to hear this encouragement and appreciation after all she had been through over the last few days and the doubts she'd had about the sanity of her actions.

Wrapping herself in the pelts, she felt safe for the first time in days. This man, strong like an ox, agile like a cat, and gentle like a deer, was a blessing. He was a sign that luck was on her side! While she listened to the measured swing of an ax splitting wood, she peacefully dozed off.

When Nayla woke up, it was already late morning. The cabin was empty. She opened the door and was greeted by a friendly Odin, who was wagging his tail in anticipation of some attention from his newfound friend.

"Where's your boss?" she asked as she rubbed the imposing animal behind the ears. She looked around outside, but there was no sign of Rowan. "I guess you are waiting for him as well."

The sun had already risen high, and its spring rays were warming up the air. She noticed one of the horses was missing. Its remaining friend was grazing peacefully.

She could hear the sprinkling of the creek and the chattering of some birds. No other sounds were to be heard, just the voice of nature. This place reminded her of the time she had spent in the United States of Bolivar. The setting was different, but this was just as much of a paradise.

"Why do I never think of Dallas, or for that matter, any of the other American cities as paradise?" she wondered while smiling at the sun.

Inside, next to the stone mason fireplace, she noticed a fresh stack of firewood. She put some extra logs on the fire while Odin made himself comfortable on the floor.

On the cutting block in the kitchen area she found some home-baked bread—something she hadn't seen since her time in Bolivar. In America all bread was industrially produced. She cut a slice and slowly chewed it, paying close attention to the tastes of this carefully crafted piece of food.

She also noticed some pots full of dried fruits, dried meat, some honey and jam. Like a curious, hungry child, she helped herself to the new tastes and textures of these unique regional foods.

After she had filled her stomach, she got her grandmother's diary and installed herself next to the crackling fire.

"This doesn't feel like being on the run. It actually feels more like vacation," she thought and smiled, happy that she was able to joke about the situation.

May 11th, 2021

There is hope for the world! I'm somewhat embarrassed to say, but it has come from the French. Or more accurately, from the Quebecois up in Canada. As descendents and cultural brothers of France, they've never lost that slightly arrogant and stubborn spirit of the French and their claim to their unequivocal rights under democracy—namely, that in a democracy the people have the power! The people have the right to a healthy commons—all those resources like land, water and air, but also the internet, road systems and cultural heritage, which sustain our lives and communities.

Actually, come to think of it, in today's world, France seems to be the only real democracy. A democracy where people use their rights to speak out and stand up for what they believe in. Where people are more concerned about what is right than what is law. They don't hesitate to shut the country down if their government or corporations act against the best interest of the people—even if that's deemed to be illegal. The results are: a great standard of living; the best healthcare in the world; waterways free of dams; a country that leads in alternative energy; a culture that knows how to enjoy life (just think about the wine, cheese and cuisine!); and an intact commons—it belongs to the people and you better not touch it.

The French who always knew how to appreciate good food, are also front runners in organic agriculture. And that was actually what I was going to write about. Not in France, but in Quebec. I get so easily distracted! Then again, I was taught that with journaling you just need to follow your thoughts. As you noticed,

63

they're not at all linear. (Smile—I wonder if I should make it clear in this diary when I am joking or laughing with my own writing. Just to make sure that you wouldn't think I am so serious all the time.)

So back to what I was going to write about: the French up north and their sustainable farming practices—something dear to my heart since I've started my own garden. The seeds have now all germinated, and I have been so excited to see these little plants grow. They also make great company. You can tell them anything and they never argue! Just thought I should quickly share that. Now back to the French (smile). No, seriously!

The Quebecois have decided en masse that enough is enough. Over the last decades several studies have demonstrated connections between the chemicals that are being used to grow our food and the chemicals that end up in the human body. We now even breast-feed our infants dioxin because their mother's milk has become contaminated. (Did I write that last time in my diary as well? Can you tell this bothers me?) So far no action has been taken to stop this chemical poisoning, because it could harm the economy. And of course, no decision or action could be taken before it has been proven beyond any doubt that the economy wouldn't be endangered as a result!

And what about the infants?! Who fights for the health of our children?! Politicians are so in bed with big business because that's where they'll find the dollars to get elected. We should have learned years ago from the French. We should have stood up for our rights as a people—our rights to healthy food, clean water and fresh air! How were we ever able to forget about those rights? Abandon them in return for some numbers on a bank account—some numbers that represented some green print on pieces of paper? How did we ever confuse money with the real resources of life: clean air, pure water and a healthy soil? But I am digressing …again.

The French Canadians have finally done what the French have shown us for years. For the last four days they've shut the entire province down and it's feared—I hope it happens—that the strike will ripple through the entire country. The protestors are demanding healthy food! Organic and sustainably farmed food! They want the government to prescribe by law that all food sold in the province has to be chemical free, organic or sustainably farmed. In addition, they're demanding that all farming practices in the province be free of chemicals, organic and done *without tilling the soil. The last point isn't only because of their food concerns, but because it helps in the fight against global warming. According to the Rodale Institute in Pennsylvania, soil that isn't tilled but instead is organically farmed with cover crops can function as a carbon storage bank and absorb up to thirty percent more carbon. If the entire landmass in the USA and Canada would apply such farming practices, the countries' annual CO_2 emissions would be reduced by ten to twenty percent.*

The Quebec farmers have blocked all highways with their farming equipment. The truckers have given them support with their big rigs, and the university students are creating havoc in the cities. Some student groups are even calling for the people to leave the cities and move into the country to live in small villages that can be sustained by the surrounding land. They argue that a society with large cities cannot be sustainable because the landmass around the metropolitan areas can't provide enough food for the inhabitants.

By the end of the first day the strike was deemed illegal. However, that didn't deter the people who had discovered their courage to stand up and fight for what should inherently be theirs. Something that democratic governments— governments that are truly by the people and for the people—should have taken care of in the first place. The police tried to break up some of the barricades during the second day, but when a farmer got killed in the skirmishes and fellow strikers rammed the police patrol with their heavy tractor, law enforcement officers across the region backed down, fearing a full-fledged civil uprising.

Sad—and somewhat comical at the same time—the media is still reporting this story from the point of view that the province is under siege. When will they rediscover their roots, and report the voice of the people? Clearly the majority of the population is behind this action; when will newsmakers take up their responsibility and speak for the people? Of course, I know, most media is owned by big corporations—businesses with an interest in safeguarding the economy and spreading chemicals on our fields. I wonder how many executives of chemical companies feed their families organic food?

How could we, in a true democracy, ever allow our storytellers to be owned by corporations? Surely we could have come up with a legal structure that protected the independence of the media—a structure that allowed the media to be the voice of and for the people.

But who knows what the future will bring? Now that a substantial group of people in North America is standing up for their rights, now that people once again are fighting for what is right—for the health of their children, for their commons, for the things that should be naturally theirs—now things might change. There is hope for the world: hope that the actions of the French up north will ripple out—not just in Canada, but all over this North American continent. There is hope for the world!

Odin suddenly lifted his head and pointed his ears in the direction of the door. He then stood up and took a step to the entrance, letting Nayla know someone was approaching.

The sound of neighing horses greeting each other upon their reunion told her that Rowan had returned. When she opened the door, he was dragging a deer to a shed. Odin eagerly went to check out the dead animal. Clearly, Rowan's hunt had been good today.

A little later he came out of the hut and smiled as he walked up to her.

"Well, that's one less headache. At least we'll have meat for the next few weeks. Let's have some food and talk. After, we'll smoke this meat and prepare for our journey. Do you ride?"

As Nayla was trying to process what she just had heard, she was only able to stammer out, "Yes!" Her heart was rejoicing, and she shouted "Yes!" again. Luck was on her side indeed!

"Let's barbecue these tenderloins," he said, holding out his hand with two pieces of fresh meat while Odin was feasting on some scraps by the shed.

Soon Nayla was enjoying some of the tastiest and most tender meat she had ever eaten.

Abruptly, Rowan started talking. This time it was Nayla's turn to listen.

"Four years ago my wife and my two children were killed. We had a small farm in the foothills just outside Huntingville. The berry season had been bad in the mountains that year, and in early fall several grizzlies descended from the Rockies in search of food. There was plenty of game for them in the foothills, and the berry and oat farms provided an abundance of feed.

"One day my wife, Heather, told me she was afraid of bringing the boys to school in the village. On the previous days they had seen a grizzly in the vicinity of the trail to the town."

At this point, Rowan's eyes flooded with guilt. He hesitated before continuing.

"I didn't listen. I told her we'd had bears around ever since we settled here. As long as man respects the bear's space, we can live together in harmony. That was the way of our culture—how we had learned to live in peace with our environment. One with nature, instead of trying to dominate it or control it!

"So like a brave woman she faced her fear, ready to learn and find peace within a new experience. She hitched up the horses and got the boys in the wagon. Ryan and Brandon waved at me when they left. Heather's eyes spoke of love, and her confident smile told me she was going to prove her bravery and independence. It was the last time I saw them alive."

Silence engulfed the cabin while the tear-filled eyes of this strong man searched the floor's wood-grains for support.

"When she didn't return, I took one of the horses and rode to the village. I wasn't even halfway before I noticed that their tracks had gone off the trail and ended at the edge of the cliff. Down below I saw the broken wagon and the three lifeless bodies of my dearest love and my two boys."

He took a deep breath, then continued, "Next to the tracks were the prints of a grizzly. Whatever happened I'll never know. The bear might have spooked the horses. A wheel might have slid off the edge and pulled both the wagon and the horses into the depths below."

Rowan paused and stared in silence into the fire. Nayla could feel his pain.

When he spoke again, his tone had changed. It had turned to ice, like the voice of a heart which, when robbed of love, takes shelter from the raw anguishing pain within cold walls of stone.

"Since everything at our home reminded me of them, I torched the place, headed closer to the mountains, and settled here. I chose a life of solitude. At first I took enormous risks when I started trapping. I had nothing to live for. I was merely a shadow of myself, an aimless soul walking around with a death wish. I killed several grizzly bears, but found neither peace nor relief of pain in doing so."

As Rowan told his story, his voice softened again, and a faint smile appeared on his lips.

"One day I found a wounded fawn. It had a huge gash in its hind leg and could not stand anymore. Based on the surrounding tracks, its mother had been killed and dragged away by a cougar. It was a miracle the cat had left the little one. I took it home and nurtured it back to health. That deer gave me life again. Once again I had someone to care for. My heart rejoiced when the fawn was able to stand. I smiled with its first steps, and for the first time in years was able to enjoy the sunrise again. I stopped trapping, and just hunted for what I needed. The forest, the hills and the towering mountains to the west gradually gained their colors back.

"I saw the beauty and perfection in nature's ways. I enjoyed the birth of a little goat, was grateful for the eggs of my chickens, talked to the vegetables I was growing in the garden, and prayed to the deer people who offered their life to feed me. A life for a life! And so I came to understand the cycle of life and death. How both are one and the same. For something to grow, for something to live, something always has to die. And through death new life is fed. My heart found peace again as I accepted the perfection of the unfolding universe, and so I learned to be grateful for the loving woman and two great boys who had crossed my path.

"During that same time Odin entered my life. A farmer's dog mated with a wolf. Afraid that the pup would be killing his farm animals, the farmer gave me the pup because I lived in the forest. I put little Odin with my goats; they ended up nursing him. Now they're his family. Odin protects this place and his pack of animals. He has been a great friend who further opened my heart and brought joy to this place.

"Since I found my peace again, I've been waiting for a sign that would reconnect me with the rest of the world, an omen for when to move on."

He looked at Nayla, determination in his eyes. "You crossed my path and can use my help. Never again will I neglect to help a woman in need."

Nayla was glad for the offered support. But she didn't want the trapper to feel obligated because of what happened to his family. When she made a move to speak, he motioned her to stay silent.

"I'm going to bring you across these mountains to the coast," he spoke steadfastly, "and if you don't mind the company, Odin and I would like to travel with you to the United States of Bolivar. I've heard of some Incan ruins high up in a mountain range they call majestic— the Andes. As a child I always dreamed of traveling and exploring the different regions of this world. It's time to follow my dream again. I'm going to help you and continue all the way south, as far as the land can carry me."

Nayla heard these words, and was glad Rowan wasn't just putting himself at risk for her. He had a personal reason to help her. The universe in its perfection had brought them together. Each one was receiving from the other what they needed at that point on their journey of life. It was serendipitous!

"We'll need the rest of the day and tomorrow to get ready for the trek. We will pack the grains and dried fruits, smoke the meat of the deer and get you some pelts to wear. There's still snow in the mountains, and you stick out in your strange outfit," Rowan smiled, laughter present in his eyes.

Wired, Dick stormed into the office.

"We got her, George! We got Nayla!"

"You got her? Where was she? Is she okay? Do you have the germinator seeds back?"

"Well, we don't exactly have her," Dick corrected quickly, cursing inwardly at himself. Once again, he'd been too excited. "We know where she is."

"So, where is she?" George demanded.

"She's far up north, in the United Canadian Communities near Huntingville."

"Well, she certainly had us looking in the wrong direction," George observed, somewhat puzzled. "I could have sworn that she would have gone south. Then again, she must have guessed we would think that. Why did she go north?"

"I've no idea. The only reason I can think of is that it was the safest place for her to go. But they don't have production seed farms up north, so she can't cultivate the seeds for large-scale distribution. My bet is that she'll try to find a boat to take her back south via the ocean. Our navy already has received orders to search any ship destined for the United States of Bolivar. It won't be easy for her to slip through that net."

"How did she get there?" George asked, curiosity in his voice.

"You are not particularly going to like this part," Dick stressed. "She hitched one of the seed trains."

But Dick was wrong: George had to smile in admiration at this brilliant escape of the woman whom he still carried in his heart despite the seed theft and her clearly different vision for the world.

"Three days ago some of the train guards saw a woman run from the train," Dick continued his report. "They chased her, but she escaped. I can't believe they didn't brief me earlier! But I'll make sure they will pay for that and learn their lesson."

"So what's next?" George inquired—interested to get the seeds back, but more concerned about Nayla's fate. He still had to work out a plan on how to save his sweetheart while at the same time maintaining his integrity as the leader of this great corporation and nation.

World control was so close! But he didn't want to lose Nayla; he wanted her by his side. After all, what was world control without someone to share it with?

Until Nayla had come along, he had been driven only by ambition. But Nayla had opened a different world to him—a world more fulfilling and colorful. He had learned to really love, and enjoyed being loved in return. Now, he wanted both to realize his vision, and to share it with his love.

To do that, he needed to resolve this situation. But Nayla had crossed the border, and things had gone international! If he could have stopped her before she had left the country, he might have been able to keep her escapade under wraps—although Dick would have given him a hard time for that. Was he about to lose both his dream and his love, all because he had feared bringing her into the picture at an earlier stage? He had to come up with *something!*

"I'll fly up north together with a team of Black Guards. Ten of us will search the area where she was last seen," the General advised George. "We'll use the new long distance, high speed helicopters which can also provide air backup for our search. Once we are there we can refuel at our base along the railroad one hour south from Huntingville. We should have her soon. I've already informed the Canadian authorities of this action. They weren't happy, but when I reminded them where they got their seed from they became more amenable. I'm leaving tomorrow."

"Just make sure you bring her back unharmed, Dick!" George said resolutely. "Unharmed!" he stressed. "We will interrogate her here. As smart as she is, she might have hidden the seeds, and in such case without her cooperation we'll never get them back." As he said these words, George thought this should sound like an acceptable reason to Dick.

"Given how important this matter is, I want to be involved in the interrogation," George continued, looking Dick sternly in the eyes to make sure he understood how earnest he was about this.

"I'll bring her here as healthy as I find her," Dick scoffed. "Now I'm going to make arrangements for tomorrow. I'll keep you up-to-date about our progress by satellite phone."

As he watched Dick depart, George didn't feel any joy over the prospect of getting the germinator seeds back. His sole concern was over Nayla's safety. The absence of information about her current circumstances and health left him with a nagging anxiety in his heart: *How was all this going to play out?*

As a leader, he was expected to be in control, but with Nayla he never was, and never would be. She always pushed him, asked questions no one else did—or dared to ask. She acted impulsively and unpredictably, in ways that forced him to explore the unknown. It was a territory for which he had no maps, nor experience. An area of new discoveries and personal growth! This time though, he felt more like he was floating rudderless on the ocean, an imminent hurricane approaching.

N ayla enjoyed the radiant heat of the fire on her skin. Tomorrow morning they would set out to cross the mountains towards the coast. She was cherishing this last night in the safety and comfort of the cabin. Rowan was tidying up some last things outside in the company of his inseparable four-legged companion.

Over the last thirty-six hours she'd learned to butcher a deer, kill and clean chickens and sew pelts. She had been surprised with the humbling and satisfying experience of providing for her own food. The food was offered by nature—as of course it always is! But in the American Confederacy it was presented like it originated from the supermarket. There, meat came out of a box—not from the muscle of an animal, or so it seemed. And when people ate steak, they typically didn't wonder which muscle it was, what kind of life the animal had had and if it was killed with respect and gratitude.

Rowan had the same connection with nature Julian had. She had never been able to feel this in her heart. But the work of the last day—the milking of the goats, the primitive butchering and the smoking of the meat—had filled her with gratitude. Gratitude for the goats' offer of milk and the deer's offer of life—it was a life given to sustain her on the journey ahead. It was so much easier to develop such appreciation while living in nature, where the daily interactions were continual reminders of the interdependency of all living things, including human beings.

For the first time Nayla felt the deep love and adoration Julian had for this earth—this paradise. The modest life Julian had invited her to in the United States of Bolivar might not be that bad and difficult after all. Julian might have been right in his observations the evening before he left. While she missed Gaya and yearned to have her with her, she now understood how the American Dream would have dimmed the light in her daughter's soul and the love in her heart for all living creatures. She wished Julian could have been here now and seen her; she imagined sharing this work with both Julian and Gaya—her family. She longed for the day of their reunion.

"Would it ever be possible for people who live in cities to develop such understanding and respect for nature?" she wondered as she opened her grandmother's diary.

June 21st, 2021

My silent, cherished hope has come true. What the Quebecois started a little over a month ago has now jumped south of the border. Today, together with tens of thousands of people, we walked the streets of New York. The same scenes were seen in five other northeastern States. If the Canadians have the right to healthy food, we want that too!

The Quebecois demonstrated that a determined mass of people always wins—something the French people have been showing the world for years. After a ten day strike in Quebec, with cars burning in the cities and a provincial government under siege, the governing powers gave in. They immediately passed new legislation that required all foods sold in the province of Quebec to be organic within five years. In addition, all industrial farms had to be dismantled and returned to independent farmers within twelve months. An immediate stop was put to all tilling of the soil, and cover cropping will be mandatory from now on—both measures to combat global warming. And last but not least, within the next three years all farmers have to adopt organic practices. A substantial budget has been allocated to facilitate this transfer of farming methods, but as one government official put it, "This is the will of the people. When our citizens desire farming practices that provide healthy produce, we, as representatives of the people, provide the laws and means for such vision to germinate. Now it's up to the people to use these laws and financial means to realize this vision of healthy food growing from a healthy soil."

Over the next two weeks, people all over Canada stood up for their rights to healthy food and chemical-free farms. All over the country provincial governments passed the same laws.

Now it's our turn. Just think of it: Why do we even have to fight for this, the right to healthy food?!

And guess who leads the struggle in this country? Guess who finally said, 'Enough is enough,' and demanded healthy foods? Women! Mothers, grandmothers and pregnant women—women who care about the future of their children! With thousands we marched as sisters, demanding that those who rule in the name of the people put the right to healthy food before the financial interest of corporations and the powerful elite of this country. Men joined too, but women led the march. Female taxi and truck drivers blocked major highways and junctions in the city; their male colleagues soon followed. Groups of women all over the city marched for their rights. I was having coffee with a friend when some women marched by. We heard their rallying cries, looked at each other, and stood up and joined them. Block after block the crowd grew like a swelling river being fed by new springs and tributaries on its way to the ocean. As news spread around the city other groups started to march.

I shouted my lungs out. It was like all my anger about the unjustness of corporate power and today's elitist governmental rule came out. All fear was gone; together we were strong! Freed of the shackles of fear and apathy, the mass was invigorated. America is a democracy, and today it was showing just that. This country is governed by the people and for the people, and if any politicians had different thoughts they were pulverized today. It was exhilarating—such an empowering experience!

The cool thing was that nothing was really organized. There were no real leaders. It was more like an organic eruption of the masses—people who'd held their voices for years suddenly came to realize that their neighbors felt the same. Their silent suffering found relief in the public display of pain and anger. It empowered their spirits to stand up and fight for what really mattered: the health and future of their children!

As we were marching and shouting our lungs out, I saw policemen standing powerless along the way. Some even joined in with us. I realized power is something that is given. We, the people, had given it for years to a government that was more concerned with the financial interests of the rich and powerful. We could have stood up years ago, but instead we worked to pay off our personal debt. We could have spoken out years ago, but instead kept to superficial conversation in fear of standing out. We could have questioned things years ago, but instead watched television to entertain us and rob us of the time to think about what really matters.

Today, all that changed. Today we took our power back! It was like how a crack in a dam allows the eroding power of rushing water to destroy the entire structure. Today this country belonged once again to the people.

The dam has cracked. Now nothing will be able to hold back the rushing water on its way to the sea. Nothing can hold back the power of people to gain the right to healthy food. Today the American people found their dream again—a dream that unleashed power and passion. Today my heart glows with pride and happiness. This is my country, a people's country! There is hope for the world!

Through time and space Nayla felt oddly connected to those women who stood up to protect their children. Her heart filled with gratitude for the words in this diary, for her grandmother's life and for the sharing of her experience through these pages. It was the voice of a young woman passionate about creating a sustainable world. The voice of a soul with purpose, but no answers—one that was searching for solutions. The voice of a heart that becomes aware of its power as it wakes up, loses its fear, and acts on what is just.

"Thank you," Nayla whispered in turn, back through the gates of space and time. "Thank you for guiding me."

Rowan's words of respect and her grandmother's struggle to make a difference and stand up for the children gave her comfort. Stealing the germinating seeds and escaping the country had been impulsive, but it had been the right thing to do.

And it seemed to Nayla that when on a righteous path, the universe became one's accomplice and offered help along the way.

When Nayla opened the door, the chilly early morning air bit her face. It was just before dawn—the twilight time before the sun warms the day with its golden rays. The cabin had been empty when she woke up, so she'd put on the pelts Rowan had given her the night before. They used to be his wife's.

"This is the only thing that is going to keep you warm. Besides, you will have to blend in as a local," he'd said matter-of-factly without displaying any obvious emotional reaction to seeing something of his late wife's.

That alone was proof of how he'd learned to accept and appreciate what life offered him. To reiterate that, though, he'd added, "I am glad they will serve a purpose again."

The fresh smell of the forest that exhaled its sweet morning dew pleased Nayla's senses, and reassured her about leaving the safety of the cabin. As she did so, she spied Rowan almost immediately.

"Good morning," Rowan greeted her while an excited Odin ran up. "Ready to ride?"

He had packed the saddle bags of the two horses with their food, pelts and some basic camp supplies. He'd also tied a pair of goats to his horse, as he planned to offer them as a gift to the first farmer they would encounter.

"If you don't mind, we'll eat later this morning while we're on the trail," he suggested. "I lived in circumstances where food isn't always instantly available. It taught me that we can get by with very little if we only eat when we are truly hungry. In my experience, the longer we let our stomachs rest in the morning, the longer it takes before we crave food. If you're all set, then we're ready to go!"

Rowan smiled eagerly with the excitement of an explorer ready to set off to where no man has gone before.

Nayla tightened her new trapper's boots and closed the door behind her.

"I'm ready," she smiled. "Let's bring these seeds to safety."

As they both got into the saddle, an enthusiastic Odin ran around the horses, jumping up and down with an untamable desire to set out on the adventure ahead of them.

"We have a choice. We can take the northern pass or the southern pass through the mountains," Rowan informed her as his horse walked around in a little circle like the needle of a compass trying to mark the right direction. "Which way do you think we should go?"

"South!" Nayla answered resolutely. "When Dick and his troops come after me they'll expect me to go further north."

"South it is!" Rowan turned his horse on the southern trail, leading the two goats behind him.

As soon as he chose the direction, Odin ran ahead on the trail with an enthusiastic bark. Nayla trotted her horse forward to catch up until she was riding right next to Rowan.

Before she left the clearing in the forest, she looked one last time towards the cabin that had provided her comfort and safety during the last few days. This had been a place of good luck for her. Not only had she received rest here, she'd found a guiding companion who now had joined her quest to save the germinator seeds.

"The southern pass is a good choice," Rowan said when she caught up with him. "There will be less snow and it's a nicer trail. Two decades ago the snow pack in the mountains would have been really thick around this time of the year. But with the warming up of the planet, spring comes earlier each year. A lot of the snow will have melted by now, and we should be able to cross easily.

"So tell me, what's the United States of Bolivar like? I better get myself a bit educated about the destination we are heading for," he smiled with a new twinkle in his eyes—the sparkling curiosity of the adventurer's spirit.

"Where do you want me to start?" Nayla laughed. "It's certainly very different from what I've seen so far of this part of the world."

"Well, just start with anything—how do the people live there? Do they have cities, or do they live in sustainable communities like here? Is the region polluted like the American Confederacy, or do people live in harmony with nature?"

"Well, the country is built on the application of sustainable technologies and a focus on the common good of its people. There are no excesses in the United States of Bolivar, and people live in harmony with their environment. The standard of living and comfort is high in comparison with this part of the world—although not as high as in the American Confederacy. Nevertheless, the society has a net zero footprint on the planet.

"The Bolivarians are a proud people for whom family, diversity and collaboration stand central. In order to understand the culture, you have to go all the way back in time to Simon Bolivar. He was a military commander and politician who liberated South America from the Spanish during the days of colonialism in the first half of the 19th century.

"Bolivar dreamed of a united Americas. It was a dream which over the years was revived by several Latin American freedom fighters. The dream wasn't realized until early in the 21st century, when Venezuelan President Hugo Chavez used the economic power of oil and mining resources to start shaping a new economy for the Latin American countries. He eventually was able to unite Venezuela, Colombia, Bolivia, Ecuador, Peru and Cuba into one United Republic with autonomous states. When Brazil decided to join a few years later, all other countries on the continent rapidly followed. The constitution was drafted in such a way that each country maintained its autonomous leadership and unique culture. Cultural diversity was celebrated, and became part of the pride of the Bolivarian people.

"Around the same time the world's attention focused on combating global warming. Chavez decided to concentrate the research and know-how of the newly united country on sustainable technology. Within a decade the United States of Bolivar had become a leader in this field.

"The air car industry is a great example of their innovation. It is also the backbone of the Bolivarian sustainable economy. The car is built completely of compostable materials like soy-based plastics, and powered by compressed air. On top of that, it's affordable for every family in the country. With its production the country has proven how their cooperative organizational institutions, their sustainable technologies and their alternative power systems can create products that enhance the quality of life while simultaneously respecting nature. Approaching economic and technological advancement in such a manner has allowed the United States of Bolivar to continuously improve the quality of life for its citizens while limiting its footprint on the planet.

"Since the use of resources has been directed to benefit the people of the country in a closed loop production cycle which allows for one hundred percent recycling of old products, the technologically advanced country doesn't have any of the health and pollution problems found in the American Confederacy. Its healthcare program, which was initiated by the state of Cuba, is based on disease prevention. The concept provides healthcare at one-tenth of the cost of the American system while at the same time delivering better results.

"The country's culture is built on four pillars: First, all organization is for the good of all. This is reflected in community ownership of large organizations—by the people for the people. It's also visible in the measurements of financial results, on an organizational, state and national level, which take into account environmental and social impacts. They call it 'True Triple Bottom Line.'

"Second, all human beings are treated as equals. This is reflected in healthcare and education for all, and a financial reward system without extremes. This last aspect is seen by some as a limit to their potential and is the reason why people like my parents have gone in search of the American Dream and the wealth and luxuries that can be found in the American Confederacy.

"Third is the recognition that free entrepreneurship allows humanity to develop faster and more efficiently. Control and uniformity have been traded for chaos and diversity, which are seen as the ultimate roots for creative expression.

"And last but not least, the Bolivarians have abandoned private land ownership. Nature, in their view, belongs to all people and other living creatures together.

"But now it is your turn," Nayla smiled at her traveling partner. "Soon we will travel through villages in this country and meet other people. And I don't know anything about your customs. If I have to fit in and act as a local, I need to understand your local culture."

"Fair enough," Rowan grinned. "Where do you want me to start?"

They both laughed. Nayla enjoyed Rowan's company. He was down to earth, relaxed and had a good sense of humor. And he made her feel safe.

"Well, why don't you start with describing the first village we will encounter and the customs of its people, so that I know what to expect and how to behave."

"The community we are heading for is called 'Davidstown.' It's a Christian community."

"Why do you mention the community's religion first?" Nayla interrupted. This felt rather strange to her. "Are there no people in the community who follow a different religious path?"

"No, there aren't. The Christian faith is what defines the community—so you need to know this first. Their spiritual belief defines every aspect of their community. It defines their values on which their laws are based; it prescribes their dress, their food, their relationships—all their customs.

"Based on that question, I've a feeling that your knowledge of the United States of Bolivar far exceeds that of the United Canadian Communities. Did you skip those history classes in school?" Rowan winked.

"Well, I grew up in Bolivar," Nayla explained somewhat embarrassed. "Seduced by the American Dream my parents moved to the American Confederacy when I was thirteen. It was their dream for me to become rich and famous. I became rich following the American Dream, and I guess I became famous in some ways."

Nayla paused for a while before continuing. "But if I succeed now, my victory will take that Dream down."

"Why do you want to take 'the Dream' down? And how would bringing those seeds to the United States of Bolivar end it?" Rowan asked more seriously.

The conversation had taken a different turn. It had brought Nayla to a point where she wasn't only thinking about the importance of saving the seeds for the purpose of diversity on the planet—for saving the wellbeing of her child and of all children of all species of all times. For the first time, Nayla was considering the larger economic and political impact of her actions. There was no way back anymore! If she failed, she most likely would be sentenced to death. If she succeeded, life as she used to know it—the American Dream she had lived, and for so long embraced and defended—would cease to exist. Either way the consequences were severe—of a magnitude that somehow did not seem to correspond with the impulsive deed of stealing some seeds. But then again, every time people stand up for what is right—fight for life itself—the outcome travels forward through time like the sound waves of a life-enthralling drumbeat.

"Well, I didn't set out to take the American Dream down, nor do I particularly want to do that," she replied thoughtfully. "But the economic power of the American Confederacy is entirely based on the production, sales and export of terminator seeds. The world's annual dependency on new seeds for its food production provides a constant flow of revenue for the country. It allows Americans to buy silk from China, diamonds and gold from Africa, and the foods they desire from any region in the world.

"The aim to control the global seed industry was a brilliant strategy to rule the world because all people are dependent on seeds to grow their food—and the terminator seeds created that dependency, in particular the mutating kind I developed for Carsanto.

"We introduced such seeds a number of years ago all over the planet. The terminator genes spread into any remaining traditional seed harvests in local regions, creating the targeted dependency on Carsanto's seed production. The only region that has refused to use any seeds with terminator technology so far has been the United States of Bolivar. While that has been a barrier to world control for Carsanto, the Bolivarians were in no position to threaten Carsanto's dominant rule in the rest of the world. The mutating germinator seeds I carry with me can change all that.

"The large-scale seed farms in the United States of Bolivar can cultivate mutating germinator seeds and sell them all over the planet. Such seeds will allow farmers to return to their sustainable agricultural methods. Once again they will be able to save seeds from their harvests to plant the following year. It will free them from the dependency on Carsanto's seeds. It will also destroy the stable and constant flow of income for the American Confederacy and therefore the entire American Dream. The country couldn't provide its citizens with an unlimited supply of products and services if its seed exports were to collapse. Neither would it be able to pay its large security force that protects its resources around the planet—resources that are needed to produce those goods and deliver them to the people."

Rowan listened intently, although he was scanning the environment continuously for any threats on the trail.

"It was never my intention to end this way of life for the American people. You know, I lived and enjoyed that lifestyle! And the Americans are good people. George, the man on top of Carsanto

83

and the effective leader of the country, is a kind man. His vision of world control has its merits; some of the most important aspects of that vision are order and peace. I have no desire to hurt him or destroy his dream. But it seems that events have pitched us against each other."

The pain in Nayla's eyes disclosed her internal struggle. The success of her mission would mean the destruction of the dream of a man she used to love, and whom she still loved in some odd way. Nayla was glad Rowan didn't query her any further on these matters, and decided to change the subject.

"Once again, I've been doing all the talking, and meanwhile I don't know anything about the village we're heading for. You've told me that it is a Christian village, and that the religion permeates the culture. That's all I know," she said.

"Well, I think it might help you if I first share some of the history of the United Canadian Communities. The great uprising of the twenties was based on a vision of community—or better, a collection of independent communities that could be sustained by the surrounding land, sea and rivers. It was recognized that technology, art and culture were important. However, it was deemed unacceptable to damage the essentials of life—a healthy soil, pure water and clean air—for the sake of progress or material value. How could anything with a negative impact on life itself even be called progress, or be considered to have value?

"In order to ensure the protection of the soil, air and water, all land, waterways, lakes and seas were all returned to the commons. It was reasoned that those elements were essential for life, and had to be equally accessible to all human and non-human life. This caused the conservative Americans to term the uprising a 'Communist revolution.' Nothing, however, was further from the truth. Still, the claim put the living fear in the population of the southern half of the continent. It was the start of a long and violent conflict in which one people fought for the dream of a harmonious lifestyle and the other part of the population tried to defend its freedom, which according to its media was under threat by the dark forces of communism.

"Private enterprise was actually pivotal to the economic life of the new settlements. Local craftsmanship and entrepreneurship became central in the newly formed society, as all industrial production was abandoned due to its environmental impact. And so it is until this day. People moved away from the cities and developed small villages, each with their own independent economies and governments. I guess you could say the villages are more like clans or tribes. They have their own specialties in crafts and food production, and an active trade takes place between them. Every village is self-governed. People founded their villages on the basis of their value system together with other like-minded citizens. As a result the country is a collection of diverse communities, each with a well-defined culture. The only thing all the villages have in common is the mutual ownership—or should I say, lack of ownership—of land, water and air.

"And Davidstown is a Christian settlement. Not all Christian settlements are the same; the rules and cultures are often different depending on how the communities have interpreted their religious texts. However, in all cases their spiritual path defines their customs. Davidstown is very conservative—"

Rowan interrupted the cultural lesson mid-sentence. He stopped his horse and focused intently on Odin. His four-legged friend stood just a short distance ahead—ears pointed forward, muscles tensed and eyes focused on the distant sky.

Seconds later, both Nayla and Rowan could hear the strange sound that had alarmed Odin. The roar didn't belong to the breathtaking landscape they were riding through, and was approaching from the south. Confusion and worry were written on Rowan's face as the sound got louder and became more distinct.

"Helicopters!" Nayla shouted as she detected two black dots in the sky. "We've got to find shelter."

"Follow me!" Rowan responded, cutting the goats loose and spurring his horse to a gallop.

Nayla prodded her horse forward to join his, and soon both she and Rowan were flying over the wide open plain towards the distant evergreen forest. The fresh spring air rushed by Nayla's face, lifting her hair.

The herd instinct of the goats had kicked in. They could not quite keep up with the horses, but they followed, running as hard as they could in fear of an unknown danger that had put their herd on the run.

As they approached the tree line, Rowan trotted along the forest edge until he found a wildlife trail. He led his horse under the protective green cover.

In single file the horses walked on the winding path that had been carved by the forest's inhabitants—deer, elk, bear and cougar. All the while, the roar in the skies had increased in volume.

Rowan finally dismounted, stroking his horse in appreciation of a job well done as he tied it under a giant spruce. The old growth canopy was large enough to provide shelter for all the animals and their two-legged companions. A restless Odin ran nervously through the surrounding trees as the thundering engines of the metal birds of doom approached fast.

Nayla peeked upward through the trees, and suddenly detected the black steel war machines traveling high above in the sky.

"They're coming after me!" she called out while her eyes locked on Rowan's to stress the danger of the situation.

"T his is where we last saw her," the train guard nervously showed Dick as they arrived on the ridge. "She wasn't running all that far in front of us. I lost sight of her once she got on top of these hills, and by the time I arrived here and could look into the valley beyond, she was gone. Vanished into thin air! My mate took a few shots at her while she was still climbing this hill, but he was far behind me and kept missing her."

The train guard kept on talking fast.

"I was closing in on her. We only noticed her when she was already halfway between the track and the hills. She was a good runner," he continued, sounding more fearful in the absence of any signs of approval from the General.

Dick didn't even hear the man anymore. His gaze had locked onto the valley and the surrounding terrain as he tried to pick up the trail of his prey.

Carefully he scanned the area. He imagined Nayla running, out of breath, reaching the crest of this hill, bullets flying around her and two men closing in on her. What would she have done? What thoughts were able to enter the mind of a fearful human being on the run? One would have expected her to run straight on, down into the valley beyond, away from the approaching danger. Had she done that though, there would have been no way to hide. She would have been in plain view of the guards when they reached the top.

Maybe she felt a little relief about being out of sight for a few minutes, out of range of the gun. She could have stopped, giving her heart some rest and getting oxygen into her lungs while her eyes examined the area around her, searching for cover.

The General had to hand it to her: Nayla was good. He was going to enjoy this chase. As he envisioned what Nayla would have done, he noticed some trees down to the south in the valley, and a creek bed running towards them. The brush there might have given her enough cover from the guards.

He also noticed a similar situation to the north. Yet while the northern group of trees in the valley was closer, it was far smaller, and the creek bed running down from the hills was located further away than the southern one was.

"Imbeciles," he thought of the guards. There had only been one logical escape route, and the shrunken minds of these useless men had been unable to detect it. They had let her slip right through their fingers.

Just when the guard opened his mouth again to continue his babbling, Dick signaled to one of his men. Promptly, firm hands grabbed the hapless man by the arm and led him towards the helicopters next to the train tracks. The man looked hopelessly over his shoulder to the General in an attempt to detect at last some sign of appreciation, but it was in vain. The General had already forgotten about the guard; his mind was focused on his prey like a bloodhound honing in on the fresh trail of a wounded animal.

Dick started to hike along the hilltop towards the southern creek bed, imagining every move of the woman who'd been on the run here just a few days ago.

"She's smart, but doesn't know the area. She'll need food and water. Such a run will wear her out; the nights are cold. She'll try to find help from villagers," his mind raced on.

Then he spoke out loud. "She must have made it to those trees," he pointed, talking to his personally selected elite guards. "Let's try to find some tracks where the creek bed enters the forest."

The appearance of the helicopters had changed the mood of the day. It had reminded Nayla and Rowan of the danger they were in, and the urgency to move on.

For the rest of the day the two rode in silence, alert and with senses heightened. Their minds, in quiet solitude, imagined scenarios of what was to come. Both realized their mission's success or failure would determine the future of the world—a future that was lodged in the germinating power of the tiny little seeds in Nayla's precious package.

"Odin, heel," Rowan ordered as the first farms came into sight.

The instant obedience of this smart animal with its wild wolf appearance impressed Nayla.

"He can really scare people, and as a result put himself in harm's way," Rowan explained in response to her facial expression. "However, when people see him walk right next to my horse, his manners give them comfort."

Nayla saw some women on the main trail that led to the village. They were dressed in long robes and long-sleeved colorful blouses.

"You never explained what I should expect, and how I should behave in this culture," Nayla whispered anxiously. "My leather pants and jacket are so different."

"Don't worry," Rowan replied. "It doesn't matter that we look different. That's because we belong to a different culture. They wouldn't expect us to be dressed like they are. Just respect their customs."

"But what *are* their customs? You never told me specifically, so I've no idea what will please them or offend them."

Her concern went unanswered, for they arrived at the first farm just when one of the local women got there. Nayla assumed this was the woman of the house.

Rowan greeted her, and asked to speak to the farmer. The middle-aged woman glanced apprehensively at Odin who stood right next to Rowan's horse, then nodded shyly, walking quickly through the front yard like a servant on a mission. She disappeared through the heavy wooden door.

The farmhouse had thick walls with rounded corners. The clay cladding gave it a light brown color. The overhanging thatched roof resembled an oversized heavy straw hat.

"The house is built entirely from straw, clay and some wooden beams," Rowan explained as he dismounted his horse. "Its thick walls provide perfect insulation from the cold winters, and aren't prone to fire due to their compact structure. As you will learn, the land, seas and rivers provide for everything in the United Canadian Communities."

A bearded man with rolled-up sleeves and a face sculpted by the elements opened the door.

"Just let me do the talking," Rowan directed Nayla before he walked up to the house and smiled at the farmer.

The man smiled back. They both shook hands and exchanged what seemed to Nayla to be somewhat formal greetings.

Rowan pointed towards the goats that were tied to his horse. The poor animals had been totally out of breath when they had joined them earlier that day under the large spruce. Not familiar with the animals' behavior, Nayla had been surprised by how stressed they'd been when left behind, and how the proximity of their familiar companions had calmed them down after they'd rejoined the group.

The farmer took a look at Nayla and the animals. His eyes stayed fixed somewhat longer on the imposing Odin, who sat upright and alertly observed Rowan's every movement. Together the two men walked up to the goats.

Nayla felt somewhat irritated since she was being ignored in the whole process. Even the dog was getting more attention. This wasn't how she was used to being treated. Where she came from, she was respected, and would at a minimum be greeted. Even when visiting the United States of Bolivar, the people had always welcomed her with genuine friendliness. Here, the farmer seemed polite, but he only had eyes for Rowan and the gift of the goats.

When he led the goats away, he signaled for Rowan to wait. A few minutes later the man reappeared with a brown fiber bag filled with food, which he handed to Rowan while expressing his thanks. The two men shook hands. Rowan returned to his horse and got back on the trail towards the village. Odin ran cheerfully ahead, glad to be able to relax and explore the smells and sights along the path.

"He didn't even greet me," Nayla complained, her pride hurt. "You didn't introduce me either!" she continued, an even more agitated tone in her voice.

"It's their culture," Rowan answered matter-of-factly, undisturbed by Nayla's emotional outburst. "As I said before, it's a conservative Christian community. Their religion permeates their entire life and culture. For starters it is reflected in the patriarchal structure of this community. Men occupy all functions of importance in politics, trades and farming. In this culture the women see it as their main task to care for the children and support their husbands—the heads of the family. They're often ignored by men, unless they're at church or in social circumstances. Pants are only worn by the men. The children are raised in a disciplined way. And on Sunday morning you will literally find all villagers in the church services in the village. No one works on Sunday, and they spend this day together, relaxing in community. That means that typically the women of the village get together and share their stories of the past week while the men talk about trading, seeding, harvesting, religion and politics."

"If only men wear pants here, I will surely stick out. Will that not offend them?" Nayla wondered aloud.

"No, it will not, since you don't belong to their culture. They would only expect you to dress like them if you decided to settle here. The villages in the United Canadian Communities all live together in peace because they respect the diversity of cultures in the country," Rowan reminded Nayla. "People from other cultures who are traveling through the area are only expected to respect the local customs. So as long as you don't do anything that's offensive to them, they will welcome you."

"So what would these people consider offensive?"

"Well, for example, you don't have to wear the same dress, but you should keep your legs and arms covered like their local women do. The village men will address me regarding such things as the length of our stay and our lodging location; you shouldn't mingle in such conversations unless they address you with a direct question."

"I guess I can do that," Nayla agreed, disgruntled. She had a hard time accepting the unequal treatment of the women.

Reluctant to give up her fight for equality, she suggested, "But if I were to set a different example, mixing in the conversation so they can see a woman is able to intelligently participate in decision making, could that not create a spark within their women to fight for their rights?"

"That's exactly what the problem was with American thinking in the first place," Rowan answered shortly. "These women are well aware of the different cultures in other villages; they choose this way of living. We should respect this. If their way of living provides them with happiness, if this spiritual practice works for them and creates harmony in their lives, who are we to judge them or try to change them? This has been the problem in the old world. Too many people tried to force their views and spiritual beliefs onto others. Change always has to come from within for it to be sustainable.

"If people in the United Canadian Communities desire to experience a different lifestyle, they move to a different village with another culture. It isn't uncommon for people when they're young to travel around, and try out different lifestyles and customs before settling down in the community that fits them best. Village government is much simplified as there are no minorities who feel disrespected in our communities. It's simply required that anyone settling in a community adapts to its culture. In most villages, a strong violation of the cultural and spiritual practices is punished by banning the person from the settlement."

"Okay, I get the fact that change should come from within and their culture should be respected. But if people don't experience something different, or if they're not challenged in their perspective or questioned in their behavior, can they ever evolve? And isn't evolution a good thing? The world evolves, the mountains evolve, relationships evolve and the collective learning of a culture makes a society evolve. Maybe if they see some different behavior, it might make them think. And wouldn't they forgive me since I'm a stranger, someone not familiar with their cultural practices? Maybe this way, I can at least plant a cultural seed. In the end, it would still be up to them to germinate or terminate that seed," she smiled at Rowan, convinced he would find it difficult to refute the argument.

Rowan only responded with a frowning look that soon transformed in a smile as he chose to simply rest his case. He respected and had come to like the tenacity of this woman of the American Confederacy. He understood why she was one of the leaders of the country, and in favor with the man in charge of the Carsanto empire.

They'd passed by a few more farms and were approaching the village when Rowan called Odin back by his side again. The fierce wolf put on his dumbest face, tilting his head with eyes that questioned, "Are you talking to me? What do you want me to do?" Rowan just frowned and narrowed his eyes, after which Odin lowered his head and moved into formation. Nayla smiled at the whole spectacle.

It was late afternoon, and the village streets were alive with the hustle and bustle of people on their way home from their daily tasks.

The village houses had the same light brown clay cladding against the thick straw bale walls. What was different from the farmhouses was that they were all row houses. They also had second floors, and green roofs made of prairie grasses. The result was lots of sheltered living space on a modest land surface.

Odin now proudly held his head up, well aware of the attention he was getting. Over the days to come, he would be the talk of the town. He knew it, and loved it.

They rode through the village until the main street gave out on a large village square; on the north end was a church with a large cross on top of its four-story-high tower. Rowan was heading for the spiritual center of the village.

"This is where we'll find the elders, the priests of the town and the patriarch of the community. These are the very people who lead this community, and whose help we need to find shelter for the night. Try at least for now to let me do the talking so that we can have a good night of sleep," he grinned.

News of the arrival of the visitors traveled faster on the voices of the children than the pace at which the horses walked. Before they'd crossed halfway over the town square, a white-bearded old man emerged from the church.

"That's the patriarch," Rowan announced.

Suddenly some havoc on the side of the market square redirected the attention away from the travelers to a handful of shouting and screaming women. It seemed they were being beaten by a man.

Nayla was appalled that the whole community just stood by and watched. Then she noticed the man was actually a woman dressed like a man, and she wasn't really harming the other women; it was all an act. Soon the woman dressed like a man was the only one left standing; the four other females were weeping on the ground.

As suddenly as the play started it ended. The women jumped on their feet again, and walked toward the patriarch determinedly, shouting from the bottom of their lungs, "Each of you is a son of God because of your faith in Christ Jesus. All of you who have been baptized into Christ have clothed yourselves with him. There does not exist among you, Jew or Greek, slave or freeman, male or female. All are one in Christ Jesus."

They repeated the same words over and over, stressing "or female" while walking proudly with chins held high towards the patriarch.

Nayla was impressed with how effective the play was in communicating their point. These women were tired of being beaten by their men, and wanted to be recognized as equals in the community. Was it coincidence that this took place while they arrived, or had they used the arrival of the travelers to gain more attention?

As the scene had started, Rowan had halted his horse and asked an alerted Odin to stay put. Together with all the perplexed villagers they had watched the somewhat surreal spectacle; it had taken less than a minute. Now that all had understood the message and recognized the protest for what it was, several men rushed towards the women, roughly grabbed them, and dragged them away from the square.

Once again Nayla was appalled, for this was not a play, but the real, forceful treatment of women who had harmed no one but only voiced their concerns. What was most disturbing was that all the people in the market square turned their attention back to the travelers, seemingly indifferent to the women's fate.

To Nayla's surprise, Rowan nudged the horses and Odin in motion, and continued their way towards the patriarch like the event had not taken place at all. A short distance away from the church, Rowan dismounted and sternly whispered, "Not a word about this. Not now! Act like nothing happened!"

"But—" Nayla started.

"Not now!" he stressed.

Nayla wasn't sure why Rowan had left Odin, the horses and herself a short distance away from the patriarch as he walked up to the old man. Was he being polite, or did he want to make sure she wouldn't cause any trouble?

The patriarch's perceptive eyes had been locked onto the travelers from the moment he'd emerged from the church. Even during the women's protest he'd kept an eye on the visitors, carefully registering their reaction to the events. In contrast to the farmer earlier, the patriarch had already acknowledged Nayla with a friendly nod when Rowan dismounted his horse. It was a greeting Nayla had returned, but her display of kindness and manners was offered somewhat reluctantly due to the confused and angry emotions raging inside her.

The old man had intently observed Odin, who lay relaxed next to the horses. Now his alert and energetic eyes were measuring Rowan as the two men greeted each other with a firm handshake.

Nayla had trouble guessing the man's age. His gray hair, carved wisdom lines on his face, and small piercing eyes that lay deep under a well-pronounced brow betrayed old age. His white long-sleeved tunic covered a tall vital body that radiated energy and created a presence more reminiscent of that of a middle-aged man.

Nayla was too far away to understand what was being said. The conversation seemed cordial, respectful but measured. While travelers always brought stories, a break from the day-to-day hustle-and-bustle, and possibly new knowledge or products, they also could pose a threat to the village. As a good father, the patriarch would protect his flock and use his wisdom and experienced observation skills to avoid welcoming visitors who could cause trouble.

When the conversation satisfied the elder, he gave some orders to some men who had gathered in curiosity around the two. One of the men returned with Rowan to the horses.

"We have been invited to stay in the village for the night. This man has been appointed as our host. We're going with him to his house to settle in, and have been invited to share our story in the community hall tonight," Rowan explained, relief written all over his face while the host acknowledged Nayla with a friendly smile.

They followed the short man, who seemed to be in his fifties. He had a round, friendly face and jovial eyes.

Nayla had been surprised by the genuine greeting of the man. It wasn't clear to her when she could expect to be ignored, and when she would be acknowledged and included in conversation. The only rule seemed to be whatever the men decided.

After they walked a few blocks through the village they arrived at the host's house. It was a two-story straw bale house in the middle of a row of interconnected houses. The children on the street all gathered around Odin, who clearly was overjoyed with all the attention. They first kept their distance, but were enthralled by the wolf's imposing size and well-behaved manner. As with all children, curiosity ultimately conquered fear, and so they moved closer.

"Can we pet him?" a small boy with excited blue eyes asked.

"Sure you can. His name is Odin. He likes to be scratched behind his ears," Rowan smiled.

And like a swarm of bees that smelled honey, the kids surrounded Odin, who relished the caressing of their hands.

"Can he come and play with us?" the same boy asked while an older boy threw a stick away to demonstrate their intentions.

Odin's eyes lit up, and with his head tilted slightly, his eyes begged to go play.

"All right, off you go. Have some fun!" Rowan conceded.

The words had barely left his lips before Odin was racing through the street in pursuit of the thrown stick. He was cheered on by a growing group of children.

The sight put smiles on everyone's faces.

"You have a well-behaved dog," the host said admiringly. "He'll be the talk of the town long after you leave," he smiled.

"He enjoys the attention and, as you can see, he absolutely loves kids," Rowan laughed.

Turning back to business, the host asked some of the children on the street to take care of the horses, and invited Rowan and Nayla into his house.

The heavy wooden door gave way to a long hallway. On the right, stairs led to the second floor.

The host invited them through an opening in the left wall covered by a woven woolen curtain into a living room where a fire was crackling in the river-stone fireplace. Some couches around a little table in front of the fireplace provided a cozy seating arrangement. Two old wooden cupboards along the wall provided storage for books and clay pottery. Further to the right in a long rectangular room was a rustic wooden table with six chairs. To the right of that was the kitchen which could also be entered from the end of the hallway. The windows in the back overlooked the communal herb and vegetable gardens, which could be accessed through the kitchen.

The host introduced his wife, who was dressed like most woman in the town.

"Nice to meet you," Nayla responded eagerly. She thought she'd finally found someone to communicate with in the community. But when making eye contact, the hostess only extended a shy smile as a sign of friendship. Immediately thereafter she submissively turned her eyes back to the floor.

"Can we get some tea?" the host asked, and his wife immediately went to work.

"I'll show our guests their rooms," he then said.

The host took them to the second floor and showed Rowan and Nayla their private quarters: two modest rooms each with a small single bed built from log timbers. The windows gave out onto the street, and in the corner was a little table with a wash basin and a clay water jar.

"You can freshen yourselves up and then join us downstairs for tea," he invited.

"Thank you," Rowan replied.

Before they did so, Rowan instructed Nayla to observe the local women and, in respect to their culture, act in the same way.

"You mean like on the market square?" Nayla snapped furiously.

"It all depends on where you want to sleep tonight—in this bed, or outside somewhere along the trail," Rowan answered undisturbed.

So Nayla did as she was told. She observed the hostess when they got together and tried to act accordingly. However, she soon discovered that it was impossible for her to watch the floor like the hostess did during the time when Rowan and the host were in conversation. And when Rowan shared the day's events of their journey to the village and the encounter with the helicopter, she found it very hard not to jump in.

When the host took Rowan outside to the communal garden, the hostess spoke to Nayla for the first time.

"I can tell you're not familiar with our culture. You seem to want to stand up to the men and engage in the conversation."

The directness of the hostess, and the acuteness of her observation skills, took Nayla completely by surprise. It was like a total personality change had taken place in this woman as soon as there wasn't a man around. Was her shy submissiveness all an act?

"You've got to know that the women in this village don't feel oppressed or anything," she continued.

"We are happy. We know our role and are grateful for it. Thank the Lord!" she then said, making a quick cross sign with her right hand.

Nayla wanted to bring up the scene on the market square, but decided it was too early.

"There's a reason God has appointed man to lead and woman to follow and serve," the hostess continued with confidence. "You're a woman yourself. You know how we can go crazy in our head once in a while, and usually at least once a month, when our emotions go all over the place. Imagine if you need to lead a family, business or a people with such an unstable nature!"

"I'm a leader in my culture," Nayla responded somewhat arrogantly, in an attempt to shock this woman out of what she considered to be a brainwashed state of mind.

But rather than continuing to justify her oppressed existence, the hostess changed the subject. "Would you like to help me prepare supper?"

Nayla nodded and was glad the hostess gave precise instructions as to what to do, so she could conceal how bad of a cook she really was.

*D*ick wasn't in a good mood. After an entire day of searching the area where Nayla had been last seen, they had come up with absolutely nothing. They had followed several deer trails for hours, without finding any sign of human travel. Not once had they come across a path created by people for travel or transportation. Nayla had gotten off the train in the middle of the wilderness, far away from any human settlements. It was like searching for a needle in a haystack.

Dick believed that if Nayla didn't reach one of the Canadian communities, it would be unlikely that she would get far, or even survive, in this place. Worries continued to occupy his mind.

What if she died out there? Further, what if she died and they failed to retrieve her body? They would never know if she was really dead and where the seeds were. And so for the rest of their existence they would have to live with the probability that at some point in time the germinator seeds could completely destroy their empire!

As the helicopter landed back at the base located south of the search area, Dick quickly banished the negative thoughts from his mind. He couldn't think like that; he could not afford to undermine his own morale! After all, they had only been searching for a day. "Tomorrow is another day," he instructed his worried mind.

"There is still some daylight left," he commanded the pilot. "I want you to fly out one more time and make a wide circle around the area we have been searching today. This time, look for any sign of human life—a village, a farm, a cabin, anything. She's going to need to find help to get out of this country."

The smell of good game stew and the sight of a bottle of red wine pleased his senses as he entered the somewhat Spartan base. Dick didn't mind roughing it for a few days. However, as compensation for the absence of the Confederate luxuries he was used to, he appreciated tasty, nourishing food, a good bottle of wine and some brandy to relax his mind and inspire more pleasant thoughts. He was particularly going to enjoy the meal tonight since he had provided for it.

Earlier in the afternoon, the helicopter pilots had detected a small elk herd along the mountains southwest of what the men at the base called Davidstown. It was more than a day's hike from where Nayla was last seen, but in a helicopter it was only a short flight. When Dick had found out, he immediately had reasoned the animals would provide an entertaining target practice for his men. So the pilots had loaded the men up, and tracked the herd down.

When they had first chased the herd with the helicopters, Dick had been impressed with the stamina of the animals. They seemed tireless and just kept on running. Eventually the animals started to show signs of exhaustion and the pilots had taken quick flights over the herd, while from each side of the chopper Dick's men had taken turns in shooting the elk. Most of his men did well. And once they had each killed two animals from the moving helicopters, they had landed along the trail of dead carcasses and taken two hind quarters for their meat supply for the next few days. Too bad there hadn't been any antlered animals worthy of a head-mount.

While Dick was enjoying the meat from the entertaining hunt, his satellite phone rang.

"How are things going there, Dick?"

It was the curious voice of his boss.

"Just fine," he answered while still chewing the delicious meat. "I'm just enjoying some tasty game. I should take you here on a helicopter hunt some time."

"What about Nayla? Any leads yet?"

Dick wasn't entirely sure if the eagerness in George's voice was triggered by his love for his girlfriend, his concern about the germinator seeds, or his interest in finding a state criminal. Somehow, though, he didn't expect the last reason to be George's driving motivation.

"Nothing yet. Absolutely nothing. It's big country out here. True wilderness. She must have found help to get out of here. Once we find the closest human settlements and get an idea of who provided her help, we'll find her. Don't worry!" he answered confidently.

"Good!"

"Why did that not sound convincing?" Dick thought.

"Remember, Dick, I want to interrogate her together with you. Make sure you get her alive!" George commanded.

But Dick heard the concern in his supervisor's order. He realized that when the time came for corrective action, he might have to stand up to his boss, who might not be able to put the interest of Carsanto and the great American Confederacy before his personal pleasures. This wasn't the time to be weak of heart.

Minutes after the phone conversation ended, one of the pilots walked in.

"We've seen a cabin in a clearing in the forest just a little further west of today's search area. It was the only human settlement in the area we flew over. The only other houses are in the villages south, north and east, and are all at least a two-day hike. We didn't see any people at the cabin, though."

"Great! Good job. We'll start our search there tomorrow morning at first light," Dick replied, satisfied. This had turned out to be a good evening after all! Good meal, good wine and good news!

The community hall was packed and abuzz with chatter. The door opened, the murmur quieted down, and all eyes focused on the entering visitors.

The children cheered on the majestic wolf who walked in a well-behaved manner next to the trapper. This was an exciting night for all, but particularly for Kate.

Her parents still called her—to her dismay—"Katie." Couldn't they understand how "Kate" was more appropriate for a grown-up young woman; after all she had just turned eighteen!

For months now, Kate had been trying to convince her parents to let her travel for a year before sending her off to Saint Helen, the Christian University up north at the foot of the Rocky Mountains. It was a good university, and she was interested in school. However, Kate first wanted to explore the world—get to know it better—in order to find out what role she wanted to play in it and what studies would be most helpful for her.

While the school system in the United Canadian Communities was free for all children, university studies were limited to those who had not only the highest marks, but were deemed most capable by their community's elders. The community itself collectively paid for a select group of students to attend university. They considered it an investment in their future scientists, leaders and wise ones.

Students weren't always selected by the elders because of their high school grades, although that was always a plus. Community engagement and emotional intelligence skills had the most weight in the scale. So those youngsters who were always ready to help their friends, neighbors or any person in need, those who cared about the animals in the village, those who were inquisitive about their environmental footprint, and those who acted as leaders and peacemakers were favored. Kate had heard that in communities with a less dogmatic spiritual path than hers, those who rebelled and challenged everything would almost always secure a place in university as long as they were motivated to study and had demonstrated that with excellent grades at school.

It was rare for the elders in her village to choose a girl to send to university—after all, men occupied all the important posts in the community. Kate was top of her class, so she certainly had proven herself academically. But what had impressed the elders most about Kate was her passion for the children of the village. She was always surrounded by them, and telling them stories. She laughed when they squeezed her fleshy cheeks, played with her long brown braided hair, or grabbed her long skirt and spun her around. She showed them the abundant everyday miracles of nature, played with them, cared for them, and vigilantly defended them if they were treated unjustly. This last trait had gotten her into trouble more than once, but it didn't deter her from taking a stand for those who were too weak to defend themselves if they were wronged.

Yes, Davidstown was a patriarchal community, but behind every patriarch and elder was a wise woman. Without female leaders who supported the patriarchal structure, order in the community would be difficult to maintain. Kate's parents were proud that their daughter had been one of the few female children chosen for university, and so now they were particularly concerned about the possibility of her traveling. They feared that the elders might see the influence of other cultures as a threat to her support for the customs of Davidstown. Such a foolish adventure could even cause her to move to a village with a different culture! And so they worried that the elders would select a different young woman to take her place if she decided to travel first.

Just last night Kate and her parents had had a fight. Usually it was Kate against her father, since her mother always took her father's side, and tried to mellow Kate into agreeing with him. In the past this had often worked, but this time Kate wasn't planning to give in. This time things were different—and more complicated. The complication gave her the extra courage and strength to brave her father's fury.

This time, there was a boy involved—not just any boy, but a boy she loved, and a boy from another culture. He lived in Al Saeed, a Muslim village a day's travel southwest into the mountains. She had met Salim when he'd accompanied his father on a trade mission to her village just two years ago.

Salim was tall and skinny, with the darkest eyes and friendliest smile she had ever seen. He smiled at her that first day. They didn't talk that day; only their eyes had spoken, and smiles had been exchanged. It was enough though to light a flame in Kate's heart and make butterflies dance in her belly.

She dreamed about the boy for months. Even when she didn't know his name yet. All she knew was that the boy she loved lived in Al Saeed, and so she prayed to God, but mostly to Mother Mary, for her love to return.

Six months later, her prayers were answered when the boy accompanied his father again on another trading trip. This time she made sure to join the villagers who were eagerly surrounding the traders to check out the wares. The boy was working hard to help his father with selling their merchandise. Determined to speak to him, she weathered the crowd until she got right to the merchants' sales tent. And there he was.

"Can I help you with something?" he asked with a voice as sweet as honey.

She lost her tongue, the butterflies in her belly dancing in joy. Her heart raced and her throat became dry.

He smiled at her, and a gentle understanding poured from his eyes. Then he offered her one of his wares.

"This bracelet of sweet-grass not only brings luck, but it's a symbol of our divine connection with all that lives," the boy said warmly.

"That includes him," she thought.

"How much is it?" she asked eagerly.

"For such a pretty young woman like you, it is free," he smiled.

"I cannot accept—" she started.

But he interrupted her, and said with a gentle firmness, "In our culture, it's an insult to refuse a gift."

She could have used the presentation of the gift to start a conversation. She could have asked his name, where he lived, how often he thought he was going to pass through Davidstown, what life was like in the village where he lived. Oh God, she could have asked just anything to start a conversation! But she didn't. She only felt how her cheeks and neck were glowing, and knew instantly that they must have been blushing red.

"Thank you," she said quickly and, a little embarrassed, turned around and left. It was only when he called after her that she realized how stupid and childish her reaction had been.

"What is your name?" he asked.

Without stopping she shouted, "Kate," and ran home disappointed with herself and convinced that after her appalling flight he wouldn't want to have anything to do with her anymore.

The following day the traders passed by her house on their way out of town. Her heart rejoiced when he smiled at her again.

"See you next time, Kate," he waved.

"He still remembered my name!" Kate thought.

Just when the visitors had almost left town, she realized that she still didn't know his name. She ran after them and shouted, "What's your name?"

"Salim!" he broadly smiled back.

Ever since that day, whenever Salim and the traders would visit Davidstown, she spent as much time with him as possible. Her parents

107

didn't approve of it. They were concerned because Salim was from a different culture, and fearful that Kate would leave God's path. But although they didn't approve, they knew that love was God's work on earth, and finally decided to let things work out in their own way.

Salim was a year older than Kate. Since he had left school last year he was following in the footsteps of his father. He had set up his own trading business. In order to see Kate more frequently he had become the most common trader to pass through Davidstown—and the one who stayed the longest.

Due to these visits their love had grown stronger, and the two had started to make plans for the future together. Salim wanted to extend his trading skills and knowledge, and travel from coast to coast through the United Canadian Communities. He'd asked Kate to join him. Kate was excited about the possibility of exploring the cultures of the other communities. Maybe in different circumstances her parents might have reluctantly approved, but a month earlier she'd been selected by the elders to attend university—a great honor, and certainly for a girl, in the community. And although Salim had promised they would be back by the start of the following year and would settle down in Saint Helen near the university from where he could make his trading missions, her parents had adamantly objected to their plans to travel together.

Just as Kate had always vehemently fought for the rights of children in the village when she thought they were wronged, she was planning to fight for her own rights this time. After all, this was her life! She was eighteen and finishing school, and while she appreciated the input and counsel of her parents, she didn't like it when she was still being told—like a child—what she could and could not do.

Last night she had stubbornly told her father just that.

"I heard your opinion, but I'm not a child anymore. I'm going to travel! I'll explain this to the elders, and will ask their permission to start university the following year."

"You shall obey!" her father had shouted back. "How dare you be so disrespectful? You are a woman!"

108

"I'm not your woman! I'm not your child! I'm your full-grown daughter!" she had yelled back, infuriated with his denigrative comment about females.

The silence that had followed the harsh fight of words stressed the tension in the room and the strength of the opponents. Her mother had been really quiet; she didn't handle these shouting matches very well.

Her mother felt a woman wasn't supposed to stand up like this. A woman was supposed to serve. But she knew too that Kate was not an ordinary woman, and it was this strength, combined with her tenderness and empathy, that gave her great female leadership potential in the eyes of the elders.

In an attempt to break the tension, settle the emotions and bring reason back to the conversation, Kate's mother had said, "Katie, we understand you want to go travel, my dear. But how many girls are selected by the elders to go study? You shouldn't waste such an opportunity. You should respect the decision of the elders."

"I am respecting their decision, and indeed I'm honored that they've selected me. But it simply makes more sense to go travel first and get to know the world before deciding what to study. It would be disrespectful to accept the money from the community to pay for my studies if I haven't decided what I want to study," she'd argued cleverly.

Her mother had never been a match for Kate's reasoning skills. Neither had her father, which is why they always ended up shouting at each other.

"I want to study," Kate had continued, "and I will explain to the elders why a year's travel will make me an even better candidate for university."

Just when she thought she'd won the battle for the night, her father had spoken in a cold and mean tone.

"You're going to study next year, or you won't study at all. I'll tell the elders that a girl who has been chosen and doesn't want to put the interest of the village before her personal romance with a boy from a different culture is not worth investing in."

Kate had choked up at the hard and cold statement. Her father's words had cut straight into her heart.

Tears had welled up in her eyes. She didn't want to give her dad the pleasure of seeing her cry, so she had stood up from the table and gone to her room without saying one more word. How could her own father abandon her like this? When you truly loved someone, didn't you help your loved one to reach their dream rather than chain them down and force them to submit to your whims?

Deep down, she knew that her dad loved her, but that he was very afraid of the dangers of the world. It scared him that his daughter could be in trouble somewhere in a different community and that he wouldn't be able to protect her. He had a huge problem with losing that control—and his ability to protect his loved ones around him. She knew that was the real problem, but had no idea how to remove that barrier. His fear was grounded in the fact that he'd never traveled himself—at least, not to another culture. A few times he had joined other community members when they traveled to a Christian conference in another Christian village in the region. But he'd never experienced any other cultures, nor seen anything from their vast country. But why cage someone so you could protect them and keep their body alive, while that very act of supposed protection smothered their dream and killed their soul?

Tonight gave her a break from all the stress; tonight was exciting! Travel, adventure and different insights and perspectives had come to Kate's doorstep. Deep inside, she also had a faint hope that the travelers and their experience might expand her father's perspectives and soften his stand.

While all the men of the village had talked to the trapper, and the children had been enthralled with the wolf, Kate was most interested in the woman. Even though she was wearing trappers' clothing, her skin was too soft, her hands too smooth and her walk too classy to have lived in the woods for a long time.

Kate suspected she was from a different culture from some distant land. She hoped the woman would get a chance to speak. It was her story she wanted to hear.

T he host led the visitors to the center of the hall where the patriarch was seated. When the patriarch stood in welcome of the guests, the whole room turned silent.

"Once again, welcome to Davidstown. We're happy to provide you with food and shelter, but all are curious to learn about your travels and experiences. Most people in this community don't travel, and it is stories from people like you, who explore and have been places, that offer us a window into other parts of the world. So please indulge us and share with us your stories and what brings you to our town."

Both Nayla and Rowan were offered a seat next to the patriarch. Odin lay down quietly at Rowan's feet.

"Thank you for your hospitality. It is well appreciated. My name is Rowan and I've lived in the forest at the foothills of the Rocky Mountains a day's ride north of here for the last four years."

Rowan had started first, as the whole room had focused on him once the patriarch had spoken. As he did, Nayla wondered if she was supposed to stay silent the whole evening. She didn't want to offend anyone and be asked to leave the village. She was curious too if Rowan was planning to tell them the whole story, and if so, would he be the one telling them her story too?

Rowan shared with the community how he had bitterly retreated from the world after his family was killed, and chosen a life of solitude at the base of the mountains. He shared the story of how the wounded fawn had been a gift of God that helped him to see beauty in life again, and how he subsequently had quit his trapping practice and had learned to live off the land, respectfully receiving with gratitude what nature was prepared to offer.

Nayla noticed that he referred to God several times throughout his story, something he hadn't done before. She assumed that he was tailoring the story to make a better connection with the people of this culture.

Lots of people nodded when Rowan talked about his respect for nature and his understanding of the cycle of life. The people here, mostly farmers, understood those things. He had connected with them and they had all felt his pain, his bitterness and the rebirth of his soul.

Rowan then continued with Odin's story, and the children hummed and cheered as he recounted how the wolf had been nursed by his goats, and from then on had protected his odd family of goats and horses from predators.

Then he fell silent. Nayla could sense his uncertainty as to how to continue. The patriarch, a master in observation, had sensed it as well.

"So what brings you here?" the elder prodded.

"In order to tell you that story, I have to introduce you to Nayla." He stood, inviting her to get up too. "She's a brave woman from the American Confederacy who has taken it upon herself to bring an important package to safety. A package that could save this planet."

A fervent murmur went through the hall.

"We will listen to Nayla's story," the patriarch announced, and the whole hall waited in silent anticipation for Nayla to speak.

So after all she was to tell her own story, and Rowan had set the stage for her to share everything! Nayla's hands tightened around the pack with the seeds. She'd taken it with her tonight—she simply wasn't planning to leave the package out of her sight until she safely delivered it at its final destination.

"I was born in the United States of Bolivar. My parents moved to the American Confederacy when I was a child in search of the American Dream," she commenced, deciding these people needed some background in order to understand the integrity in which she was acting and the seriousness of the situation. She shared with them her role in Carsanto, her marriage to Julian and the birth of her precious Gaya, the mutating terminator and germinator seeds she had developed, Carsanto's goal to rule the world by controlling the entire seed production on the planet, the plan to spray seeds over the United States of Bolivar, her escape, and how Rowan saved her from the hands of the train guards.

"I have to bring these germinator seeds to the United States of Bolivar so that they can mass-produce them and distribute them around the world," she ended. "It's a dangerous mission, since it threatens Carsanto's control of the world. No doubt there is a price on my head in the American Confederacy, and this morning we saw two helicopters flying overhead. I'm sure they're part of the search team that's trying to capture me."

Nayla then took the pack out and unfolded it. She lifted up the little bags, carefully tagged as they contained seeds of hundreds of agricultural species. She put some seeds of barley, oats and corn in her hand, turned to the patriarch, and stretching her hand out said, "This is my gift to you and your people for providing us shelter. Let these seeds germinate. Save the seeds of their harvest until you have enough to spread them across all your fields. It will liberate you from the dependency on Carsanto's seeds that are delivered annually by the seed train."

Nayla sat down and a murmur welled up in the crowd. Lots of faces nodded in approval; on others she saw sheer terror.

The patriarch stood, stretching his arm out to the crowd while now holding the precious seeds in the cup of his hand. The people quieted down as he began to address them.

"Life! Seeds of life, returned to us in the way the Creator had given them to us. God wanted men to be good stewards of the earth, but not meddle in His Creation. These travelers are doing God's work and restoring His Creation in all its beauty. Once again we will be able to save the seeds of our harvests to plant the following year just like our ancestors used to do."

He turned to Nayla and continued, "Thank you for this precious gift. You are a brave woman," he said, his eyes moving to Rowan, "for whom God found a courageous man to lead you to your destiny."

Nayla wasn't quite sure how to interpret this last statement. Sure, Rowan was a great help, but this sounded like she couldn't have survived without a man. She decided not to make too much of it, and to respect the culture of these people. Maybe the patriarch's words were not intended to sound denigrating.

"You are welcome to stay here as long as you want, and we will keep your stay here a secret even long after you leave. Your struggle is not unlike that of our ancestors, who freed themselves of the delusions of the American way of life and returned to the land. It is only by living in communion with the land—by being a good steward—that we honor God's work and allow His beautiful Creation to provide for us all. It is in that humble relationship with the land that we find happiness and are able to cherish the little things—the smiles of the children, the germination of the seeds in the field and the rising of the sun in the morning.

"Since God gave earth to all people, we are supposed to steward it as a community. The cultures of the past mistakenly carved the land into pieces that were sold and could be 'owned' by individuals. Often people or organizations possessed more land than they needed to provide for themselves—or they owned land far away. But how can you care for the land as a good steward if you are not dependent on that land and therefore don't rely on its long-term health? It is only the people—as a community—who are living from this land that will be responsible and good stewards. Their children are fed from this land, and so will their children's children. The continuity of the very community depends on good stewardship and therefore ensures it.

"Our ancestors fought for the right to proper land stewardship when they founded this country. It's that very caring for the earth— the right and freedom for people to enjoy the soil, water and air that God has given them—that binds the diverse cultural communities of

115

this country together. Our local living economies respect God's Creation and allow us to live comfortably, in harmony with each other and our environment. The American Confederacy in its aim to gain control over all of Creation and the world made us dependent on their terminator seeds. Your gift of germinator seeds will allow us to return to a life in harmony with the Creation which God has given us.

"Let us thank God together in prayer for sending us these travelers with this treasure, a treasure of Creation itself."

The patriarch led the community in prayer before adjourning the meeting.

N ayla and Rowan returned to the home of their host, but Nayla found herself unable to sleep that night.

Alone in her room, she reflected on the events of the day.

The helicopters were most certainly looking for her. How long would she have before Dick would track her down? Her mind wandered to her initial discomfort with the religious culture of the community which she had come to appreciate in a short period of time. Here people were friendly, hospitable, and lived in harmony with each other and their surroundings. The children seemed happy and healthy. The only thing that really bothered her was the oppression of the women, even though they seemed happy and accepted their role.

Or did they? What had that protest been all about?

Nayla still hoped to be able to plant a seed for equality before leaving the village sometime the following day. She took her grandmother's diary and decided to read some more.

July 4ᵗʰ, 2021

Today the world changed! What's happening to my country? Not that we were not warned, but come on; who would have believed this could happen in the country of the free? Thousands of environmental and social activists were rounded up today and arrested all across the country, including Jensen, the author of Endgame, *and writer Naomi Wolf, who has been warning our citizens for years that the American government was executing a blueprint that turns democratic* *regimes into dictatorships. She claims it's the same blueprint Hitler used in the thirties to eliminate democracy in Germany before he started the war and the slaughter of the Jewish people and other minorities. I never read her book, <u>The End of America</u>, but I saw her present a few years ago at the university I attended.*

The activists weren't just arrested today; they were actually taken to an undisclosed location for interrogation. The evening news announced the capture of thousands of 'disruptive elements' who formed a terrorist threat to the country. It hailed Whitefog, who was contracted for the task, for having saved the country from a looming terrorist attack on home soil! What has happened to free speech, to the right for a fair trial, to liberty and free press? Why is it that the press always sings to the tune of big corporations and the government? They really must think we are all morons—too stupid to understand what's really going on.

And what does it take to enrage a population to the point that they'll fight back? Will they ever? (Or should I say, we?) The Germans never did. They were too afraid of their own government. Same for any of the people that Alejandro talked about who lived under dictatorial governments in Latin America. They also were too scared to stand up and fight for their dream. They all stood by—and sometimes even helped—while evil executed its plan. I was too scared a few months ago when I was pondering this question in my diary, and after today's events, I'm terrified. I'd better go tend my nice growing organic garden and keep my mouth shut …but I sure hope someone else will be braver than me and stand up and fight.

"Is that how women in this community of Davidstown feel?" Nayla wondered. "Are they too afraid to stand up for their rights, and instead pray in silence for someone with the courage to stand up and change things for them—or at least, to demand the change?"

With those thoughts Nayla finally drifted off to sleep.

The following morning Rowan and Nayla packed their horses early. When they were leaving they noticed the streets were empty, with the exception of a few people who barely paid attention to them and hurried in the direction of the market square.

"What's going on?" Nayla asked Rowan, who in turn inquired the same of their host.

"The women that disturbed the peace yesterday are being sentenced," Rowan informed her as soon as he found out.

"You mean they're being punished for protesting being beaten by their men?" Nayla snapped, appalled.

"It's their culture…"

"It might be their culture, but it doesn't make it right, does it?" she interrupted Rowan. "I have to see this. Let's get over there."

"But Nayla, we should get moving if we want to reach Al Saeed before nightfall," Rowan objected.

"I've got to see this. We'll just have to ride faster today," Nayla retorted.

Nayla didn't wait for Rowan's approval, and rode in the direction of the town center.

When she arrived at the market square, the female protestors stood on one side of the patriarch in front of the church, their faces down, their shoulders drooping forward in defeat. Behind each of the women sat a man, back straight and chin held high.

Seated on the other side of the elder were four old men and one gray-haired woman.

The patriarch was addressing the crowd.

"…and they shamed our entire village by their insulting display when visitors arrived."

Nayla heard him finish before he was able to note her arrival.

"They insulted their husbands, and failed to find an amicable solution to their marital challenges that might exist from time to time."

Nayla had the distinct feeling that the patriarch was simply repeating this last statement for her ears only—as justification for what was to follow.

"The elders have spoken and sentenced these women to be shunned for two weeks. They're not allowed to talk, nor should anyone see them, hear them or speak to them. During that time they will be allocated the most labor-intensive work in the fields. Their husbands will supervise their work and period of silence, and are tasked with taking corrective measures in case the women do not abide by the ruling."

The patriarch's hard and commanding words carried across the market square.

"If there's anyone who has anything to say on behalf of these women or who doesn't agree with this judgment, now is the time to speak," he directed.

But when his eyes crossed Nayla's, she understood the flame behind his gaze, and knew her words wouldn't be welcome.

Nayla felt Rowan's eyes piercing into her back. She knew he too didn't want her to speak out. But how could she stay silent, how could she walk away from the injustice that was taking place right before her? What if she was up there, being sentenced because she was tired of being beaten, because she'd stood up for her rights? While a country, a culture or a community always has certain rules, it doesn't mean that the rules are just. If she herself had lived by the rules, she wouldn't have been here, trying to save seeds for the sake of the planet!

In her case, the deed was punishable with the death penalty in her country.

Nayla looked over the crowd. She noted that most women had their eyes locked on the ground in defeat, while most men were nodding in approval. It appalled her that no one was speaking out.

"They're afraid," she thought. Were they all waiting for someone brave enough to speak, someone they could shelter behind?

The patriarch continued, "If all are in agreement with the fairness of the elders' sentence—"

"I don't think this is fair."

Nayla's voice interrupted the elder, whose eyes shot fire as a murmur went through the crowd. Many women on the market square lifted their heads up, and she could see a glimmer of hope in their eyes. Even the women on trial had shifted their defeated body language. Would it turn out that their courage and actions were not in vain after all?

"Nayla, don't!" Rowan whispered demandingly from behind her.

"I don't think this is fair at all!" Nayla repeated in defiance of the patriarch's look. "These women desire the right to not be beaten; they simply desire the right to be treated with respect. I'm not raised in this culture, but is that an unreasonable request according to your spiritual texts and values?"

"You raise a very valid point. However, as you said, you were not raised in this culture, and therefore have no right to speak in this matter," the patriarch responded in an attempt to take back control.

But Nayla ignored him, just like he had ignored her question.

"Have you investigated if these women have been beaten?"

The patriarch's eyes were fuming as she publicly questioned his authority and the judgment of the elders.

"You are not from our culture, and shall stay out of this!" the patriarch's voice thundered out over the market square.

The women on trial took on their defeated pose again, and most present on the market square lowered their heads as their newfound hope faded away.

"But the traveler is right and so were these women yesterday!" A female voice rose from the crowd. "Paul writes in 3:26-28: Each of you is a son of God because of your faith in Christ Jesus. All of you who have been baptized into Christ have clothed yourselves with him. There does not exist among you Jew or Greek, slave or freeman, male or female. All are one in Christ Jesus.

"What gives men the right to beat their women? Why are women not treated as equals in our culture if the Bible says we should be treated as equals?" a young woman called out, a tremor in her voice.

A member of their own community had spoken out—and Nayla noted the courageous female was visibly shaking as the crowd's eyes shifted from the patriarch to the young woman.

"Katie, don't be so disrespectful! You have no right to speak like this," the girl's father commanded.

Nayla was struck by the hypocrisy that was playing out in front of her. The young girl had spoken out by invitation! And, how could it be disrespectful to speak out when an injustice was taking place? How could it be disrespectful to stand up for the rights of the oppressed or for one's own rights?

Clearly agitated by the turn of events, the patriarch then said, "The elders will give thought to what was said here today. We will reconvene tomorrow to present a final verdict."

It was obvious to all that this was a smart move to get Nayla out of the picture, so that the patriarch could regain control over the judging process.

To stress his intention, the patriarch addressed Nayla and Rowan.

"We wish you well on your journey. I appreciate your gift of seeds and your courage, and I respect you for that. But don't claim to understand and be able to judge a culture by visiting for just one day. Our ways work for our people, and any changes to them have to come from our people. That's why our rulings are public. We invite the community to participate, for we seek the input of those who have a deep understanding of our culture. Go now, and may God guide you on your path."

"Thank you for your blessing," Rowan jumped in.

Then he took Nayla's horse and started leading it away before she could say anything more.

Nayla was enraged. The patriarch had sidelined her, and there was nothing she could do anymore on behalf of these oppressed women. It was difficult to accept and deal with such feelings of powerlessness.

As Rowan was leading her away from the marketplace, she sought the eyes of the brave girl. However, the young woman's face was directed to the ground as her father made dramatic, angry gestures towards her, and spewed out his anger.

Nayla questioned her actions; had she been wise to speak up? Did she cause more harm than good? She probably would never find out.

T he crowd started to disperse, the women looking even more defeated now than before.

"You're *done!* You are not worthy of studying, or of leading the women in this community. What were you thinking?" Kate's father shouted while he grabbed her by the arm. "I'm going to speak to the elders right now and put an end to this university nonsense."

Kate pulled herself loose and ran home, heavy tears running down her cheeks. She felt abandoned and powerless.

Was it only the night before that her soul had danced wildly as she listened to the story of the brave woman of the Confederacy? She'd hoped that a spark of Nayla's courage would rub off on the women of the village; it certainly had on her! Today Kate had felt empowered to speak up when the female traveler questioned the patriarch, and she'd hoped that following her words, more voices would rise from the crowd to stand up for what was right.

Of course, she hadn't expected any support from the men, and although she wished things were different, she had known too how her father would react. But what had hurt the most was that none of the women had supported her. She'd seen the hope in their eyes when she spoke, but it had been like a hope that had already been defeated before it found root. The other females simply didn't believe they could succeed. They didn't believe that things could change. As a result, they had given up. Maybe some, just like the women on trial, had tried to stand up for their rights when they were young. But the multiple failures, the absence of any progress at all, had completely erased the real possibility of achieving those rights in their minds.

Salim had once told her why elephant trainers could tie such strong animals with a chain around their leg to a simple log. Certainly the elephant was powerful enough to simply walk away, dragging the log along with it. But the trainers had started with tying the elephants onto a log when the giants were just little baby elephants. At such time the log would prevent their escape. They would struggle to gain their freedom, but to no avail. Eventually they would give up trying. As they grew older and stronger and could easily break free from the log chained to their leg, the idea of trying to do so had been erased from their minds. The log represented a reality so strong that it wasn't worth challenging anymore.

"That's really what's happening in our community with the women," Kate thought. And by the time she got home, her sadness had changed into anger. She resolved not to ever abandon her hope, and to strive for justice.

"I have to get away from here," she thought. "I don't want to become like the elephants or all the other women in this town. I will not allow my spirit to be broken."

Abandoned by her community, her mind drifted to Salim. He was the only person in the whole world who would understand her and support her. "I have to get to Salim," she decided.

Then she remembered the travelers were heading for Al Saeed. She quickly grabbed some of her things, some food and water, and her horse. Then she rode out of town.

"If I keep my distance, they won't even know I'm following them, and they will lead me to Salim's village," she thought as she saw the travelers in the distance along the trail heading west towards the mountains.

Rowan and Nayla had been riding in tense silence since they left Davidstown. Rowan was angry because Nayla hadn't respected the culture and ways of the community. Nayla in turn felt bitter because she had failed to make a difference in the fate of the women on trial—and in the overall oppression of the women in the village. Neither of them wanted to talk about the event, as they both knew it would lead to a fight. They needed each other on this journey, and needed to maintain the peace. Besides, the events had taken place already; they belonged to the past, and couldn't be changed anymore. The journey ahead was what counted.

Odin was clearly happy to be traveling again. He would run ahead, then stay busy sniffing all kinds of smells until Rowan and Nayla caught up, at which point he would race ahead again to indulge in the discovery of more odor stories and traces. At one point he just stood in the middle of the trail watching Rowan and Nayla approach.

"What's up? Aren't we moving fast enough?" Rowan laughed.

But as they caught up with Odin, the wolf stayed fixated on something in the distance far behind them.

"He's not waiting for us, he's looking at something behind us," Rowan said, glad Odin provided a reason to talk—something to break the tension and focus their attention away from the morning events.

He turned his horse and gazed into the distance. Quickly he spotted what had caught Odin's interest. Someone was following them—a single rider. Why?

"I don't like this," he said to Nayla. "This could be trouble. Once we reach the next hilltop, let's gallop ahead to the closest point of shelter so we can shake whoever that is from our trail—or at least, confront them and find out why we're being followed."

A t first Kate had been careful to stay out of sight, but the further away she'd gotten from the town, the more she'd become concerned with losing her guides ahead and getting lost in this big country. After a while she'd just started following in full view since neither one of the travelers looked back anyway. Besides, at times there wasn't any cover, leaving her with little choice.

She'd noticed that just before the travelers crested the next hill, they had stopped and looked in her direction. She'd kept on riding in order not to look conspicuous—she would be just another traveler on the trail.

When she finally reached the top of the same hill, she couldn't see the travelers or the wolf anywhere in the valley ahead. Her fear had been realized: She was all alone in the wilderness!

What should she do? Well, somewhere ahead of her in this big country was Al Saeed. And returning home was not an option. She wasn't going to grant her father that satisfaction.

When she looked closer at the grass in front of her, she noticed a faint trail where the horses had walked through the dry brown grass. Determined to get to Salim, she forged ahead, limiting her vision now to the grass in front of her.

At one point it seemed the tracks had veered off towards some spruce trees a little ways to the side of the trail. Kate stopped to examine the ground better, and then peered into the darkness of the forest. Why did her guides seemingly decide to ride into the forest here? She felt nervous about entering the woods, afraid of getting really lost.

"Hello," she tried, feeling a little anxious. "Anyone there?"

The forest was eerily silent, and Kate felt that she was being watched.

Next Kate's eyes caught some movement. She felt a sigh of relief as she noticed it was the wolf running towards her. Soon after, the woman on horse followed. The man came out a moment later.

"Hi," Kate offered with a smile. "I thought I'd lost you," she confessed.

"I'm Nayla, and this is Rowan," the woman answered in a friendly manner. "You're the girl who spoke up this morning, right?"

"Yes. My name is Kate."

"So where are you heading, Kate? It seems you have been following us," the trapper broke in, suspicion in his voice.

"Well, yes, I have been. With no bad intentions, though. I want to get to Al Saeed, where my boyfriend lives. However, I didn't know how to get there, and when I heard the two of you were traveling there, I decided to use you as my guides," she explained, feeling both excited and somewhat apologetic.

"Do your parents know of your travel?" Rowan continued his query in a stern manner

"Mmmh … not exactly," she mumbled.

"They do, or they don't?" Rowan insisted impatiently.

"No, they don't," Kate answered directly in an attempt to regain her normally grounded manner.

Then she recounted the events of that morning and the previous day: the fight with her father, her plan to travel with Salim, and how speaking up earlier had completely shattered the possibility of her studying at the university anyway.

"You can't come with us," Rowan responded harshly. "We can't get involved in your community affairs."

"Sure she can," Nayla said, jumping eagerly to the girl's defense. "That was very brave of you this morning," she commended Kate. "It was the right thing to do."

Then she turned to Rowan and explained, "Kate is clearly a very bright and conscientious student. Her future of studying is being threatened because this morning she stood up not only for what she believed in, but for what is right and just. I was partly the cause of that, and got her into this situation. Therefore, I'm going to stand by her and help her to get to her boyfriend."

"But—" Rowan protested.

Yet Nayla continued in a determined fashion, "I'm not taking one further step in the direction of Al Saeed without Kate."

Rowan looked Nayla in the eyes, and for a few seconds a silent duel took place. But when the brave woman from the Confederacy didn't shrink back, he spurred his horse and galloped ahead.

Nayla smiled in the direction of Rowan. "I guess we better follow him, or we'll both get lost," she winked at Kate.

Kate smiled and proudly rode alongside this courageous woman from the American Confederacy whom she now admired even more. Nayla had listened to her. She had treated her like the adult woman she now was. She had understood her and offered her support. Kate suddenly didn't feel all alone in the world anymore. There was hope, and soon she would be able to find more comfort in the arms of Salim.

She could have argued with her father, or defended her position to the elders about her worthiness to study. However, in doing so she would have confirmed their authority and the control they had claimed over her life—something she was just not prepared to do. Instead she had drawn a line in the sand, cut the ropes of dependency and reclaimed the control she'd given to all these people. She had demonstrated that she was an equal and should be treated as such. As she was pondering those thoughts, Kate realized that taking control—and responsibility—over one's life was the pinnacle of adulthood. She had become a woman!

Control was something that was given. Children give it to their parents, and in turn, parents provide education, the necessities of life, and coaching on the way to adulthood. But there's a point when the teenage girl becomes a woman. That point isn't marked by age, school graduation or any other special ritual, but rather by the moment when the teenage girl takes full control and responsibility of her own life—in essence, removing that control and responsibility from her parents.

Pondering this insight further, Kate concluded that most women in her culture never came to that point. Rather they transferred their dependency from their parents to their husband, and with it control over their lives. She rejoiced in her newfound freedom, shaking her hair in the wind and smiling. It was like being born all over again. Rebirth! She was the master of her own destiny. She was a free woman with the whole world in front of her to explore.

She felt a slight sadness too, because she would never be able to share this feeling with her mother or most of her friends. They simply wouldn't understand this until they took control and responsibility of their own lives—like Nayla, the woman who had inspired her, who had shown her it was possible for women to lead, be independent and even determine the course of the world.

Rowan slowed down and stopped. His gaze was concentrated on a large number of ravens that were circling in the distant sky. Odin too had his nose in the air. His sharp sense of smell had no doubt already told him what they would find ahead.

"There must be a dead animal over the next ridge, so we should be careful for bears," Rowan warned.

As they reached the top of the hill, the view unveiled a massacre. The grasslands in front of them were dotted with the bodies of at least twenty dead elk. The scene unleashed in the trio of travelers strong emotions of disgust, outrage and shame at being part of the human race.

The animals had clearly been on the run, and had been finished off one by one while trying to reach the cover of the forest. Ravens and coyotes were feeding on the bloated carcasses, which were spread over the plain all the way to the trees on the next ridge. At a safe distance to the west a grizzly bear was burying a carcass to forage on over the days to come.

At the sight, Rowan's face betrayed his deep pain. For the last four years the animals had fed him, and offered their lives for him in a sacred ritual called "the hunt"—the universal cycle where each death transforms into new life. He had cared for these animals, respected them, and loved them. They were like family, his brothers and sisters. They were one. He was elk. He was deer. They lived on in him—

through him. So when his sudden scream of "Why?" tore through the macabre silence, it was heartrending.

Just like with the loss of his family years ago, he felt his heart turn to stone as he walked to the first elk carcass and respectfully knelt down next to it. Putting his hand on the bloated bullet-ridden body, he whispered coldly through his teeth, "I'll kill whoever did this if they ever cross my path."

As for Nayla, she had a pretty good idea who was behind this massacre. There was too much respect for life in this country for such a wasteful and disrespectful act to be perpetrated by its inhabitants. People here lived in balance with their environment. They were part of it, were fed by it, and as a result respected it. Such waste, such display of the lowest qualities of humankind, could only come from someone who had no notion of the possibility of such a relationship between man and his environment—someone who had reduced this miraculous planet to a collection of resources to be controlled, used and abused for man's pleasure and comfort. But how could anyone find pleasure in such destruction, in such waste?

The carnage made her even more determined to bring the seeds to the United States of Bolivar. It seemed that the whole world—with the notable exception of the American Confederacy—understood the interdependence of man and nature. For Nayla, the massacre proved it was time to break the stranglehold her sick culture had on the world. While she had struggled with abandoning the American Dream, viewing the disgusting sight of blatant disrespect for other living things on this planet made it an easy choice. Now, she felt ashamed for having been part of the American culture for so many years.

She wasn't quite sure what it was or how she had come to this point, but for the first time in her life a heartfelt connection with nature touched her soul. This was something that had eluded her throughout her life, but something she had seen in her husband Julian, and in this hunter who was now helping her.

133

Nayla could feel Rowan's pain. She could feel the waste and the senseless destruction of life. She could feel the sorrow of the elk people—who were confused about man's breach of the sacred tradition. She could feel how the blood-soaked earth was crying for its children. And as Nayla opened her heart to nature, she allowed the appalling display before her to cut painfully deep into her heart. Tears streamed down her face.

Kate's elation with her newfound freedom became short-lived at the sight of the animal massacre. There was ugliness—evil in this world. Maybe, she decided, what she had observed in her community wasn't all that bad—or at least, unusual. Maybe evil and injustice were just part of the world. Or maybe, it existed to call out the best in those who believed in a better world, to test their courage to stand up and fight for freedom, respect, equality and love.

Rowan's voice interrupted the women's thoughts.
"Let's circle around this valley."
His suggestion was welcomed by all except Odin, whose hunting instincts were awakened by the smell of the bloating carcasses.
The trio rode on in silence, each contemplating the lessons the elk had taught them in death.

*D*ick searched the bedroom in the trapper's cabin. Finally, he found what he was looking for. Female clothing that was most definitely from the American Confederacy. A solid lead! Nayla had been here. She was alive, and had found help.

Based on the absence of any decoration in the cabin and the small bedroom, he concluded the place must have belonged to a single trapper. "She probably used her seductive skills to get him to help her. The whore! I should tell George when the time is right; it might help him to see Nayla for what she is: a traitor!" he pondered while fantasizing about how she'd gained the favors of the trapper.

He noted that the corrals outside the cabin had been home to some horses and goats. All the animals were gone, but based on the freshness of the manure and the still-soft deer hide they found in the little shelter, the fugitive had only left in the last couple of days. Dick also found wolf tracks, and assumed the animal had passed through, attracted by the deer remains.

Since the place was deserted just recently, it seemed likely Nayla wasn't traveling alone. The trapper must have become her companion—her personal local guide. They were traveling by horse, and Nayla was likely dressed as a local since she had left her Confederate clothing behind. Due to the many horse trails going in and out of the clearing, his men were not able to determine in which direction they had left.

There was, however, no time to lose. Dick had enough clues to continue his search. He could already smell his prey; victory was near! While Nayla had been smart in her escape from the American Confederacy, she'd made some important mistakes here. It was now only a matter of time before he would track her down. Horseback wasn't a very fast way of traveling—certainly not compared to the helicopters he had at his disposal.

"Where would she be going?"

Dick closed his eyes while trying to put himself into Nayla's shoes. North would only get her further away from her final destination, which must be the United States of Bolivar. South would close the distance between them so it would be unlikely for her to do that. But then again, she went north last time while they all expected her to go south.

Going east she would find some of the major rivers that would bring her eventually via the Mississippi river to the Gulf, which she could cross by ship to the United States of Bolivar. That route would be risky though, since she would have to enter the American Confederacy again. However, he couldn't exclude this travel route—it could be another brilliant escape move from Nayla.

Now, if she went west she could cross the mountains and try to find a ship that would sail from the United Canadian Communities to the United States of Bolivar.

"What would she have done?" he wondered frantically.

"The closest village is Huntingville to the North," one of his men happened to inform him.

The news was all he needed to make his decision.

"All right, let's start there. If we don't find anything there, let's check out the closest eastern community, then the southern one and last, the closest western village. Now, let's get back to the helicopters and get those birds in the air. We have a prey to catch."

Dick grinned. He could smell blood, and the trail was fresh.

he path along the river climbed higher as the group got deeper into the Rocky Mountains. Over the years a persistent flow of water had conquered the rigid strength of the rocks and carved a canyon that gave way to the plains.

The narrow pass the travelers were riding through gave access to a valley behind this first mountain range. By the time they reached the top of the pass the river was running deep below them in the canyon. From their vantage point they could overlook the sheltered valley ahead that stretched towards the west.

Al Saeed was bathed in the golden light of the last evening sun and nestled along the river against the flank of the northern mountain. This provided the community with natural shelter from the polar winds.

The northern bank of the river provided fertile farm land while the southern bank was home to a lush forest. As the sun started her descent behind the mountains in the west, the temperature fell quickly.

Rowan shared his relief at the sight of the village. "I am glad we reached this place before nightfall. The nights are still cold at this time of the year."

Just like in Davidstown, the arrival of the travelers was first noticed by the village children, who made sure the news spread fast. It was still early in the year, the snow had just broken, and Al Saeed's villagers didn't normally see any travelers crossing the mountains until late spring. Winter was a time of rest in Al Saeed, and visitors were a welcome break from the hibernation time.

At the entrance of the community, a large carved wooden sign next to a decorated chest invited all women, in respect of local custom, to cover their hair. The crate contained scarves of various colors to aid amenable female travelers in respecting the request.

Nayla and Kate both honored the petition, and each draped a brightly-colored shawl over their hair.

"Al Saeed is a Muslim village," Rowan explained to her.

Nayla knew this meant the community's laws and customs were rooted in the Muslim religious texts. It was, however, a religion she was unfamiliar with. This visit would offer yet another cultural exploration.

"How do they treat their women?" she asked Rowan jokingly.

Rowan didn't laugh though. "Please don't ruin things here as well. Just try to respect their culture."

Maybe the women are treated the same as in Davidstown, Nayla worried, regretting her bad joke.

They rode down one of the main streets leading to the market square.

"This town design makes it easy for arriving travelers." Nayla pondered the concentric community layout, which had been similar in Davidstown: a central market square to which all main streets from the different geographical directions gave access. The houses were all connected again, but this time built from logs and river stone. Their architecture was characterized by one or more minarets that formed the second or third floor of the homes.

As the children were spreading the news rapidly, the street was filling with friendly faces of men and women greeting the travelers with broad smiles. The women all had their hair covered and wore long tunics that covered their entire body, but none of them had the submissive look Nayla had observed among the women of Davidstown. These women all held their heads high, and she could read genuine smiles of welcome on their faces.

Once again, the massive black Odin was getting the brunt of the attention. Just like in Davidstown he was walking proudly, and obediently, right next to Rowan's horse.

"Kate! Kate!" a voice shouted over the crowd as they approached the market square.

A tall and slender young man with dark skin came running towards the travelers.

"Salim!" an overjoyed Kate responded.

In the blink of an eye she'd dismounted her horse and was racing towards Salim. The young couple now captured the attention of all people in the street. When they fell into each other's arms, loud cheers echoed through the streets. Who wouldn't be touched by two souls, deeply in love, who reunite after a long separation? Even Odin wasn't a match for this scene.

Kate proudly introduced Salim to Nayla and Rowan. A tall, skinny man dressed in a rich blue robe approached from the market square. The way others were making way for the man indicated his importance in the community.

Salim introduced the man as his father, the master trader of the community.

"Welcome to Al Saeed," the trader gestured with a bow. "You are braving the mountains early in the year. Good you got here before nightfall. It's cold out in the mountains after dark.

"Friends of my son Salim are friends of mine. My house is your house. We'll talk tonight over dinner, after you've had time to unpack and refresh. Salim, please show our guests where they can stay, and ask your mother to prepare some extra food."

Salim led the travelers to a large, freestanding mansion on the market square. The log work of the house was decorated with delicate carvings. Each corner of the mansion had a minaret built from river-rock. The house was spacious, and in the center of the large living room was a stone masonry fireplace. The circular seating area around it was decorated with colorful cushions and blankets, all of which had unique designs embroidered on them. A polar bear hide dating from a

139

time before the animals became extinct—a courtesy of global warming—was draped against the wall. Several wooly bison hides functioned as soft rugs on the polished wooden floors.

Clearly the trader was a wealthy and important man in the community; it was reflected in the delicate design and decorative ways in which the various local natural materials were used in the home. To develop an elegant home there was no need to import marble from China or hardwoods from the rainforests around the world—like they did in the American Confederacy. It wasn't the material or its origin that made the home stand out, but rather how man had used the material to provide class and comfort to the home.

Nayla soon discovered that each of the travelers' rooms looked out on the communal garden behind the house. The use of that central space within the housing blocks was similar to Davidstown, but here the garden took the form of a park with large trees, communal seating areas and a playground for children where they could climb on a wooden structure and crawl through tunnels.

As in Davidstown, Nayla was struck by the harmony between the community and its natural surroundings. It all came down to innovative design that used nature as its teacher. The design was respectful of the environment and employed local natural materials for its construction.

During dinner Rowan and Nayla shared the story of their journey and informed the trader about the importance of the mutating germinator seeds for the future of the planet. The trader listened attentively and thoughtfully, without interrupting.

In turn the travelers learned that Salim's father was one of the most revered and successful traders of the western United Canadian Communities, and an important member of the town council. He had been a trader and traveler since he'd left high school, and knew all about the product specialties of all the western United Canadian Communities. He was a man of the world. His travels and trading had taught him about human desire, greed and revenge, but also about human love, kindness and harmony. His experience with different

140

cultures had provided a rich foundation from which to interpret the ebbs and flows of the world. As a result, his wisdom was often sought in the community for everything from marital disputes to serious communal affairs.

"Your success in trading is reflected in your beautiful home," Nayla complimented him.

"I'm afraid you have that wrong," the trader politely smiled. "It's true that I have been very successful in my trading. But I never aspired to enrich myself through it. What my success and acquired resources allowed me to do was to be a better servant. That's, after all, what's expected of every Muslim: to serve God and his Creation. Everything that I earned was because of the will of Allah, and therefore it would only be right for me to serve his Creation with these earnings. I served my community with my success, and gave what I earned to the needy. I gave it all away. Everything you see here, including this house, has been given to me. Some of these have been gifts from people whom I helped during my travels. Others are from people whom I've been of service to in this village. The house has been given to me by the community."

Nayla was perplexed by the simple concept of service, and how the gift of time and money had returned to the trader in the same form: that of gifts.

The trader read the surprise on Nayla's face.

"I know this concept is unusual within your culture and might be difficult to understand. Somehow in the American Confederacy they held on to the old belief that one had to acquire things in order to be rich and find happiness. But I tell you, the opposite is true. It's by being of service, by helping others, that one finds meaning and happiness—lasting happiness. And that's what ultimately makes a man truly rich.

"Think of it; what are you personally gaining in material value by putting your life at risk to save these seeds? Why are you doing this? My guess is that it doesn't bring you any material possessions; on the contrary, it may be depriving you of them. However, I do expect that your quest truly gives meaning to your life, and that when you turn the germinating power of seeds back to all farmers in the world, it will provide you a satisfaction and happiness you've never known before. It will truly fulfill you. This is your purpose—the purpose of your life! In this context, all the money and gold of the world have no value. If it did, you would sell the seeds to the highest bidder. No, you already know that true meaning and happiness are found in what you give, in how you serve the world, and not in what you take or control."

Grateful for the insight, Nayla smiled and looked into the dark wise eyes of the trader. Eyes that had seen the world—or at least, a vast part of it—and had absorbed and learned without judging.

"So after all your travels, which village has the most attractive culture in your opinion?" Nayla questioned.

"Al Saeed, of course!" he broadly smiled. "That's why I live here and not anywhere else!"

"And why is the culture of Al Saeed superior?" she questioned.

"Well, I wouldn't say it's superior to any of the other cultures; it's just right for me. For one, I was raised Muslim. The Qur'an provided spiritual guidance to me as I grew up. Second, and equally important, I grew up with the people in this community. They're my friends and family. All cultures have strong points and some weaker features. If we would all pick and choose the things we like and develop our own personal culture, we would all live in communities of one," he smiled again. "There are always compromises that we need to make to our desired individual behavior to fit into a culture and respect its communal customs."

"But some cultures are more respectful of nature, like the ones in this country for example—at least in comparison with the culture of my country. Other cultures have more respect for human rights," Nayla insisted. "We just came from Davidstown, and women are really oppressed there."

"But it works for them," the trader replied more seriously.

"That's what Rowan keeps telling me as well. But the way I see it, it works for the men, not for the women."

"I can understand your struggle, but I would argue that it works for the women there as well. The United Canadian Communities are built on four pillars that are respected by all communities. First is the recognition that the land is sacred. We need fresh air, pure water and healthy soils to live as human beings. Everything else is mere detail and becomes irrelevant if those essential elements aren't in place—something some countries have forgotten. As a result, all land here belongs to the commons in our country. We don't own it! We can use it—all of it—as long as we live, but we cannot possess it and withhold it from the rest of humanity by owning it, destroying it and robbing it from future generations. We care for it collectively as a community, and leave it to our collective children from whom we are really borrowing it.

"Second, every community is independent in its government and cultural development. That includes its customs, laws, economy, communal resource management—land, water and air—and judicial system.

"Third, all citizens are free to choose the best fitting culture for themselves. They can seek out a community that lives according to their desired culture, or start a new one.

"Lastly, all people are treated equally within the cultural practices of the community. That means that all people have equal access to healthcare, all children have equal access to education and the villages select the most qualified students to be sent to the various universities in the country. Every person in this country knows these pillars, and so every woman in Davidstown understands that they have the right to leave in search of a new community. There are no walls built around Davidstown, yet most of the women choose to stay. That means it works for them. If the culture wouldn't function for them—if they were truly unhappy—they would leave."

"But with all your cultural experience, do you think it is just?" Kate jumped in.

"Justice is always a matter of context. My values are inspired by the Qur'an and it clearly states, 'Men are a raiment for women as

143

women are a raiment for men.' That's why I live in a community where women are treated as equals to men. But it's not up to me to judge the laws of another culture since I don't understand the roots of their values. We can question the culture and challenge it, but we shouldn't judge it. All change has to come from within the community, and each culture evolves based on the very questions and challenges of travelers or inquisitive minds from within the community."

"So you wouldn't judge the laws of my country either?" Nayla questioned

"Well, that's a different story, since your country violates the four pillars that our country is based on. It doesn't respect the soil, water and air, and therefore doesn't respect life itself. That's a violation of the values of any religion on this planet and of pure common sense. It's just plain wrong!" the trader said forthrightly. "Actually, I would go further and say that robbing future generations of clean air, water and soil is nothing short of criminal. It kills life, for now and into the future. This country was built by people who fought for these rights, and as diverse as our communal cultures are we would take up arms again if our key pillars were to be threatened."

"Well, if I succeed in getting these seeds to their destination, the controlling power of the American Confederacy will be broken and their culture will be doomed."

"Surely, the powers-that-be won't let that happen without trying to stop you," the trader observed wisely.

"You're right. Carsanto's security forces are already searching for me. The General, who leads them, will do anything to track me down and recover the seeds. We saw two helicopters the day before yesterday on our way to Davidstown."

The trader's face turned serious and concerned. "Did they see you?"

"No, they did not. We took shelter among the spruce trees," Rowan replied.

"That will give us a little more time. But we should act quickly. It's not going to take long before they will be visiting this village then," the trader pondered aloud. "The men that are after you know that you won't make it in this country without help. They'll start making inquiries in all communities in an ever-widening circle from the point where you were last seen. You can bet they're doing just that today, and given what is at stake, I know they will not do this kindly. I'll call all the villagers together in the morning and prepare them for evacuation. *In sha' Allah!*"

Nayla apologized for the problem she was creating by traveling through the village. She felt guilty, and now regretted their stop in Al Saeed.

But the trader comforted the visitors. "Don't feel bad. We're better off now. The Confederate troops would have paid us a visit anyway. It's true that if we were to tell your General that we helped you, he would likely harm our people as punishment," the trader agreed. "But if we were to tell him we never saw you, he would likely use force—or even torture—to see if he might get a different answer. So your stay here doesn't make a difference. Either way, there will be a visit—and accompanying trouble. At least now we know enough to ready ourselves for it. It was Allah's will for you to inform us so we can prepare for what's to come," the trader explained calmly.

"Young lady," he said as he turned to Kate, "we all have shared our wisdom and stories tonight. Before going to bed and preparing for a busy day tomorrow, I would like to hear your story. I know you love my son. But what made you decide to join the travelers and bless us with your visit?"

Kate shared everything: her wish to travel with Salim, their plans to delay her studies with one year, her fights with her father and the events of that morning on the market square.

"So why did you come here?" the trader persisted.

"Because Salim is the only person who understands me. No one in Davidstown understands me!" Kate blurted out. "You said cultural change has to come from within, but I can tell you that it doesn't. The issue of equal treatment of women has been raised over

Hugo Bonjean

and over by different women in my community, and each time it has
fallen on deaf ears."

"Well, I didn't say change is easy, or that it happens without
disruption, trials or even conflict. That's all an intrinsic part of it. A
community needs to go through such turmoil to evolve, which is
exactly why such change cannot come from the outside. The values
and customs of a culture are built on the scars and efforts of the
members of that culture. You're a brave young woman," he observed.
"It takes courage and perseverance to challenge tradition and pave new
ways for the future. It's a lonely task only carried by the most
passionate and persevering of souls. The trials on the path are also
testing your convictions of what is right, and your skill in explaining
and convincing others of it. So don't give up your quest. Follow what
your heart tells you to fight for. That's your purpose!

"However, tomorrow I have to send you home. Your parents
don't know where you are. They love you and will be very worried.
You have to go back and talk to them. If you then decide to come
back, you're welcome here. They don't have to agree with your
decision, but at least they should know.

"You're eighteen, a young woman now and ready to explore
the world on your own terms. You should learn from other cultures
and decide what's right for you. I too think it's wise to travel first.
Your experience will influence your choice of study. You are right; it
shows more respect for those who are supporting your education to
wait until you have a better understanding of what you want to do with
your life. And if this morning's events have destroyed your current
chance for funding, do not abandon your dream just yet. Allah works
in mysterious ways. Other funding might come forth once you're ready
to study. Salim will be your guide and protect you on your return
journey to Davidstown tomorrow."

Disappointment could be read on Kate's face, but she sought
strength in Salim's supportive eyes. She didn't speak, but merely
nodded politely.

146

The trader closed the evening by thanking the visitors for sharing their stories. Before leaving for his room, he turned to Nayla.

"Thank you for being here, and for all you're doing. It's my honor to serve your cause. I hope you will succeed. *In sha Allah!*"

Nayla looked out at the moon high above in a black sky dotted with trillions of twinkling stars. The night skies were so much prettier here than in the American Confederacy where all the city lights stole the stars from the heavens. Yet she couldn't sleep. Despite the comforting words of the trader, she felt guilty for having endangered the lives of the people in the surrounding communities, and particularly the lives of those whom had helped her.

"Why does change always have to be accompanied with trials and tribulations?" she wondered. "Is it really a test of how strongly we believe in our vision, like the trader suggested? Are our dreams only granted once we demonstrate that we're prepared to put everything on the line for them? When we can get up after we fall down—over and over again—because we've discovered in the depths of the silence within us the ever-burning flame that keeps us going when all else falls away?"

These questions raced through Nayla's restless mind. She knew she was doing the right thing; she just wished no one would get hurt in the process. Once again on this journey, she decided to read some more in her grandmother's diary. It was becoming an evening ritual in which the guiding words of her ancestor, at the right moments, taught her what she needed to know.

September 20, 2021

Today we gave new meaning to the American Dream of liberty and freedom. In some sick way the meaning of the American Dream has been raped over the last few decades and become synonymous to unbridled consumption and the destruction of our environment. We often call it now the American way of life. A way of life which our government defends by all means—even war. But the right to unbridled consumption was not what our dream used to be about. It wasn't about the freedom to buy the stuff we want and destroy the planet in the process—the very essentials for life itself, our water, soil and air. The founding fathers of our country, the very men who gave birth to our American Dream, wanted to provide all Americans with the freedom to pursue their dreams. What's curious is that most people I know dream of a just, peaceful and sustainable world, and when we try to work towards such a world we're not given the freedom to do so. They say we inhibit economic progress and negatively impact the profits of corporations. Since when are the interests of intangible paper persons like corporations—who do not have the ability to dream but only can post bank accounts—more important than the interests of real people?

Here's how bad it got. On July 4, those who actively spoke up and took action to create the world of their dreams got all rounded up and put in mega-prisons. It was all done, of course, to protect the people and the American way of life. Our country had been invaded by thousands of insurgents who were poisoning the minds of the American citizens and planning multiple terrorist activities. Of course, no formal trials have been held; who would expect that these days? Thousands of people are now locked up with no due process, no justice, and no legal defense. What has happened to my country?

My organic garden has done well. I grew my own lettuce for most of the summer, and even now I still have some standing. My tomatoes also fared well ...and my herbs. Broccoli and Brussels sprouts were a huge disaster. Some type of bug got into them and ate all the leaves. I could hear the guys from Carsanto say, "You should have used our pesticides. We told you so." Alejandro teased me and told me the bugs were answers to his prayers since he hates broccoli and Brussels sprouts.

Anyway, I'm jumping all over the place again. Don't think I'll ever get rid of that habit. But then again, who cares. This is my diary, written for …I guess me.

Well, when I said today 'we' gave new meaning to the American Dream, I really meant Alejandro and some of his friends. I guess I acknowledge the value of Alejandro's perspective now, but I don't have the guts to do what they did. I'll stick to my organic garden, although I actually took my next step this summer. There wasn't much to do with the garden, just some weeding and watching the seeds grow, so I started my recycling program. I really ramped it up fast. Now I even produce my own compost which I can use in my garden. I'm so proud.

But you know what I learned yesterday? For every bag of garbage each of us produces, there are seventy garbage bags produced in creating the junk we are throwing out in the first place. It gets even worse. Of the products we buy, only one percent is still in use six months after we've bought it. In essence we're ripping the planet apart to produce stuff. Then we throw ninety-nine percent of that stuff away within six months. Every one of those garbage bags on the curb needs to be multiplied by seventy to incorporate the waste created during the production and extraction process in order to get the true picture of our wasteful culture. If that doesn't sound like madness to you, there's a good chance you're really crazy.

This knowledge brought me to my third project, and that is to cut down my consumption drastically. Every time I have the urge to go out and buy something, I ask myself, do I really need it. Is it worth the true cost to the environment in the world? Most of the time I've found the answer to be "No." I got the information from a website that got me really thinking. It explained the problem of our linear consumption society in an entertaining but very clear way. It was called "The Story of Stuff."

But I'm off topic—again. I was going to write about Alejandro today, and his brave action. I would never do such a thing myself, but I'm sure glad that someone else is doing something that can shake up the status quo. Sometimes, I fear, he might be right: Maybe the things I do are only to comfort my own conscience, like raindrops on a hot plate. But then I remember that many little raindrops can form a mighty ocean. And as I remember that, I look for the next positive thing I can do to work towards my dream of a sustainable and peaceful world.

We make quite a pair, Alejandro and me—the revolutionary and the pacifist. What we have learned from each other is that although our chosen course of action is different, each of our actions is driven by a deep love and passion for a dream of a better world. And maybe, both of us, each in our own way, have our role to play. Certainly now that America is starting to look more like the dictatorial regimes of the world—or like Naomi Wolf pointed out, like Germany in the thirties—it's more difficult to imagine that the powers-that-be will change or leave without a fight. Yes, I still have the freedom to grow my organic garden ...and to recycle. But what about my freedom of speech? If I say something that's deemed inappropriate—these days that means something that could be a threat to big business—it's unlikely to get any media attention at all. And if I take a grassroots approach to spread my message, I might end up in one of those mega-jails—to protect the American population from my subversive talk.

Freedom used to have a different meaning. Actually, I think it's exactly the removal of our liberties, the paranoid striving for control and security which rejects any notion of change or sustainability and defends the 'American way of life' beyond reason, that has driven the sustainability movement underground—to a point of more drastic action. In the end, I don't really care how we're going to realize our dream anymore. As long as I can grow my vegetables organically and more people can start doing the same, it's all good. And if big chemical corporations or bureaucratic government officials are standing in the way of that, then we need people like Alejandro, people with the guts to push them aside, people who have the courage to fight for their dreams. Who knows? One day, I might get there.

Alejandro always says that we're being tested. It's all a trial to see how firmly we believe in our dreams. Are we worth the paradise we all dream of? Are we prepared to put everything on the line for it, even our lives? As he keeps pointing out, the keepers of "the dream of world control" sure do ...and as long as we're not prepared to do the same to see our dream of the world come to fruition, it will just stay a dream, an aspiration rather than a reality.

I guess I still haven't told you why I'm writing today, and how Alejandro gave new meaning to the American Dream. Anyway, today Alejandro and his friends took a step towards creating a more harmonious society by blowing up an old dam and giving the river its freedom back. No one was killed or wounded in the action. But it was an important first step. They returned freedom to the river, *freedom to the salmon so they could return to their spawning grounds, freedom to the people who want to live in harmony with nature. When he came home he was all emotional, telling me about their gift of freedom to the salmon, which in return provide us with their gifts of life to feed our people. It made him realize how we all live in one interconnected system where it is our service to one another, as humans and as living beings on this planet—fish, birds, plants and mammals—that allows for the giving to continue in a never-ending cycle of life and death. If we stop serving the salmon, their gifts will diminish and eventually cease completely. If we stop serving the soil, it will reduce its gifts to us and eventually be unable to produce anything for us. If we stop serving our fellow human beings, they will be unable to give anything to us and be only concerned with their own survival. None of us can survive on our own. Only within this magically interconnected universe can we all exist, so therefore we should measure the justness of our actions with how well we're serving our interdependent eco-system—the expression of Divinity itself. Today, for the first time, Alejandro felt he'd done something worth living for. It gave him a deep sense of satisfaction and happiness.*

I had never considered the perspective of being a servant to my organic plants, to the soil, to this miraculous planet. But I like the perspective. If only we could all just focus on what we have to give to one another, not just between humans, but also the giving between species. Think about it; how much have all the other organisms on this planet given us over the last decades—actually, ever since we started to walk on Earth? And what have we given in return? It's time we start to give and find our happiness in the process. It makes us feel of value, gives us purpose—at least that's what I observe in Alejandro. And that awareness of being a valuable link in this bigger-than-life play of the universe leads to a deep and lasting feeling of happiness.

Seeing him like this makes me yearn to discover such a feeling of value with what I do. Am I really doing all I can, or is there more? Do I have to overcome my fears first, before I will be able to share such a sense of purpose? What am I prepared to offer, to give, for my dream?

he early morning sky above the mountains was colored bright pink and purple as the sun was rising. "What a great day to go hunting," Dick thought as he entered the chopper at the base. This morning they were heading for Davidstown.

The previous day they'd paid a visit to Huntingville. At first none of the villagers had talked. But Dick had sensed they'd held some information that they were not sharing with him. So he'd changed tactics, dropped his friendly, polite strategy and did what he did best: squeeze things out of people. He'd known his instincts had been right. Their faces had told him they'd known something.

They'd rounded up all the villagers at gunpoint in the community square. With his thundering voice he had commanded the villagers to share their information and warned them about the consequences of withholding anything. While he had done so he'd observed them all closely.

One farmer in particular had caught his attention. His eyes had descended in fear to the ground when Dick had looked at him. This man knew something; the General had seen it in his eyes. His men had removed him from the crowd. He'd accused the man, warned the village that this man—by not speaking—was threatening the safety of the entire village. The farmer had still denied knowing anything.

His men had held him while Dick punched and kicked the farmer until his face was bleeding. When Dick had cocked his gun and told him to say goodbye to his family, the farmer had finally spoken:

"No one traveled through here, but I do know the trapper who lives in the forest. It's Rowan. He lives alone. We've not seen him for weeks. But it must be his cabin that you visited."

Dick had been delighted he'd been right about the farmer. Damn, he was good at his job! He had given the farmer one last brutal kick while shouting over the marketplace, "You should have answered me immediately. You could have avoided all this hassle. Remember that when we ask you any questions in the future."

It hadn't been much information, but at least he had known Nayla hadn't gone north and she was traveling together with a trapper named Rowan.

Next they'd visited Plainview to the east. He'd tried the friendly way with just two people, and when he'd noticed the same response as in Huntingville, he'd decided not to waste any more time trying to be the nice guy. His men had brutally rounded up all the villagers as well as their livestock. Then he'd declared to the villagers that he was going to keep killing until someone shared information about the two travelers he was looking for.

His men had lined up the goats and cows. One by one Dick had started shooting them. Each time an animal had been shot, falling to the ground, and letting its life's blood spill over the marketplace, Dick had looked sternly at the fear-filled crowd.

The General had finally decided he had to increase the stakes in order to find out if these people really knew nothing. Maybe these animals weren't important enough; after all, Nayla's package of the mutating germinating seeds was of much more value.

So he'd grabbed a little four-year-old boy from the crowd. Both the boy and his mother had made a terrifying scene as they clutched at one another. His men had to club the father down to the ground to keep him back. The boy had screamed loudly as Dick took him to the same place where he'd shot all the animals. The close sight of dead corpses had silenced the child. When Dick had put his gun against the boy's head, only silent tears ran over the child's face.

"I'm asking you one last time; tell me what you know about the two travelers!" he had heartlessly commanded the crowd. "As I said, I'm going to keep killing until I know. The children are next!"

But no valuable information had come forward—only pleas from begging mothers and the elderly. His men had needed to restrain some village men who were trying to charge him.

The General knew Nayla hadn't been there. The people hadn't known anything. He had coldly dropped the boy, walked to the chopper and returned to the base just before nightfall.

It had been a productive day. He knew Nayla hadn't gone north or east. So that left south or west.

If today he interrogated as efficiently, he would be able to track Nayla down before the sun set. That would be good, because he was already looking forward to returning to the order and comfort of the American Confederacy. How could people stand such primitive lifestyles as those in the United Canadian Communities? They were missing out on all the good things in life. But then again, all that good stuff was reserved for those who had the brains, organizational skills, and talent to rule and control this world. That's the way God had organized things. The smart and disciplined stewards of this world received their rewards for organizing and employing the lesser beings in a controlled and orderly way—for creating a civilized society from this world of primitive chaos.

K ate and Salim had left Al Saeed right at dawn. They planned to be on top of the pass that gave access to the plains by sunrise. The first few minutes they rode in silence, but then Kate couldn't hold in her disappointment.

"Why, Salim? Why do I have to return? What do I have to tell my dad?"

"Well, you heard my father …and honestly, I think he is right. Your parents should know where you are. Just go tell them, and we can return together. As my father said, they don't have to agree."

"That's easier said than done. You don't know my dad," she sighed as she lost heart.

"No, but I do know you."

That last comment made her feel somewhat better. That's why she loved Salim: He always stood behind her and believed in her, but he also still gave his honest opinion. He was right: She should tell her father, and then they could leave again. It was just that she'd never been able to have a decent conversation with him. Sometimes they had started off well on issues of importance, but once she disagreed with him, he raised his voice, started shouting, or threatened to make her life more difficult one way or another.

"The problem is that when I start talking with my dad," she confided, "it almost always ends up in a shouting match. He doesn't seem capable of understanding, or is totally unwilling to see, my point of view."

156

Salim considered her words before he responded, "I would say that's because he considers himself to be in a power position. The first rule of good trading negotiations is to position yourself as an equal to the opposite party right from the start. If you position yourself in an inferior role, the other party will be inclined to use power techniques to dominate the trade, or in this case, the conversation. If you position yourself as superior, the other party will quickly take on a defensive role. In either of these two cases, there is no hope for good communication or trade, since there is no mutual respect. In such case the interaction becomes all about fear and control."

"That's exactly what happens when we talk. He always acts like he owns me!" Kate agreed heartily.

"And what signals do you give with your body language?" Salim asked.

"How do you mean?" she asked, confused.

"Well, body language is probably even more important in communication than the actual words that are being said. If, when you address your father, your chest caves in, your eyes focus on the ground, and you feel anxiety about what you want to say or ask, you're taking on the inferior role and are confirming him in his power position.

"On the other hand, if you stand straight and hold your head high, you're not giving him power. That in turn though might be a problem, since he might feel threatened in his role by such posture. Therefore, it's important that you address that in the way you talk. The tone of your voice and the expression on your face should find root in strength and empathy rather than in arrogance and rebellion."

Kate loved how smart Salim was. Everything he was saying was so true. He had deduced accurately how she'd started all her conversations with her father; they began either in fear or from a position of rebellion. Hearing his analysis increased her desire to travel with Salim and learn the things he'd learned during his trading journeys.

"So how should I start the conversation?" she quizzed further.

"By acknowledging you made a mistake. It will disarm his anger. But as you do that, make sure your body language doesn't take on a submissive posture."

"So, something like: 'Hi, Dad, I am sorry I ran away. I didn't want to upset you and Mom. I realize you must have been very worried,'" she ventured.

"Exactly! That acknowledges the emotions of the other party. By doing so, you disarm their anger and open the way for an equal-footed conversation," Salim encouraged with excitement.

"Okay, I get that. So what do I do next?"

"Well, you explain that you returned to come and talk to him. Early on you tell him you're not there to ask for his permission, but that out of respect for him and your mother, and in gratitude of how well they raised you, you want to inform them about what you've decided to do over the next year."

"I don't think that's going to go down very well. I can almost guarantee you that he'll start shouting again right there," Kate predicted.

"It's very important that if he does so, you don't take on a submissive or rebellious role. He can only enter into a word fight in an attempt to control the conversation if you're willing to enter into that battle with him. You have a choice: to oppose and retaliate or to deflect that attack and disarm the emotion once again by simply acknowledging it."

"You mean, continue along the lines of the way I started, for example: 'I can see you're getting upset, Dad. I'm sorry for that; I don't want to make you angry, but it's important to me that you understand what I'm trying to share with you. If you could just hear me out, I would be glad to listen to your concerns.'"

"If you keep learning that fast, I'm going to let you do the trading on our travels," Salim complimented her with a broad smile.

Kate's feelings of anxiety had changed to those of excitement. She was proud of Salim's important communication insights, and his compliments made the butterflies dance in her belly.

They had reached the top of the pass and were treated to a wide panoramic view of the plains in front of them. They could see for miles. Far in the distance was Davidstown, their destination. They stood in silence letting the magic of the moment, this display of God's beauty and perfection, touch their souls.

However, a faint distant roaring sound was out of place.

"What's that there above Davidstown?" Kate questioned.

Two black dots were descending from the skies towards the community.

"That must be the helicopters Rowan and Nayla talked about last night," Salim gasped. "We must return and warn our people in Al Saeed. It might not be safe to travel to your village today. Let's get back."

In a hurry they turned their horses and rushed down the pass, back to Al Saeed.

All the villagers of Davidstown were gathered at the marketplace to hear the judgment of the female protestors. The turnout was larger than usual. Word about how the female traveler had boldly challenged the patriarch, and how Kate, this sharp-tongued teenager, had revoked the judgment by referring to the Bible itself had spread quickly. The townspeople had streamed to the market square to personally witness any other disturbances, or at least the punishment of the women and possibly Kate. However, Kate had been missing since the previous day. Her parents, who were extremely angry were now also worried; they had no idea where she was hiding. Still, most women in the crowd hoped she would show up, including her mother, who deep down inside was proud of her daughter's bravery.

When the patriarch addressed the crowd, the silence was so pervasive you could hear a pin drop.

"We debated late into the night," he started, lines of intense thought carved into his face. "The challenge to our way of life by one of the young potential leaders of this community found its root in our own scriptures. They do indeed say: 'Each of you is a son of God because of your faith in Christ Jesus. All of you who have been baptized into Christ have clothed yourselves with him. There does not exist among you Jew or Greek, slave or freeman, male or female. All are one in Christ Jesus,' as written by Paul in 3:26-28.

"All are one in Christ Jesus," the patriarch repeated, emphasizing these words. As an experienced orator, he waited for a few seconds to allow silence to do its work and let the words sink in—not only into the minds of the audience, but into their hearts as well.

"When we cannot look our young people in the eye and explain to them how our cultural practices are rooted in the scriptures, how can we expect them to embrace our culture? How are we demonstrating our integrity to them? How are we being an example to them so they can walk with integrity through their lives? How can we sleep in peace at night when we know about the discrepancy in what Jesus taught us and our cultural practices?"

Again after each question, the patriarch left a measured pause.

"As with all rulings, we—the elders—seek your input, and we do so now as well. After debating until late in the night, we've come to the conclusion that Kate's questions were justified. Maybe it's time to change our ways and treat our women as equal citizens in this community."

A clamor spread through the crowd. Some men were nodding; others were vehemently shaking their heads and shouting aggressively in protest of the proposed change. Passionate discussions rose up among small groups of men. The women stayed silent. With eyes filled with hope, they observed their husbands and the other men of the community.

Kate's father was fuming. How could the patriarch insult him in such a way? How could these elders suggest that his daughter with all her crazy ideas was still worthy of future leadership? How could they take her words under serious consideration? What was happening to the respect that men deserve from their women! This was not acceptable! He wouldn't support this!

He should have dealt with his subversive daughter a long time ago. It was always her mother who'd deterred him from it. But now, Kate had divided the entire community. And the elders had lost their minds.

Just at that pivotal moment of change for the community of Davidstown, something else captured the attention of its villagers. It was a roaring, threatening sound that came from the sky.

Some men yelled, "Listen, God doesn't agree! He growls at this proposed change."

But then someone saw the two black dots in the eastern sky approaching. "Helicopters!" one of the elders whispered.

Silence and fear paralyzed the villagers, who anticipated what was to come next.

They knew these helicopters housed the men of the American Confederacy who were looking for a brave and generous woman, Nayla, who had given the germinator seeds to their patriarch. They were seeds that could make their village independent from the seed train and Carsanto's empire.

The patriarch had hidden the seeds in the church. As long as no one would talk, no matter what, they would be fine.

As the helicopters flew over the market square, Dick laughed. God was on his side; he didn't even have to round the villagers up in this town—they were already gathered at the square!

"This should make things easy," he thought. "Yesterday's technique worked well. I'll repeat the same here."

As soon as the copters landed, Dick's elite guards, armed with machine guns, took positions around the square.

"Just get me five animals; it doesn't matter where you find them. When people see some killing take place before I hold my gun against a child's head, it will loosen their tongues," he ordered a few guards.

Dick walked up to the patriarch and introduced himself loudly enough so that all the people on the market square could hear him. When he asked about Nayla, he could see nothing in the patriarch's eyes.

"I wouldn't want to play poker with this man," he mused.

"Does anyone have any news about a dangerous female fugitive called Nayla who is traveling together with a local trapper named Rowan?" he repeated louder, addressing the crowd in the hope of reading some clues on people's faces. "These people have stolen state secrets of the American Confederacy, and are dangerous. If you know anything about them you should tell me now, as we will consider their friends our enemies."

His sharp eye detected anxiety among several people. For sure they knew something in this village.

"Well, I've invited you kindly to share with me what you know about these fugitives. I know some of you here have knowledge about them—I've seen it in your eyes—and I am going to start killing until I receive that information."

A dog was brought to him by one of his men. He put his gun against the dog's head, but before he could pull the trigger, a voice from the crowd spoke.

"They were here yesterday."

That was the news Dick had hoped to hear, since starting his interrogations the previous day. Nayla was just a day ahead of them, and since she was traveling by horse, he could catch up to her before nightfall. He let the dog go and turned towards the man.

The crowd held its breath. The patriarch's eyes stared in defeat at the ground. In the center of the crowd, one man stood with his head held high, proud to be of help.

"They arrived two days ago. They stayed here overnight. We didn't ask any questions—just provided food and lodging—and they left yesterday morning," Kate's father spoke loudly.

"So you didn't ask any questions?" Dick responded sarcastically. "You always let any traveler stay in your community, including potential criminals that could harm your kids? I guess my men and I might want to stay for the night," he laughed cruelly. "Well you said A, now you better give me B as well. Where did they leave to?"

"They left for Al Saeed, another village just a day's travel southwest from here," Kate's father responded self-assuredly.

"So you did talk to them?" Dick continued his interrogation play. Things were going fast here, and this man who was giving him answers was no match for his cunning mind.

"Well, they told us where they were going," Kate's father replied, sounding a little less sure of himself this time.

"...and I assume where they came from," Dick prodded.

"Uh. Yes, that too."

"Well, what else did they tell you?"

"Nothing."

"Of course. And why would I believe that?" Dick suddenly snarled. "First you said you didn't ask questions, then you tell me they told you where they were traveling to, and only after I prompted you again did you tell me they shared where they came from."

In the blink of an eye, his face turned terrifying and he shouted from the top of his lungs, "If I were a betting man, which I am, I'd say you know much more and are withholding information from me. I told you before: We'll treat whoever protects this woman as our enemy! Now, what was she wearing?" Dick continued in his stern but unpredictable line of questioning.

"Uh, she was dressed like a trapper's woman," came the voice of Kate's father. It sounded somewhat subdued now.

"...and she told you she came from the American Confederacy."

"Well, yes."

"And you didn't think that clothing was odd, or ask any further questions about why she was traveling through here, dressed like that, far away from home?

"What about you; did you ask her any questions?" he suddenly turned to the patriarch.

The patriarch didn't flinch at the change of address. He responded in an attempt to take control of the situation, "You know what you need to know. You have the information you were looking for. Our people helped you in your search. Why does it matter what we talked about? Of course we had some conversations. I wanted to know if these travelers were a threat to our community. They seemed quite harmless to me and caused us no trouble. So please go now and let us continue our community affairs."

"Did she tell you anything about seeds? Did she trade any seeds with you in return for your help?" Dick's voice thundered while he carefully watched the crowd and paid particular attention to the man

165

who had spoken before. And yes, there in his eyes, he could read the answer. These people knew the full story and quite possibly had some of the seeds, which if they did, they surely had hidden in a safe place. But he had to continue his hunt, there were other ways of making sure that the few potential seeds they might have would never germinate. Now, there was no time to waste; he was getting close.

"You're right," he turned to the patriarch. "I did get the information I was looking for, and should not waste any more time here to find out what exactly transpired."

Without a further word he signaled his men towards the helicopters and left.

K ate's father felt relief as the choppers rose into the sky. It had worked. He had saved the village!

When these men of the American Confederacy were threatening to turn the village into a bloodbath and the patriarch had not been fast enough to act, he'd seen his chance to turn the tables and grab control to save the village from these soldiers and from the insanity of the elders. How could the so-called wise ones even consider treating women as equals?

But once he had answered the interrogator's first few questions, Kate's father had doubted that he'd made the right move. This evil man hadn't been appreciative of the help he had offered. This brute had shown no respect at all. When the intruder had asked about the seeds, Kate's father had felt his knees shake and had been certain that things were going to turn out for the worst. But then all of a sudden, the soldiers had left.

God had been on his side. Now people would listen to him when he spoke and demanded that the traditions be honored.

But just when it seemed that the helicopters were going to disappear, they suddenly returned. Confused, the people looked towards the two approaching black war machines. Then all hell broke loose as rattling automatic machine guns opened fire.

Bullets were hitting people everywhere. Those who were hit in the head were lucky; they died fast. Children's arms were shot off; a pregnant woman was hit in the belly; the patriarch died from several shots in the chest.

Panic took hold of the crowd as people ran screaming all over the village. Fathers were trying to save the wounded; mothers began crying over their dead children. Some people tried to run for cover, only to trip over wounded or dead bodies.

Kate's father screamed, fist in the air toward the helicopters, "Why? We helped you as friends! I did as you asked!" Then he collapsed, hit by a bullet to the head.

Next two rockets hit the village, wiping out entire streets and spreading fire throughout. Those who were left alive in Davidstown didn't care anymore. They had lost their loved ones, their homes, their lives. They wandered helplessly, aimlessly, through the burning streets.

"That will teach them to help any of our fugitives," Dick commended his men as the helicopters headed away. He was satisfied by the success of their mission so far.

"Now let's go find the little Latin cat and recover the seeds she stole."

Voices rose up from the crowd in support of Nayla's and Rowan's cause. No one seemed at all in doubt of the righteousness of their mission. That they would help them was simply a given—Allah's will.

In appreciation of the community's hospitality, Nayla had, as in Davidstown, presented some germinator seeds to the Al Saeed community council.

Men and women were talking energetically about the practical arrangements when Salim and Kate galloped onto the market place.

"We've seen the helicopters above Davidstown," Salim warned his father.

"It was a wise decision to return to tell us this news, my son," the trader complimented him before addressing the crowd. "We don't have much time. Just take the absolute necessities and let's spread out in the mountains. Remember, no fires, so make sure you all dress warmly enough and take pelts for the cold nights."

He then turned to Nayla and Rowan.

"Thank you for your visit, for warning us, and for these precious seeds. You should leave as soon as possible. May Allah be with you!"

Within the hour that followed, the villagers left in small groups, together with their horses and goats, in all directions into the mountains. They only carried the bare essentials to survive over the next few days.

When the trader left with his family, the eastern wind carried the smell of fire. The smoke was fogging up the blue morning sky above them with a pungent brown haze, a sign of a large fire on the plains. He could only imagine the terrible ordeal that was playing out in Davidstown. He was glad his son and Kate had interrupted their journey and returned safely.

The trader took a last look at his own village before getting onto the forest trail. Would he ever see this town again, or would they have to resurrect it from the ashes?

"*In sha' Allah*," he mumbled, putting his faith and trust in Allah.

*O*din kept a good pace in front of the horses. He had traded his inquisitive, playful behavior for a more serious guarded one, almost like he sensed the danger that was closing in on them. The group had left immediately after the trader had wished them well.

They rode in silence. Nayla knew Dick was closing in on her. How could she bring these seeds to safety? She considered splitting up from Rowan, and handing him the package. But would he make it to the United States of Bolivar? Would the precious package be as important to him as it was to her?

When they saw the eastern winds carry the smoke from the plains, feelings of guilt captured Nayla's heart. What trouble had she brought onto these people? Had her actions led to their demise, the destruction of their village and disruption of their lives? What could she do to stop Dick's evil? She should have convinced George a long time ago that Dick was a threat, not only to this planet, but also to the reputation of the American Confederacy.

"I've led all these people to their death and misery," she whispered mournfully.

"No, you haven't. Don't forget, you're not carrying out the destruction or the killing," Rowan resolutely corrected her. "You cannot think that way! You have a mission to fulfill. You didn't force anyone to do anything. You shared your story, and because of the important thing you are trying to do, all these people have chosen to help you, including myself."

"I know," she said miserably, "but because they followed my dream to save these seeds, and helped me, they've put their lives at risk, have had their homes burned down or might have even died. I know Dick: Evil does not exist in his book! He thinks every action is good—acceptable—as long as it leads to world control," she insisted.

"So because you decide to take action and someone else chooses to support you in your cause—follow you—it suddenly makes you responsible for them? Is that what you're saying?" Rowan questioned, deciding to help Nayla find her way out of the darkness that had surrounded her heart.

"Yes, that's what leadership is about, right? You carry responsibility for those who follow you."

"So because I have chosen to help you in your cause, you are now responsible for my life?"

"Well, if you were to get harmed, then I would feel responsible, yes," Nayla responded.

"So if I don't get harmed but find a new place to live in the United States of Bolivar, find a new wife and happiness for the rest of my life, would you take responsibility for that?"

"No, of course not."

"So you're only responsible for the bad things that would happen to me? But is it not I who is leading you through these mountains? So doesn't that make me responsible for what happens to you?"

Rowan's words had totally confused her. Feeling a bit disoriented, Nayla found her emotions of guilt making place for curiosity and a quest to understand the responsibility of leadership.

"Well, I decided to trust you and follow you through these mountains," she replied slowly.

"Exactly! It was your choice, your decision to follow me. So why would that make me responsible for you?"

"It doesn't," she corrected. "I'm my own person."

"Exactly my point," Rowan replied contentedly. "Leaders are merely leaders because others choose to follow them—with an emphasis on 'choose.' True leaders are people with a vision who have decided to pursue that vision. They don't force anyone to follow—they merely share their vision and set the example of walking towards it. When others choose to follow and make them their leader, it's their choice. The outcome of that choice is still the responsibility of the person who makes such a choice."

"But what if these people—the people of the villages—were not aware of the danger they got themselves into by helping me?" she wondered.

"You walked with integrity, spoke with honesty, and shared all you knew—including that those of your country would be searching for you, the importance of these seeds to the American Confederacy, and the fact that we saw the two helicopters the day we left. If you had intentionally withheld information from them, and therefore manipulated these people into helping you, things would be different. But you didn't. You acted with integrity. Therefore you carry no fault and shouldn't be carrying the burden of the consequences. The only things you're responsible for are yourself and those seeds, since you made it your mission to bring them to safety."

Rowan's logic made sense. It was a perspective on leadership that Nayla had never before considered. It certainly wasn't how she was raised within the American Confederacy, and how she had seen George carrying out his responsibilities. But maybe that burden of responsibility came from a leadership style that was based on control—a position of authority that used control, fear and dependency to protect the status quo of existing power positions. Setting out on a mission to realize a vision, and leaving others free to choose to follow you, was a totally different type of leadership.

Nayla wondered how many people would follow George and Dick, or the Carsanto management in the execution of their vision of world control, if they were given the freedom of choice—without rewards or repercussions.

"So what's my responsibility as a leader in bringing these germinator seeds to safety?" she questioned in an attempt to further understand this new perspective.

"To give your very best in your efforts to succeed. To put everything you have on the line for your vision. Nothing more, nothing less, and the outcome is up to God, Allah or the universe—whomever you pray to," he answered straightforwardly. "When you fight for something, you better fight to win! Anything less will hold you back from victory. Too often people have a dream but are not prepared to risk all they have to reach their vision. They simply play not to lose, and that doesn't deliver success. As they say, 'No risk, no gain.'"

The pounding sound of helicopters arrived in the valley.

Nayla, Rowan and Odin had made good headway into the forest. However, if it were not for the shelter of the evergreen canopy, they would have been an easy catch. From the opposite mountain flank they saw the two choppers come down above Al Saeed.

"Let's stop and wait here," Rowan suggested. "The trees provide us shelter. Besides, we will be more difficult to spot when we sit still than if we keep moving. We have a good vantage point from here, and we can observe what the General's next step will be."

A s the helicopters were descending on Al Saeed, Dick thought it was odd that there was not a living soul in the village. After all, it was a nice, sunny day, and just past noon. There should have been activity in the community.

"Just wait a second before setting these birds down," he instructed the pilots.

Looking past the borders of the village, he couldn't detect anyone in the fields either. Nor was there any livestock around.

"Just fly low around the village and the surrounding forest areas. Something isn't right," he said, evaluating the situation.

As they did, he noticed in various places in the forests on the mountain flanks small groups of people fleeing with their animals.

"They were warned about our visit. The smoke from the Davidstown fire might not have helped our hunt."

Dick realized they couldn't put the helicopters down in the forest, and that it would be too time-consuming to track the villagers down to question them. Besides, it might not be of help in finding Nayla. He concluded that she'd been there; the question was where she had gone.

Once he was convinced there was no ambush lurking in the village, he ordered the pilots to land at the marketplace in Al Saeed. Dick and his men then searched the village, but could find no one, nor any clues about Nayla's presence.

"Should we torch it?" one of his men asked, gesturing to the town.

"No. Let's leave and check out if there is a place on the western pass where we could set up an ambush. Nayla and her trapper are probably somewhere up in those forests heading west, trying to get to the coast. With the tracks of all these people fleeing in different directions, it's as good as impossible to find them. If we leave the town as it is, the villagers might come back. That might offer us a chance for a visit tomorrow, or the day after. Meanwhile, we can try to make Nayla come to us instead of chasing her down," Dick said, strategic and calculated in his approach as always.

They hovered low over the valley in their choppers a few times in an attempt to see any sign of the fugitive. Eventually they flew west and inspected the terrain beyond the western pass.

The river that found its origin in the lake just east of Al Saeed flowed west towards the Pacific. It had carved a deep canyon which couldn't be traveled. The terrain would force the fugitives first up the mountain pass preceding a descent into the next valley. Before that valley opened up, the terrain formed a natural bottleneck, where the forest slimmed down to a narrow strip high above the river. It had a steep rock cliff running up on the other side.

Dick decided this would be the perfect place to set up an ambush. The mountainous terrain to the east functioned like a great funnel, and would force any traveler through this narrow strip of forest above the river. Dick estimated it would take a day's travel by horse from Al Saeed to reach this point.

"Let's get back to the base and relax. They'll think we left. Tomorrow morning, we'll fly south across the mountains so they won't hear the sound of the helicopters. Then we'll travel north again to the ambush point. The clearing west of the forested bottleneck is perfect to set down the choppers."

Content with how the day had developed, Dick returned to camp. It was time to celebrate. Tomorrow Nayla would be in his hands.

ayla and Rowan had stayed under their cover until the helicopters had circled the valley and left. From the point where they were observing the village, Nayla had recognized Dick as he got out of one of the helicopters at the market place.

There he was, the stocky, muscular, bald-headed General of Carsanto—a man she'd worked with, a man who had been her peer in the boardroom. Now he looked anything but the business executive, dressed as he was in khaki military camouflage.

She knew he was cunning and ruthless …and way too close for comfort. Whenever he would give an order, his men would obey expediently and without question. Would she and Rowan be able to outsmart him?

When Rowan sighed out loud, "They're leaving," a tone of relief was in his words.

"Mmmh, don't get too comfortable," Nayla responded. "I'm sure Dick knows we were in Al Saeed. He doesn't give up that easily. He's up to something."

They continued their journey upward to cross the next pass in a westerly direction. The peace and quiet of the forest nurtured Nayla's soul. She was running from a cruel man, but the timeless forest seemed to absorb all her worries. She treasured the moment, connected with the trees, and in silence, celebrated creation and her very own existence.

When the sun was setting above the snow-capped peaks in the west, Rowan suggested they make camp. This would be their first night under the open stars. It was going to be a cold night, and one without fire. A fire was too risky in the event some of Dick's men had been following them on foot.

They shared a meal of dried meat, fruits and some grains.

"Kate picked a good man in Salim," Nayla smiled, attempting to bring up some lighter conversation to steer the attention away from their precarious situation. "If you look at his father's wealth and knowledge, not only did the boy have a good teacher in his dad, he will eventually inherit lots of wealth."

"I agree that he's a good man and has had a smart teacher in his father, but you're mistaken with regards to the inheritance of the gifts his father collected," Rowan replied.

"How do you mean?" Nayla questioned, confused.

"Well, in this country there's no inheritance law that benefits someone's children. When someone dies, all their possessions stay at first with their spouse but eventually return to the commons. It's a direct extension of the fact that people cannot own land, water or air. Everyone has equal access to all necessities to build a living, and people's status and wealth is a direct extension of their value to the community, to what they have given. So in the context of providing all children with an equal start, children can't inherit anything from their parents. Once both partners die, their belongings return to the community, which decides how to use them best."

"Wow! That *is* unusual. In the American Confederacy, people inherit the wealth of their parents."

"I know, but your way is unnatural to us. Your inheritance law is a major cause of inequality; through it, not all children receive an equal chance at life. Attaining wealth in the Confederacy is what provides security for your children.

"But in the United Canadian Communities, all children are treated equally, and have the same access to healthcare, education and support to reach for their dreams. Our security isn't based on the material possessions we obtain and gather for our children, but rather on the community. It's by belonging to a community, by delivering value to it, that people create security, because in turn the community will take care of them."

"Sounds like such a system could be heavily abused by lazy people," Nayla theorized. "They could live on the back of the community."

"No, they cannot. Social pressure is much more effective than pyramidal control. When people don't contribute to the community and take advantage of others, they'll hear complaints about it fast, and if they don't start contributing, the community can expel them. It's one of the things that make communal living and rule so effective."

"It's such an uncomfortable notion for me—having been raised in an orderly society that's managed by top-down control—to imagine the concept of unstructured group management. It isn't that I'm that unfamiliar with it; in the United States of Bolivar most companies are cooperatives, or companies under communal management. However, I've never seen it applied on such a large scale," Nayla explained. "I remember from the time I spent in Bolivar and from talking with Julian that the key to their way of cooperative management is the absolute transparency of all operational and financial matters of the companies."

"That's right. Same here," Rowan nodded. "All the operational and economic affairs of the community are totally transparent."

"That's something not a lot of people in the American Confederacy would be able to get their head around. Such a notion of transparency would be impossible for a company like Carsanto to administer."

"That's because there isn't a communal security net. Everybody needs to fend for their own interests in the American Confederacy. As a result, you have to acquire as many material possessions as possible, be able to protect them, and keep lots of secrets in the interest of guarding your wealth and the way in which you achieved it."

"I guess you're right. Everyone, in a way, is on their own in the American Confederacy. That might be what my parents meant when they told me they felt no sense of community there."

Nayla sat in silence for a while, letting these new insights sink in. She'd never really understood why her parents had left the American Confederacy until now. She'd blamed it on the fact that they had missed their family, but now she understood the root of their unhappiness and the reason they'd returned to their country of birth.

"But how do you protect intellectual property?" she questioned, still not fully convinced of the benefits of management by social pressure.

"You don't."

"How do you mean, 'you don't'?"

"We don't protect intellectual property. How can you own an idea in the first place? Ideas find their roots in what we learn from parents, teachers and life's events. Any new idea always grows from the ideas of all past generations. What entitles you to withhold an idea from the rest of the population and all future generations?"

What an incredible, thought-provoking perspective! Nayla had to think about this. It was a lot for one evening, but then again, she was unable to read her diary without having a fire or using her lamp. This conversation challenged her perspectives and certainly allowed her to concentrate on something else. Come to think of it, she was actually enjoying this. "So, if I'm an artist, a singer or a writer, how do I protect my trade? How can I ensure I can live from my creations?"

"Our communal life celebrates storytellers and musicians; they are our only form of entertainment. They actually share their music and stories with one another so that they have a wider selection to entertain the community with."

"It comes back again to your community structure. That's why it works. Okay then, how do you create an environment that stimulates research and development without the protection of intellectual property rights? How does an organization make a return on the time and effort involved in scientific research, a field I'm well at home in?"

"All of that work takes place at the universities, which are funded by the communities collectively. After all, the results of such research benefit all the citizens in the country. Companies or community cooperatives have access to the research results and a chance to commercialize the inventions in their communities. If more than one organization is interested in a particular idea, we let free market economics take its course when they bring it to market. Ultimately that's how the community benefits most."

"Interesting indeed! Society takes on such a different dynamic if it's focused on 'we' rather than 'me,' " Nayla said out loud. "It actually makes so much sense to me to focus on the value one creates for the community rather than the things we acquire. Even if I look back at my own life, it's those times when I've been able to help others that have given me the most satisfaction and pleasure. Those moments have been much more important than all the money I gathered in my bank account. In fact, until now, I've not even once thought about the millions of dollars I left behind the day I ran from the Carsanto building!"

"We should try to catch some sleep. We have a long travel day in front of us tomorrow," Rowan said while he rolled out the pelts that were to keep them warm for the night. "I suggest we share this hide. If we sleep close together, it will be easier to stay warm," he invited as he lifted up the soft bison hide.

When the moonlight on Nayla's face betrayed her concern, he added laughingly, "Don't worry, I'm not planning anything. If this offers any comfort to you, Odin will sleep with us as well."

At these words, Odin started licking his neck.

Nayla noticed that the cold night air was starting to bite at her face. She knew that throughout the night the chill would crawl through her clothes and enter into her bones. Rowan's invitation sounded reasonable.

Minutes later she found herself nestled under the protection of smooth bison fur between a trapper and a wolf. Rowan had been right:

Both of them were shielding her from the cold and keeping her nice and warm.

Rowan fell asleep right away, but Nayla watched the moon high up in the dark crisp sky. Her neck was being stroked by the relaxed breaths of the man who'd rescued her just a few days ago, a man who had left his life—his home—to help her on her journey, a man who now walked with her without asking anything in return, a man who could not be bought, a man who acted merely on what he considered the right thing to do. She felt blessed, and his close proximity not only provided warmth to her body, but also to her heart. Gratefully she cuddled closer against him, and allowed the night sounds of the forest to whisper her to sleep.

Dick was enjoying a good glass of whiskey in celebration of the progress he'd made and his anticipated capture of Nayla the following day. As he rejoiced in how skillful and clever he was, the satellite phone rang.

"Dick?" George's voice questioned.

"Yes, it's me. How are things going at home? Anything exciting? I'm planning to return in the next few days."

"Oh!" George responded, surprise coating his voice. "Do you have Nayla?"

"No, but I will tomorrow," Dick assured him. "I know exactly where she is. We will be ambushing her in the morning. If it's early enough, I might be home tomorrow evening. Otherwise it should be the day after."

"Dick, I appreciate your good work, but I have to reprimand you," George continued in a seriously concerned tone. "I've been contacted by the central administration of the United Canadian Communities. They're complaining about brutalities. You harassed one of their farmers, and killed a bunch of livestock. And for crying out loud, what were you thinking when you put a gun against a child's head?"

"I wasn't thinking about the kid," Dick shot back, "I was focused on getting information. That's why you hired me, right? It's only because of my intelligence-gathering skills that I know where Nayla is at the moment and will be getting the seeds back."

183

"Dick, Carsanto has had good relationships with the United Canadian Communities for years. You know how difficult they can make life for us if they start sabotaging the pipeline and rail transport between our country and the oil-sands up north."

"Let them try! When we burn a few more villages down, it will sober them up quickly."

"What do you mean, 'burn a few *more* villages?' You didn't do that, right?" George choked out in utter disbelief.

"Yes, I did," the General staunchly defended himself and his actions. "We torched Davidstown today. You probably didn't get that news yet, so prepare for it. And we killed most of the villagers. That will teach these bastards to provide help to one of our fugitives and then lie about it when we question them."

"Dick, you're out of your mind!" George shouted furiously.

"No, I'm not! What I'm doing is getting you your seeds back—hence, your chance to gain world control. Remember that! And tomorrow, because of my efficient way of working, I'm going to catch your little whore!" Dick responded, enraged. "Instead of giving me a hard time, you should be thanking me. Where would you be without me keeping you and our company secure?"

"Don't ever call Nayla a whore again," George hissed. "And don't even think about hurting a hair on her head, or I'll have yours."

It wasn't time yet to enter into this power struggle with George, but the day to remove this man from power could well come soon. So Dick didn't hesitate to throw a spear into George's heart.

"Well, what should I call her then? I found her clothes in a trapper's bed. He's the very man who protects her now. He's leading her through the mountains. It seems she's using her female assets to buy her help in this country."

George got very quiet.

Dick rejoiced in the silence, knowing it was only letting the image of Nayla selling her wares become even more distinct in George's mind. Oh, how he loved taunting others. "Let's wait a bit longer and see if this great leader recovers from this," his cruel mind contemplated.

"You're making assumptions," George finally responded. But the tone of his voice betrayed his doubts and pain. "Just get some facts, Dick."

"I don't need facts, George. I only need clues, some imagination and knowledge of human nature. That's how I always get ahead of my prey and catch them. And that's something I'm about to do with Nayla and her newfound lover. Should I keep the man alive for you, or should I just shoot him?"

Dick kept rubbing it in. When there was no response from the other end of the phone, he continued, "Human nature works very simply, George. People use and get used. They sell whatever they have to get ahead. There's nothing noble about human beings; you of all people should know that, George. Did you really think Nayla was any different? Did you trust her honesty? She stole your seeds, remember! Honesty doesn't exist. It's just an illusion, George."

Dick enjoyed the control he'd taken of the conversation. He had successfully wounded his boss. Moreover, he was one step closer to getting total control of Nayla, and fulfilling his wildest dreams.

As he was drooling on that thought, he heard a click.

George had hung up the phone.

owan and Nayla were making their way down into the next valley. The rising sun had warmed them when they had been climbing the eastern flank of the mountain pass. However, it wasn't high enough yet for its rays to nurture them on their western descent.

Nayla was surprised she hadn't heard Dick's helicopters so far this morning. She'd been convinced that he would return at daybreak. But there had been no sign of him or his men. Could he really have left? She was still expecting the sounds of choppers behind her at any moment.

Their trail through the forest was easy to travel. Odin was his relaxed, exploring self again, running back and forth, eager to discover the various smells along the trail. Once in a while he would stand alert and motionless, watching the trail behind them for a long time—like he was expecting someone or something to show up. His behavior worried Rowan, who was expecting the General's men to appear on their trail. He waited several times to see if anyone would show up, but no one did. After that, Rowan just kept increasing their travel pace ever faster.

The forest was now being forced through a narrow funnel with a huge rock cliff on the left and the river canyon on the right. On the other side of the river was another steep rocky wall. The sun's rays had made it over the mountain, and threw their light onto the trees, turning the forest into a painting of shadowy strokes and colorful light.

Suddenly Odin froze, his ears pointed forward, and his coat stood upright, almost doubling his already impressive size.

"He has smelled something, something that's not friendly to us," Rowan warned as he halted his horse beside his canine friend.

"What's up, boy? What do you smell?" Rowan asked as he peered ahead into the small piece of forest they would be riding through. He didn't see anything.

"What do you think we should do?" Nayla asked nervously.

"Not sure. Sometimes he picks up the scent of a bear or cougar even long after they visited a spot. I don't see anything, and there isn't a lot of terrain to inspect. The rock-wall is just over to the left, and the river runs on the other side.

"Let's go, boy, maybe the animals are long gone," he prodded Odin as he spurred his horse forward.

Nayla followed, but Odin stayed put.

After a short distance Rowan stopped again to look around, but couldn't detect any danger.

"Come on, Odin. It's all fine," he reassured him and took a few more steps.

Nayla moved along right at Rowan's side. But still Odin wouldn't move.

Rowan decided to forge ahead in the assumption that Odin would eventually follow.

When Rowan stopped again some distance ahead to check behind him and see if his worried wolf was following yet, it happened. Seven men zipped down from the tree canopy and made a circle around Rowan and Nayla, machine guns pointed at them. The two travelers shrunk together in fear and defeat.

"Ha, ha, ha," the voice of Dick Duke, the General, boomed a short distance ahead of them. "You should have seen your face, Nayla," he sneered. "I wish I'd had a camera, so I could send a picture to George. I'm sure he is going to like your new lover," he mocked while he approached through the trees, relaxed and broadly smiling.

As planned, he and his men had avoided flying over the Al Saeed valley on their early morning journey west. They'd arrived at dawn on the green field below the narrow mountain pass and sought cover high in the trees. Then they had waited until Nayla and Rowan had simply walked into their well-planned trap.

Dick stopped right in front of Nayla, and in a threatening, quiet voice got straight to the point. "Where are the seeds, Nayla?"

"What seeds?" she responded defiantly.

He pulled her roughly from her horse, threw her to the ground and shouted, "Don't you play these stupid games with me, woman. You're nothing more than a fugitive now."

He raised his hand to hit her in the face, but before he could strike, the sharp teeth of a black, intimidating wolf pierced through his arm's skin right into his muscles. The wolf dragged the muscular man to the ground. The domesticated Odin had transformed into a terrifying, fierce, wild animal.

Before any of the guards could act, Odin mauled Dick on his arms, face and shoulder, removing significant chunks of muscle in his rage.

Dick's men moved in a panic to assist their General.

Suddenly. A shot.

A heart-piercing yelp.

"Odin," Rowan screamed. "Odin!"

Rowan threw himself into the fight to save his canine friend. He fought like a wild man, but four of Dick's men wrestled him to the ground while their fists pounded all over his body.

When his eyes met Odin's, he saw a broken gaze that spoke of pain and failure. Blood was gushing out of Odin's right shoulder as one of Dick's men walked up to the wolf at the edge of the cliff and aimed his gun at Odin's head. In a last desperate attempt to fight for his life, Odin launched at the man's neck, pushing the barrel of the gun to the side as he moved up. With one calculated bite, he ripped the guard's throat out.

"Bang!"

One last shot hit Odin in his hind leg. Through the impact of the bullet and the burning pain in his hindquarters he lost his balance, and plunged into the depths of the canyon towards the river.

"Odin!" Rowan screamed at the loss of his beloved wolf.

The whole event had taken less than a minute. One of the guards was dead and Dick badly wounded. His men were confused, unable to comprehend what had just happened.

When Dick got up, his cheek was torn open, there was blood on his shoulder and right arm, and from his left arm blood was spraying everywhere. Odin had ruptured a major vein in Dick's arm. As his men saw their General bleeding, they hurried to his assistance.

Rowan took advantage of the confusion and wrestled himself free from the two men who were left holding him. A well-aimed kick in the neck of the guard holding Nayla down freed her.

Nayla grabbed the gun of her offender and jumped to her feet facing Dick, the gun pointed straight at him. Here was her chance to pull the trigger, to rid the world of this evil man, to secure her safe voyage to the United States of Bolivar, to possibly convince George to drop his plan so she could return to Carsanto. She saw no fear, no remorse, and no emotion at all in Dick's heartless eyes. The guards were all frozen, paralyzed in fear that this woman was about to kill their leader.

The whole world disappeared into the piercing gaze shared between Nayla and Dick. A cold, calculated and heartless mind dueled with a passionate, confused mind with a conscience.

"Nayla," Rowan shouted, breaking her trance.

She turned. He was sitting on his horse, the reins of the other one in hand.

"Get on!" he directed.

She turned and jumped on her horse. The next minute, they were racing downhill through the trees.

The guards aimed their machine guns.

"Don't shoot!" Dick commanded. "We have to get her alive!"

189

As Rowan and Nayla approached the clearing below the narrow pass, the pilots and a few more guards aimed their weapons.

"Nayla, throw me the gun," Rowan shouted.

Instantly she obeyed. Rowan dropped his reins and aimed while keeping his horse at a full gallop. Before they reached the clearing, he fired off two consecutive shots that echoed through the mountains.

Two soldiers grabbed at their bleeding chests, and the pilots ran for cover as the trapper and the runaway woman galloped through the clearing and disappeared into the deep, large forest to the west.

The horses were breathing heavily. The pounding sound of their hooves was muffled by the soft forest soil. Suddenly Rowan stopped.

"Listen, the helicopters are leaving. Let's find cover in case they try to find us from the air."

They took shelter under some large spruce trees, got off their horses, and waited until the sound of the choppers disappeared entirely.

Resting under the large evergreens calmed them both down. Nayla's adrenaline rush was ebbing, her mind starting to grasp what had just transpired: Odin was dead.

Then she noticed Rowan's face was bleeding. Blood was running from his nose, and he had a deep cut next to his eye and on the side of his chin.

When she took a step closer towards him, she felt a deep stinging pain in her ankle. It hurt so bad she could barely stand on it.

"I'm so sorry about Odin," she consoled him.

"So am I, but he died fighting for what he believed in, for what he loved. He had a good life. I'm grateful for the years he has given me. Feeling sorry for ourselves isn't going to help us now. We've got to clean our wounds and get going before they return. Let's make sure Odin didn't die in vain."

Nayla was at first surprised by Rowan's response, which seemed somewhat cold, but then she remembered how this man lived from the forest, and had been for years a very conscious part of the never-ending cycle of life and death. Odin had given his life for them; in Rowan's mind, questioning Odin's death would be to question their lives, and be disrespectful of Odin's brave fight.

She noticed how Rowan—in stark contrast to the tradition of mourning she'd grown accustomed to in the American Confederacy—shifted instantly to a deep, respectful feeling of gratitude for the time and life Odin had given him. The more time she spent with this trapper, the more her respect, understanding, and connection with nature—that interdependent oneness with all that was—intensified.

"Let's get to the river so I can clean up my face and have a look at your ankle," Rowan suggested.

On their escape into the valley they'd descended to a point where the canyon had given way to wide river banks covered with old-growth spruce forests. Having made its way down the steep rocky canyon, the river had transformed itself from wildly thundering between the rocks to gently meandering in its widened bed through the trees.

They staggered through the forest like two wounded, exhausted warriors. As they neared the river, Rowan signaled her to stop. He listened alertly.

Very faint, at times, they could hear a high-pitched moan.

"What's that sound?" Nayla whispered quietly.

But Rowan didn't answer. He was completely focused on the sound.

Suddenly he tied up his horse and lightly moved through the trees in the direction of the moaning. As he got near the river, he started running towards its bank.

"It's Odin," he shouted back to his traveling companion. "Odin's here. He's wounded ...but alive!"

Nayla tied up her horse and ran as fast as she could towards the trapper and his injured wolf.

There was a gaping bullet wound high on Odin's shoulder and another on his hind leg on the same side; this made it impossible for the wolf to stand. He was moaning in pain, lying helplessly with his hind legs in the river.

"Help me to get him out of the water," Rowan instructed.

As soon as they had done so, Rowan ran for the horses and soon came back with them. He took the hide they'd slept in the previous night and covered the wolf with it. Next he opened one of his saddle bags and got some herbs from a leather pouch.

"What's that?" Nayla questioned curiously.

"Yarrow. It has been used through the ages to stop bleeding and disinfect wounds," Rowan said without interrupting his care for Odin. He put lots of the dried herbs into the wounds and covered them up with lichen which he had pulled from a nearby tree.

"What's that for?" Nayla queried, impressed with Rowan's pharmacy—the forest.

"It's Usnea, a lichen that kills bacteria and fungi."

Next he stripped some bark from fresh willow twigs along the river and used it to tie the herbal bandages into place.

"How do you know all this?" Nayla inquired, impressed.

But instead of answering, Rowan froze and stared intently into the forest towards the trail they'd been following.

Nayla immediately spotted what concerned him. Someone was moving through the trees on horseback—two riders. Could this be some of Dick's men? If so, where did they get the horses?

But as they got closer, she suddenly recognized the two figures.

"Kate, Salim, we're over here," she waved in relief.

The two young people sped towards them.

"Are you both okay? We heard rifle shots," Kate called out.

As they got close, they saw the wounded wolf covered by the heavy hide.

"Odin!" Kate cried as she jumped off her horse and petted the massive black head of the wolf.

"He needs help as soon as possible," Rowan said, looking to Salim, who'd grown up in the area and was well-traveled.

"There's a medicine man who lives in the mountains a few hours south of here, near the hot springs," Salim said decisively.

"Great! That's where we'll go."

Rowan immediately started to gather together various sizes of sticks and two large poles.

"What are you doing? Can I help?" Nayla tried to assist him.

"No, just stay with Odin. Comfort him; he's in pain. I'm going to make a travois to pull behind my horse so that we can transport him. Salim can help me."

A little while later the four travelers were making their way through the valley in a southerly direction. The black wolf was resting on a makeshift bed of sticks behind Rowan's horse. One end of the bed was tied to the back of the horse; the other end was dragging over the ground.

"Why were you guys behind us?" Rowan finally asked.

Salim explained that once the helicopters had left the previous day, his father had sent messengers to the surrounding villages. He had wanted to warn them about the possible visit of Confederate troops, but the wire system that connected one central phone in each village had been damaged by a winter storm, isolating all the mountain communities from the country's central administration and any news announcements.

Salim had volunteered to warn the Bluewater village to the west. Together with Kate he'd started climbing the pass late in the afternoon.

"When we made it to the top this morning, we heard rifle shots," he recalled excitedly. "We descended as soon as possible. When we were halfway down we saw the helicopters leave. We were afraid that you had been captured. We're so glad to see you. Can you tell us what happened?"

Nayla and Rowan took turns, each recounting a part of the story.

"When we were traveling this morning, Odin kept looking back on the trail. I knew he sensed something. It must have been you guys following us," Rowan said as he concluded the story.

On a regular basis they stopped travelling so Rowan could check on Odin.

The big wolf lay seemingly lifeless on the makeshift bed. In truth, he was silently fighting to hold on to a last glimmering flame of life.

They made good time. A few hours later, the trail took them through a narrow canyon. At the end of the canyon, a new valley opened up. The pungent smell of sulfur announced the proximity of the hot springs. On the western mountain flank above some steaming pools was an old log cabin. Two large bear skulls decorated either side of the door.

"That's where the medicine man lives," Salim confirmed to everyone's relief. Odin was still breathing, but his breaths were very shallow.

Skulls from a variety of animals—elk, deer, moose, cougar and wolf—were strung on various trees surrounding the cabin. Various bird feathers were dangling in the wind from some of their branches. The place gave Nayla a creepy feeling.

A sinewy, old, but clearly fit man with a weathered face appeared from behind the cabin carrying a load of firewood in his arms.

"Hi, there," he greeted the travelers as he put his heavy load down and approached them.

To Nayla's surprise, the movements of the old man were as supple and graceful as that of an agile mountain lion. Some owl feathers were woven into his long braided grey hair. His eyes glowed and sparkled, carrying in their depths joy, magic and wisdom.

It only took the medicine man one quick glance over the travel party to know exactly the purpose of their visit.

"You need my help," he said before anyone had spoken.

He headed straight for Odin, whose life was hanging on a thread. The medicine man removed the bison hide covering the wolf and eyed the wounds while putting his hand on Odin's chest.

"Get the wolf into the cabin. Make room in front of the fire and put him on the floor. Then take my wood inside, put some logs on the fire and heat water in the kettle. You dressed his wounds well. It may have saved his life—the next twenty-four hours will tell. There's no time to waste. We'll have to act quickly."

Without any further ado he disappeared into the forest.

The travelers did as instructed, and soon were all sitting around Odin on the wooden floor in front of the fireplace. The only thing they hadn't removed from the immediate area in front of the hearth was a low and long polished rock.

"That must be his altar," Rowan had said.

The cabin's grace was in its simplicity: log walls, furniture made from forest woods and sticks, a small cooking fire and a rock fireplace. There was no artwork on the walls. Some rustic racks next to the kitchen area were stocked with several dozen clay pots. In the corner next to the fireplace hung a vest and a hat made from hides and decorated with feathers. Beside them lay an eagle fan, a drum, a rattle, a staff, several decorated leather bags and a few crystal stones.

The door swung open and the medicine man walked in with a pouch made of a beautifully tanned coyote skin. Without a word he headed for the kitchen area and started to mix several herbs and pastes. Some came from the pouch he'd brought in; others he took from the clay jars.

It struck Nayla how focused and driven he was as he worked, without giving the feeling of being rushed or concerned. The medicine man was totally dedicated to his tasks, and nothing—not even their presence—caused any distraction to his undertaking. It was like the man was an integrated part of the medicine he was creating.

When he finished preparing the medicine he put on the unusual vest and hat in the corner. The top of the hat was graced with the head of a mountain lion. A cape was hanging off the shaman's back and was decorated with long owl feathers. He took his drum and turned to the visitors.

"It's time for you to leave. I suggest you camp near the hot springs. You'll find some warm soil surrounding it, which will keep you warm for the night. There's a wood pile next to the rocks to make a fire."

He turned to Rowan and continued, "If you hunt something for supper, save some food for me in the morning. I might be hungry by then," he chuckled, and his eyes twinkled with laughter.

In the blink of an eye, though, he changed from being a joker to being the magic man as he turned his attention back to Odin.

The travelers left for the night. They discovered it was becoming dusk outside. Rowan located some comfortably warm flat spots between the hot pools and the rocky cliff nearby.

"This is a good spot to camp for the night," he confirmed. He instructed Salim to make a fire, and asked Nayla and Kate to unload the horses, get the pelts and prepare their beds for the night. Then he took his bow and disappeared into the darkness of the forest.

When Rowan returned, the full moon was already rising above the mountains. He carried two grouse and a rabbit. Nayla, Kate and Salim were sitting by a warm, crackling fire.

Rowan cleaned and skinned the rabbit, while Kate got up and skillfully plucked the birds.

Nayla felt useless. It struck her how these young people were skilled to live off the land, while she couldn't even cook properly! Julian had done the cooking when they were married, and with George she ate out most of the time—or one of the maids cooked for them. While Nayla had great scientific knowledge, she couldn't even provide for her basic needs. Her survival depended on a sophisticated distribution system that delivered goods and services to her country's stores. It was a system that was based on electricity and oil. Without either of those resources, she was helpless, unable to live off the land.

What would happen to all the people in her country if ever those resources weren't available anymore? Would they all perish?

"We should always teach our children basic survival skills, or the knowledge to live off the land," she thought.

A little later they were enjoying a meal of tastefully roasted meat which Rowan had spiced with some herbs he'd picked on his hunt. Besides the meat, he'd cooked some potatoes, onions and garlic which he'd borrowed from the medicine man's food supply. In return he'd saved a large leg of the rabbit for the elder.

"Why didn't you shoot the General when you had the chance?" Rowan asked, breaking the silent enjoyment of their meal.

"I don't know."

"You could have freed yourself and everyone else on this planet from a ruthless and evil character. You had the chance."

"I know," Nayla acknowledged with some regret. "I guess I was so stunned by his cold, unremorseful eyes that I didn't even think about the gun anymore. In them there was no anger, no rage, no fear, no love—not even for his own life—just the ice-cold absence of any emotion at all. It scared me—paralyzed me.

"What frightened me most then was the realization that Dick was a human being just like me. He had a heart and soul, but somehow it had turned so cold and icy that he was entirely incapable of any feeling at all. What does that to a man? And how many other human hearts have turned to stone? Would it have made a difference if I had shot him, or would there simply have been another heartless bastard who would have stepped into his place? And would killing Dick have turned my heart to stone—made me like him?"

"I know the kind of events that turn a man's heart into stone. I know how it feels to be unable to experience joy, love or any feelings at all," Rowan answered. "My passage through the darkness of the soul has taught me that only the miracles of life and nature can bring light to such a wounded, shriveled heart. And those miracles are much more difficult to find in your country among your concrete cities.

"However, I'm not surprised by his fearlessness or absence of remorse. The man simply believes in what he's fighting for. He believes it is just, that the goal justifies the means, and he's prepared to put everything on the line for it—even his life...and that deserves nothing less than our deep respect. It's just like what you are doing: putting everything on the line to save those seeds and fulfill your purpose. He's only doing the same, which makes you worthy opponents.

"Still, you had the upper hand; you should have taken him out. He wouldn't have hesitated if he had been in your place; remember that. You'll never share his vision, for your heart connects with the Creation, but to prevail you must want to succeed just as strongly as he does."

Rowan's insights helped Nayla see Dick in a different light, one of respect and empathy. With that perspective, she felt oddly more comfortable with the thought of pulling the trigger if she was put in that position again. She recognized, somewhat uncomfortably, that she would have no feelings of anger, revenge or remorse at such a time— only gratitude, respect and the deep satisfaction that comes from fulfillment.

As they lay about the fire, at regular intervals they heard a monotone drumbeat from the cabin which seemed to synchronize with the pulse of life on earth itself. At other times the old medicine man would sing out weird nasal songs in a language Nayla didn't understand.

While the others went to sleep after this harrowing day, Nayla took her grandmother's diary, curled up with her back against the rocks in front of the fire and started reading. Maybe her grandmother would share some insights tonight that would further assist her on her journey.

*N*ovember 11, 2021

  Alejandro celebrated today. I'm not sure if I should, or if I even could, cheer about today's events. Truthfully, I feel more like crying, although I'm not sure what I would be crying for.

  So far, I've shared his joy with the successes of the random acts of sabotage and civil disobedience. A lot has happened since that first illegal dam removal in September. When Alejandro and his friends put the explosions on that very first dam, they left a note behind and signed it, 'Sacred Earth.' The intent was to leave a clue with regards to the motives for setting the river free and the reason why the salmon should be able to reach its spawning grounds.

  The media turned it into a huge act of terrorism and depicted Sacred Earth as a new terrorism organization that needed to be quenched. What started out as a harmless act of bravery by some young people who believe in a dream—after all, the dam was out of use, obsolete and far away from any human settlements—got transformed into a threat to state security. Soon homeland security and Whitefog were searching for members of Sacred Earth throughout the country. Several activists disappeared. They probably call the new mega-prisons home now—if they're lucky enough to still be alive. Due legal process doesn't exist anymore in this country, or what's left of it is just a charade, a poor attempt to fool a not-so-dumb population.

  To all of our surprise, just a week later, right on the other side of the country, a dam was blown up. A note left on site was signed, 'Sacred Earth.'

  Over the weeks that followed, right across the country, dams were blown up, the electricity grid was sabotaged by unbolting the main poles so that the wind could blow them over, and the assets of oil and gas companies—their offices, distribution pipelines and gas stations—were vandalized and often permanently destroyed. Each time a note was left inscribed, 'Sacred Earth.' So far, no one has been killed. Regretfully, though, a few people were wounded.

The effect on the country has been devastating. The relatively simple actions of sabotage have affected the supply of electricity, oil and gas—the key pillars on which our society is based.

Alejandro has been overjoyed with all the action. Everything has been completely unorganized—hardcore activists around the country have understood that they don't need to organize, but are able to act as independent units with the same goals by adopting the same name. As a result the security forces are in effect chasing a phantom. There simply is no organization called 'Sacred Earth.' This is something the well-organized and strongly controlled leadership in this country is unable to comprehend.

An open source website has been developed where people from all across the country have been defining the values and vision of Sacred Earth. As the internet debate was taking place, the values and vision rapidly shrunk in size to the most common denominator. Now a vision of independent sustainable communities has taken shape—communities that would all live in harmony with the land, each with their own unique culture and independent government and judicial system.

The rapid growth of this organic movement, with no leadership, no guiding structure, and no organization, has made it impossible for the authorities to gain control. At times Alejandro has encountered other people who have joined this chaotic movement. He has found Muslims, Christians, Hindus, Pagans, company executives, plumbers, teachers, and even government clerks among them. They all had concluded that the current structure of society was not only unjust but destroying life itself. They were driven by a dream to create a better future for their children. They were sick and tired of corporate power and control, and despised how government officials bent over backwards to please their powerful and rich business friends. They had abandoned their respect for mainstream media, and had finally started to think for themselves.

Today though, things have taken a whole different turn. The stakes are escalating.

A few years ago Las Vegas—arguably the most unsustainable city on this planet, given its use of water and electricity in the middle of a desert—completed its 2 billion dollar water pipeline which pumps water from rural Nevada to the wasteful entertainment city. The project had been fought during its planning process, and was sabotaged several times during its construction by the local farmers and ranchers of the area, whose water supply, lifestyle and means of income—ranching—were threatened by the project. Eventually, though, four years after the planned completion date and well over budget, the pipeline opened, and the ranchers had to watch in defeat how their water supply dwindled.

What the rich casino barons of Vegas and their political puppets had forgotten was that these ranchers are the pioneers of the west who built this country. They built it by believing in their dreams and their skill to stake out a new life. They built it because they acted on their beliefs and always kept thinking for themselves. They loved the land that provided for them, lived in harmony with it, and could still judge for themselves what was right and what was wrong. And this project was, in their book, pure robbery. These pioneers and ranchers were men of action, just and courageous men, men you could count on, men you could trust, men you could build on. These were the cowboys of the west. They were not always the best talkers, but they sure knew when they saw something that was right and something that was plain wrong.

The Las Vegas city officials should have thought twice before messing with such men. This past summer, several ranchers in the Snake Valley saw their cattle perish from drought while their water was lavishly wasted in useless Las Vegas fountains. Yesterday, they spoke. They spoke with action.

This morning the police found two casino barons and the mayor of the city. Dead, all shot—assassinated. Now this in itself wouldn't be unusual in Las Vegas if it weren't for the notes found on the bodies. They read: 'Sacred Earth.' And then continued: 'Don't mess with our water.' A few hours later the water pipeline was blown up in three different locations, causing millions of dollars in damage. The repairs will take at least a year.

The police have arrested a sixty-seven-year-old farmer who'd been ranching for the last fifty-two years. He had lost the majority of his herd this summer to the drought, and all three of his sons were struggling to survive the large losses of cattle they endured. While the farmer didn't confess to the murders, he didn't deny his *involvement either. His only defiant comment for the media was, "You won't be able to stop us all. Victory will be ours. Remember the Alamo!"*

When the news was announced, Alejandro called some friends, uncorked a good bottle of Argentinean wine, and started to celebrate that the settlers of this country, the very men who'd unlocked the American West, had joined their cause.

When I questioned the murders of the men—fathers of children, husbands of wives, sons of mothers—Alejandro just said, "These are casualties of war. Did you really think that we were going to win our liberty and independence, our birthright to access clean air, water and soil, without spilling any blood?"

When he saw the confusion and disgust on my face, he said something that's going to occupy my mind for a long time. Yes, once again he managed to challenge my perspectives and make me really think. I sure cannot dance and celebrate on this day, but there's truth in Alejandro's argument.

What he pointed out was that those currently in power didn't hesitate to kill to realize their vision. He told me about pulp companies clearing the Tasmanian rainforest with napalm and murdering every animal that makes their home there in the process—all so that some powerful and rich men could realize their vision of large monoculture plantations of fast-growing eucalyptus trees that were better suited for their paper mills. He accused the electricity companies of damming rivers, drowning vast areas of land, and preventing the salmon from reaching their spawning locations. He accused the mining companies of moving entire mountains without consideration for the people who lived on those mountains, and in the process polluting the rivers and soil. He continued his rant by explaining how numerous corporations were exploiting people in the most outrageous working circumstances in Third World countries, all to provide us with another cheap gadget so they could make another quick buck—another number on their bank account. "Those in power have been in power because they robbed the gold and land from the rest of us during the days of colonization, and then they bought out the rest of what we had left with the gold they stole from us in the first place," he raved. Then he dropped the bombshell, the words that have me thinking now: "We will only be able to realize our vision of the world if we are prepared to sacrifice and kill for it, just like they do. If not, they'll just keep on winning their battles until they destroy the last one of us. Until they destroy the last hope for the planet…and only at that point will they realize they have effectively destroyed themselves, as no money in the world will be able to buy a new planet with clean air, water and soil."

I questioned if we really had to become as heartless as our opponents in order to create a better world, and if it would even be possible to create a better world under such a premise.

"We don't have to become as heartless. We only have to believe as strongly in our vision as they do in theirs," he simply answered before returning to his friends.

These words will keep me awake tonight. What am I prepared to sacrifice for a better world? Am I prepared to fight for it? Or would I sacrifice my dream in order to keep on living in a world of limitless consumption that is slowly— although more rapidly lately—but surely destroying our planet? Would I give up my dream of a sustainable society to maintain peace with those in power who don't hesitate to remove any obstacles to their beloved lifestyle—even if it means going to war, destroying the planet or killing innocent human beings? Is Alejandro right?

Nayla looked at the stars above her. She wished that there was a way for her to communicate to her grandmother, to go back through time and explain how her words were affecting her, comforting her ...and how timely they were in presenting themselves. In some strange way, she felt her grandmother was guiding her, supporting her on her mission.

Drumming and chanting sounds still came from the cabin. Nayla wasn't one for prayers, but this night was special and so was this brave wolf Odin, who had saved her today. And so she prayed. She prayed for the majestic animal to live.

She didn't know to whom she was praying, but the star-dotted heavens were so vast that she knew her prayers would be heard. Besides, her experience over the last few days had taught her that it really didn't matter who she was praying to. The name given to Him or Her was not important. In the end all prayer was just a language to connect with the Creator.

Nayla also thanked the spirit of the wolf, and asked her ancestors to assist in saving him if they had the power to do so.

The fire and the heated ground easily could have kept her warm for the night, but she crawled back under the hides with Rowan and gently curled her back against him. She enjoyed his close presence, his body heat and his restful, calm breathing. It gave her comfort and peace of mind.

George was on his way to the hospital. They had flown the General home the previous day due to his severe arm injury.

Dick's men had stabilized his health at the base near Huntingville. However, he'd lost a lot of blood, and they couldn't fix up his wounds properly there. So Dick's lieutenant had been left in charge of tracking and capturing Nayla.

George had received another official complaint from the United Canadian Communities, this time about the torching of Davidstown. He'd assured the authorities that this was all an accident due to a rogue guard patrol, and nothing to start a war over. He'd promised to rebuild a better village and pay compensation to the community members. He was furious that the international stability on which the Confederacy had thrived for years was being threatened, all because they were trying to get control over that one last continent to the south, the United States of Bolivar.

George wondered if he'd made a really serious mistake. Maybe he had already achieved his vision of world control, order and a thriving American Confederacy! Maybe this plan of secretly spreading the mutating terminator seeds over the continent hadn't been such a great idea. After all, in the process he'd lost the only woman he'd ever truly loved, a woman who had treated him just like she would have treated any other man. Nayla was unique from other females in not being impressed with his titles, money and power.

Now the relationship with their neighbor to the north was strained. And what if Nayla succeeded in delivering the mutating germinator seeds to the seed farms of the southern country? In a few years the United States of Bolivar could start selling those seeds to Asia, Europe and the United Canadian Communities, and the economic trading power of the American Confederacy would start to crumble. His attempt to get these last crumbs on the table had actually destabilized his vision, and even threatened the current status quo. In hindsight his latest strategy had turned out to be a huge mistake.

Neither had it been a good idea to send Dick on an international manhunt to capture Nayla. How could George recover from this? His life's work, actually the life's work of all his ancestors, was at stake. Could he win Nayla back by promising to never spray mutating terminator seeds over the United States of Bolivar? Maybe he could make the promise to never even try to sell terminator seeds to that country. They didn't really need to; the company could manage just as well without, for Carsanto already controlled the rest of the world.

The past few days had been horrible. He missed Nayla so much. He'd tried to concentrate on running the company and the country, but had not been able to banish his constant concern about Nayla's safety. He so wanted her back securely by his side.

"So, was it Nayla who bit you?" he smiled cruelly as he walked into Dick's hospital room. This was his time to regain control and rein the General in. After that last phone conversation, he wasn't going to hesitate to rub his finger in Dick's wounded pride. He noted with some satisfaction that Dick had stitches running in the shape of a half moon over his left cheek. His shoulder and right arm were bandaged up, and his mauled left arm had harvested tissue from his leg so that he still would be able to use his hand.

Dick's eyes shot fire. He obviously hated that George had gained the upper hand again due to the embarrassment of his injuries and his failure to keep Nayla from escaping again.

"It was a wolf. This stupid wolf came out of nowhere! I had her in my hands. Who would have thought the trapper lived and traveled with a wolf?" Dick cursed. "Good thing my men shot the wild animal."

"Was Nayla harmed in the struggle?" George asked, concerned.

"No, don't you worry. Your Latin cat has no scars on her pretty body," he sneered. "You would have had your seeds back though if we could simply have shot her."

His next words showed his eagerness to return and complete the mission.

"I plan to return tomorrow. We have a pretty good idea of where she'll be going. She's in the mountains, and the trails lead only in a few directions since the rest of the terrain can't be traveled easily. That will make our lives much easier. My men will keep pursuing her until my return."

"No, you can't go," George said resolutely. "I need you here to oversee the security of this country."

He was lying, and even though Dick probably knew it, he really didn't care.

"If Nayla succeeds with delivering these seeds to the United States of Bolivar, the world economy, which we now control through terminator seeds, will be destabilized. Our entire basis of existence would collapse, George ...and you think there are more important security issues for me to take care of?"

"You had your chance, Dick, and you didn't deliver. Maybe it's time for a different approach. Maybe I can reach out to Nayla and bring her in under friendly terms. You can keep your men following her, but there are to be no more brutalities in the United Canadian Communities. Understood?" he said sternly.

When Dick didn't respond but his face got red and his hands clenched, George said, "From a distance, things sometimes look different, Dick. It allows us to take another perspective and come up with alternative solutions. That's what I want you to focus on doing now."

As he finished these words, he was surprised to see a smile appear on Dick's face. How could what he had said possibly make Dick happy? The General must be up to no good.

"What are you smiling about?" George asked.

But Dick would only say, "You're right, George. From a distance we have a different perspective that allows new solutions to surface. Thank you for your insight. Now I need to be alone, to rest."

With a slow, somewhat reluctant step, George left the hospital room.

Nayla woke up when the sun was throwing its first rays across the mountains into the valley. Rowan was gone—likely hunting. The pelts that had covered both Kate and Salim were also empty of their occupants. Anxiously, she looked in the direction of the cabin. She noted the drumming and chanting had stopped.

"He will live!" a deep wise voice comforted her from the direction of the hot pools.

There, through the thick steam in the hot water, she recognized the old medicine man.

"Why don't you join me?" he invited. "The hot water is invigorating. I noticed you were limping yesterday. The healing properties of the springs will be good for your injury."

For a moment Nayla hesitated. Then she took off her trapper's clothes and entered the water in her t-shirt and underwear. The water was hot.

She thought she saw a faint smile on the elder's face. It made her a little uncomfortable since she didn't understand what was humoring him.

"If you move to the side there you will find a nice rock to sit on," the shaman guided. "What's your name?" the old man then asked.

His casual, friendly manner relaxed Nayla. She introduced herself and shared every detail of her entire story. She got emotional when she recalled the events of how the brave Odin had kept her out of the hands of her pursuers the previous day.

The old man listened to the whole story without interrupting. When she finished, there was only silence and the steaming water of the pools.

"They call me Screeching Owl," the shaman broke the silence. "I'm glad you found your purpose and stepped into the flow of life."

The shaman moved closer to Nayla. She felt his hands grab hold of her ankle.

A strange, tingling energy from his palms was penetrating the injured joint. He sat right opposite her, performing his magic healing on her ankle while intensely staring in her eyes, reading her soul. His eyes were strong and spoke of deep wisdom. They were balanced, loving but detached, grounded in the magnificent cycle of life and death.

In order to hide her discomfort with the intensity of his gaze and the stillness that had descended over the steaming pools, Nayla broke the silence.

"What do you mean with the flow of life …and why do you think this is my purpose?"

"I know this is your life's purpose," the old shaman said decisively. "I know because the universe is collaborating with you."

"I…I don't understand," Nayla responded, thoroughly confused.

"Life is a mystery. The Creation is magical and miraculous; I certainly don't claim to understand it. I'm not sure the human mind is even capable of understanding it, nor do I think it's necessary.

"But life has lifted the veil on some of its aspects to me," he explained. "It's nothing that cannot be observed by anyone else on this planet, it's just that I've taken the time and interest to notice them."

Nayla listened intently to the humble elder as he shared some of his hard-earned wisdom with her. His eyes were still as strong and focused on her, but it didn't bother her anymore. Her walls had come down, and she'd noticed the faint smile on his face—a light smile that seemed to be ever-present, a reflection of his joy of life.

"If you observe little children, toddlers, you can observe human nature before any of the cultural habits start to inhibit it. Based on such observations, and that of any of the other animals, I know that curiosity is an innate aspect of life itself. By its very nature, life means change, a continuous progression from one moment to the next. None of us can predict or control the reality that will be presented to us over the next few seconds. The only thing we can do is choose how we react to it and learn from the process. We are here to learn; that's why all living creatures are curious. That's how we are evolving and progressing throughout time.

"Now, in some odd, twisted way, many cultures teach their people to fear this change rather than embrace it. It really starts with parents who are overprotective of their children; they get too attached to that precious new life that they are given to guide to adulthood. As a result, lots of people kill the innate curiosity in their children, and with that the dream that every human soul carries inside since birth. We need to nurture that curiosity for people to at least explore their dream and turn it into reality.

"Driven by our fear of death, we teach our children to make their life's decision with their minds rather than their hearts. But it's the heart that carries the voice of the soul. The mind doesn't hear that voice. The brain is a great problem-solving tool, but lacks the intuitive sensitivity to connect with the voice of the universe. As a result, many people live their lives disconnected from their purpose and from the flow of the universe.

"In that moment when you impulsively grabbed those seeds and ran from the Carsanto building, it was your heart that was driving you. At that moment you stepped into your purpose, you stepped into the flow of the universe."

Nayla nodded. "I know that was a life-changing moment for me—one that I've questioned more than once since then. But I still don't understand why this is my purpose, and what this 'flow of the universe' is?"

"I've concluded that we're all born with a purpose. It's something our early learning and development prepares us for. Our parents, the people who cross our lives, our education, our skills, the things we are naturally good at and our passions all prepare us for the time when we are invited to create ourselves and shape the future of the planet. The question is, are we still open, curious, and ready explorers by that time, or have our minds, shriveled by fear, taken control of our lives, thereby presenting us rational reasons to justify our inaction? In the latter case, our dream dies and the rest of our existence becomes a mere shadow of the true potential we carry inside of us.

"However, when people listen to their heart, and act—often in very irrational ways—to realize their dream, they set out to fulfill their purpose. In doing so they step into what I call 'the flow of the universe.' You're in such a flow when the universe becomes your collaborator, when you tend to attract your luck, when the omens are in your favor—helping you to realize the dream, execute your mission.

"Think about how the taxi appeared as you reached the street when you were running from the Carsanto building, how the location where the train stopped brought you to Rowan—a local trapper who could guide you, and who lived with a wolf who saved you. Think about how you spoke up at the trial in Davidstown. It provided the spark for Kate to follow you and introduce you to Salim and his family, who ultimately led you to this place. The synchronicity of all these events tells me you have stepped into the flow of life. The universe is collaborating with you."

"It seems to me that the universe is also collaborating with Dick," Nayla mumbled. "Look how fast he found us."

"You escaped, right?" the old shaman replied.

"Yes, but still…" she objected.

"You're probably right!" the unexpected answer from the elder came. "This is where the mystery of Creation will always stay a mystery. It's not up to us to even try to understand the larger plan—if there even is such a plan. And if the General believes as strongly in his

214

dream as you do, the universe likely collaborates with him as well ...and the future of this planet will be determined by who will win the battle. In this case though, I would like to believe your chances are better since your dream supports life itself, the very essence of this universe. The General's dream is based on chaining—controlling—the very nature of Creation. It's a struggle between dreams of germination and termination. The key question that will determine the outcome of this battle is: What are you prepared to offer to realize your dream? How hard are you willing to fight for it? The fact you didn't shoot the General when you had the chance tells me you're still at risk of losing. I've a feeling he wouldn't have hesitated if the roles had been reversed."

"That's what Rowan said last night as well," Nayla said regretfully, amazed at the mutuality of their perspective. "And in fact, ever since that evening when I ran, I'm discovering new pieces of myself, some of which frighten me. I'm not sure if I'm ready to carry this responsibility. What if I fail?"

"First of all, we're not here to search or discover ourselves," the elder quietly corrected. "We're here to create ourselves. Ever since that night when you ran, you've set out on a journey of creating yourself with the guidance of your heart, freed of the inhibiting chains of your mind.

"With regards to your responsibility, the only responsibility you have is to listen to your heart, give everything you have, and be open to whatever the universe presents you in return. Often people get too attached to their vision, or their ultimate goal. When they do so, they become afraid of making mistakes or failing. What you need to remember is that the end result of your actions isn't within your control; only your actions towards that goal are! It is only when we stay detached from the outcome of our actions that we'll have the perseverance and flexibility to continue our journey and overcome the challenges that are presented to us along the way."

While they had been talking the medicine man's hands had remained on Nayla's ankle. She suddenly noticed her injury had started to feel a lot better.

"How do you do that? That stuff on my ankle and the healing of Odin?" she wondered curiously.

"It's something we all can do. I just practiced it as much as most people practice walking. The universe consists of energy—the energy that permeates all things, that gives existence, moves things, flows through us. I've practiced working with that energy so that I can guide it and use it for healing purposes. I'm not really sure if I'm using it, or if it's using me—but that I leave to the mystery."

The elder let go of Nayla's ankle and looked in the direction of the cabin. "I should go and check on our friend."

The old man turned around and walked out of the pool. To Nayla's utter surprise, the elder was completely naked! She'd shared the pool with a naked man! Embarrassed, she didn't know where to look and felt her cheeks blushing.

The shaman saw the embarrassment on Nayla's face and laughed out loud.

"Never seen a naked man? Now don't get any wrong thoughts. Remember we are all born perfect—without clothes. Maybe we should all bathe like this rather than with our clothes on. Now stop looking at my butt," he chuckled.

At that moment Rowan returned from another successful hunt with some more birds. Nayla wasn't sure what amused Rowan the most—the naked elder, or the look on her face. But now that she was learning more about living in balance with nature, she was guessing it was the latter.

*O*din's life-energy sparkled in his eyes again, even though he was still unable to get up. He wouldn't be able to walk for a while.

Rowan had made the decision to leave him with the medicine man. Years ago, Odin had given him a reason to live again. Their life paths had run together since that time, and allowed them both to grow. But life's circumstances were separating their paths. Maybe it was time for both of them to create space for others to become part of their journey and offer their gifts of learning.

That morning Rowan spent a lot of time with Odin. They simply took joy in each other's presence. As Nayla observed the brave trapper with his caring heart sharing his friendship with his trusted wolf, she felt her heart glowing. Had the universe put Rowan into her path for more than just guiding her through this country?

It was time to say goodbye to Kate and Salim too. A man of his word, the young trader wanted to honor the promise to his father and travel to Bluewater in the west to warn the villagers of the raiding American Confederate troops.

"Thank you for bringing us here. It saved Odin's life," Rowan said as he embraced Salim.

"We'll come and visit him from time to time," Salim answered. "May Allah be with you on your journey!"

"Thank you for giving me the courage to follow my dreams. Thank you for setting the example," Kate sniffed in an emotional goodbye as she tightly embraced her heroine, tears running down her face.

"I think you're giving me more credit than I deserve," Nayla answered. "You're a brave young woman. You found the courage to follow your dream much sooner than I did. Hold on to it! Live it! You'll be a great leader. Now, travel safely."

"I'll pray that you will succeed in delivering the seeds to the United States of Bolivar. Write me; who knows? We might come and explore that area of the world at some point. It might be a new trade route for Salim." Kate smiled between her tears as she glanced towards her boyfriend.

"May God be with you!" she added.

As they were saying their goodbyes, the sound of distant helicopters reminded them all of the urgency to move on.

Rowan expressed his gratitude to the shaman, and thanked Odin for the good times they'd shared.

"Pay attention to the omens," the medicine man advised Nayla. "Now that you've stepped into the flow of life, the universe talks to you all the time. Little things, the appearance of animals, things that are being said multiple times by different people, repeating images: all are messages to guide you on your journey. Don't ask me how it works, because I truly don't know. It belongs to the mystery. But I do know—beyond any doubt—that the Creator has Her means to communicate with you, and is doing so all the time. Be open to it and let the Creation itself be your guidance."

"Thank you for saving Odin and for sharing your wisdom," Nayla answered respectfully.

As they all rode off, the medicine man shouted, "Remember, don't look at old men's naked butts."

His booming laugh echoed through the valley as he returned to his cabin.

"Where are we heading?" Nayla asked once they had picked up a good pace riding south. She'd left all the decisions with regards to the choice of trail up to Rowan. He'd consulted with the old shaman and Salim while she was breaking up camp.

"We're heading for Sequoia, a pagan community," Rowan informed her. "The elder and Salim thought it was a better choice than retracing our steps and heading further west to Bluewater. We should reach Sequoia tomorrow, in the late morning. Another day's travel south from there is a river which can bring us far to the southwest."

"Tell me about this pagan village. What's the foundation of their culture?"

"The pagans follow an earth-based spirituality. Their culture is not dogmatic like other religions, and finds its roots in a deep reverence for Mother Earth and Creation itself."

"What is Sequoia like? How do people dress there, and make a living?"

"I have no idea. I've never visited the community before. Based on my experience with other pagan villages, I expect the culture in Sequoia to be less structured than in the previous communities we've visited. On the whole, pagans cherish organic growth and networks. To outsiders, things can look really chaotic in their communities, but to them they are honoring a natural unfolding of Creation. There are fewer rules; actually, often there's only one guiding principle, and that is a reverence for life and Creation. This is reflected in everything they do—their way of using colors to paint their houses; their use of flowers and other earth materials to create all kinds of artwork; their way of celebrating their women—the bearers of new life for the community; their unbridled curiosity; their way of dancing and celebrating; and their view on sexuality."

"So what's unique about their perspective on sexuality?" Nayla questioned curiously.

"For pagans, the sexual relations between men and women are like a sacred ritual, the celebration of the life-giving powers of the Goddess. Most of them don't connect the naked body with sexual behavior. When the weather permits you'll see men and women walking around naked, doing their daily chores. Clothing to them is functional—something to keep them warm, something that covers them from the rain or allows them to carry certain items with them. Since man is born naked, they celebrate their bodies and are proud of them—no matter the size or shape."

"And walking around naked isn't sexual?" Nayla remarked in disbelief.

"It only is if your culture considers it to be," Rowan replied with certainty. "As a young man, I lived in a pagan village down south for a few years. No one wore clothes for most of their existence due to the warm climate. I learned within days that any sexual connection disappeared once you became accustomed to seeing people walking around and performing their daily tasks in the nude. I've actually come to believe that it is exactly the covering of the skin that gives sexual meaning to the uncovering of it. The more the religious text of a certain culture requires their women to cover up a particular body part, the more the mere sight of that skin, when uncovered, turns on a man from that culture. For instance, if the religion requires the ankles to be covered, the sight of a bare ankle will be arousing to a man and therefore considered to be sexually provocative. In pagan communities, the site of a naked butt wouldn't be considered a sexual turn-on. Nor would it arouse anyone in particular. It's only erotic behavior that would be considered sexual, and in most pagan communities that's kept private."

"We can keep our clothes on, right, when we visit?" Nayla asked in a teasing manner, but her hopes were hinged on a positive answer.

"Yeah, don't worry. We're just visitors. Just don't stare at anyone, particularly the butts of old men."

When Rowan picked up on the shaman's joke, they both broke into laughter.

Apart from Nayla's interesting education on pagan life and the fact that she had a new perspective to ponder with regards to sexuality, the day passed uneventfully. With the exception of the helicopters they had heard in the morning, they had neither heard nor seen any sign of Dick and his men. Rowan expected them to be searching west of the ambush point.

They came upon an overhanging rock along a cliff with a view of the river valley below. The valley side of the spot was partially sheltered by some evergreen trees. Rowan decided this was a good spot to spend the night and decided it was safe to make a fire. He was planning to keep it on during the night as a deterrent for predators now that they'd lost the protection of Odin.

Nayla relaxed against the rocks. She admired the colors the setting sun was painting in the sky. The river valley below them took on a serene, peaceful atmosphere. Some deer left the protective shelter of the forests and started grazing at the edges of the pastures. A wolf was howling at the rising moon. Nayla drank in the magic of the scene and allowed it to touch her heart.

Rowan was relaxed and skillfully preparing some food above the fire he'd lit. For the first time since they'd met, Nayla saw this grounded, caring man with different eyes. She felt attracted to him. She admired his strong arms, his determined, supple movements, his handsome face and his deep blue eyes.

She wasn't quite sure what had caused her to view Rowan in this new way. Was it sleeping in his proximity, the harrowing escape from Dick's men or the relaxing day spent in each other's company? She wasn't sure why, but she loved to be close to him, feel his presence, hear his voice, and see him laugh.

"What's that book you're always reading?" he asked as she opened her grandmother's diary after supper.

"These are the words of my grandmother talking to me through time. Most curiously, her words reach me daily with messages that are relative to my journey and help me grow through it."

"Well, I am not going to stop your ancestor from conversing with you, certainly not when she might offer you clues for the road ahead.

"See those elk along the river bed?" Rowan then pointed.

Nayla could barely make out the animals with the dusky light—the white rays of the moon were helpful.

"Yes." She saw a small herd of somewhat larger animals grazing on the river bank.

"See that group of trees close by?"

"Yes."

"That's where I'm going to be for the next hour or so while you do your reading. I just love to spend time in the proximity of those animals. Not sure what it is, but it feels like magic; it brings me closer to the Creator. The elk people feed me. In a way, that makes me elk. Elk are majestic animals with an endurance and tenacity like no other. Just call me when you feel uncomfortable—and keep the fire going."

Without a sound Rowan disappeared into the darkening forest.

December 6th, 2021

I'm pregnant! It didn't take long to get to my reason for writing today. I'm pregnant! I'm pregnant! I'm pregnant! I'm going to give life to a child! Creation, the miracle of life, is growing inside of me. The love I've shared with Alejandro, a love we celebrate when we're making love, has been the spark for a miracle of Creation. I'm going to be a mother!

Some people warned me to keep things silent. "In case something goes wrong," they said. I know it's only just a month, but why would I keep this magical moment hidden from the world? I'm pregnant! I want to shout it from the rooftops, dance to the beat of the universe and make love over and over again with Alejandro.

We found out this afternoon. Alejandro called all his friends and has been boasting like a proud peacock. We've celebrated (and did make love). We briefly talked about the idea of marriage, and then decided that no official piece of paper really has any relevance or meaning when it comes to love. So we went to Central Park, and by the waterfall in the ravine officially declared our love for each other (like we didn't know ☺). Now we are married! We are husband and wife, and I'm expecting a child. In eight months time we'll be mother and father to our little baby!

Life is just so great, it's beautiful—full of surprises, precious, something to be cherished, nurtured and defended when the need arises.

Every few minutes I'm holding my hands on my belly. I just can't wait until I feel movement and can communicate with my little baby. We'll be able to push each other's hands. I've been told such movement will still take a while—but it's fun to imagine it now.

Talking about imagining: Tonight, I stood in front of the mirror and tried to imagine myself with a big tummy. It was kind of difficult to picture it. So I took a pillow and put it under my sweater and there I was, nine months pregnant. Proudly pregnant! Alejandro was watching me. When I asked him if he still was going to love me, he walked over, got on his knees and started to kiss my belly (well the pillow on top of my belly). Then he went lower (no further details here, but it was then that we made love). We tried to keep the pillow between us to imagine how the huge belly would feel. It was kind of difficult in the passion of our play, but very amusing. We loved, we laughed, we cried.

Alejandro is sleeping peacefully. He's drooling again, though. Every time I tell him he does that, it embarrasses him. I guess drooling isn't worthy of his macho image.

I love him so much. The father of my child! The seed of the little miracle growing inside of me. Our love!

223

The excitement of her grandmother's pregnancy brought back memories of Nayla's mother. Nayla's mother certainly had been a welcome child, born out of the love of two excited parents. But it had been years since Nayla had seen her. Even though their love for each other was deep and they could have maintained contact via the internet video means that were available to them, just like she kept regular contact with Gaya, for some reason they didn't. It was almost like their worldviews had grown to be so different that it was easier not to talk at all.

Reading her grandmother's words also rekindled Nayla's feelings of motherhood. How had she been able to live, continue her work without her precious little Gaya for all those years and be content with some internet video calls? Was Julian right? Did all that stone of the cities harden people's hearts, make them incapable of establishing a deep connection with the magic of Creation?

Nayla realized that she not only had to get to the United States of Bolivar to deliver these seeds—she had to reunite with her family. Visit her mother, and find her precious baby again. She was a mother. It was time she was living that reality—giving her love to Gaya rather than sending her money. What else could be more important than raising a child … loving a child …and loving a man?

She'd been blessed with two caring, good men in her life—no, actually three. She shouldn't forget George; in his own way, he was kind and caring. He'd loved her differently than Julian, but certainly he'd loved her, and he had always treated her like a princess. Now that she'd finally connected with paradise—the way Julian had tried to teach her—now that she'd unchained her heart, was able to feel the world and be part of paradise instead of just observing it, maybe it was time to really love again.

Her thoughts were interrupted when Rowan arrived back from his visit with the elk. As he invited her to share his pelts again, she noticed that he was looking at her differently. He cared for her, wanted to take care of her, keep her warm, protect her …maybe love her? She curled up against this strong hunter and realized that she loved this man, just like she'd loved—and still loved—Julian.

With George though, things had been different ...and George wouldn't be able to understand or experience her newly discovered embrace with nature and the universe itself. But if she returned to the United States of Bolivar, would her feelings for Julian be rekindled? They had never really left. In fact, she'd never talked with Julian since he left—it seemed too painful for both of them. He simply had made a commitment to keep Gaya in contact with her.

Could she love both Rowan and Julian? It probably would be too complicated. Maybe Julian had completely changed ...or gotten remarried.

Anyway, this would all have to wait until they arrived in the United States of Bolivar. In the meantime, she'd better enjoy the pleasure of Rowan's company.

They continued their journey to Sequoia at dawn. Rowan found a wolf print close to their camp. He thought one of Odin's kin had smelled Odin's scent on their belongings and had come by to check things out.

"Maybe Odin sent one of his family members to watch over us," Nayla smiled.

The conversation that morning had turned to the United States of Bolivar. Rowan had a great interest in learning more about the region, and in some unspoken way they'd both decided to focus on their ultimate destination in an attempt to forget their slow progress and the terrible odds they were facing.

Nayla explained in more detail different aspects of the country. She decided first to cover the nation's green energy production since it formed the basis for all other sustainable technologies. Something the United Canadian Communities simply hadn't developed.

Given that the United States of Bolivar had mostly consisted of developing countries during the time of the oil crisis early in the century, the Bolivarians had looked for solutions to their social and environmental challenges in the direction of new technologies. As a result they'd become leading producers of biodiesel and ethanol.

The South American coastline was dotted with windmills and tidal wave spiral electricity plants. In addition, they had huge solar power farms, and had become leading producers of photovoltaic roofing shingles. They had embraced sustainable and organic farming practices similar to those in Rowan's country, but their knowledge was more organized and readily available through the internet and their extensive fiber system. The communities and cities had been developed with sustainable materials, and in such a way that most of the goods and services people needed were available within walking distance. As a result the bicycle was the main vehicle of transportation next to the air car.

The country's larger companies were mostly structured as conglomerates of smaller entrepreneurial enterprises, and functioned on a completely virtual basis. No office buildings had been built like in the American Confederacy; as real estate which was only occupied during the daytime, and therefore had only limited use, was considered a waste of resources and time. A building had to be of use twenty-four hours a day in order to justify its construction. All business and research interactions took place virtually, via the internet through instant video connections. It allowed people to work from their homes—and even the beach, if that was the place they hung out for the day!

Rowan said he couldn't wait to explore the new continent. And he kept repeating that he wanted to travel to the Andes and visit the famous Incan ruins of Machu Picchu—just like he'd always dreamed of doing as a child.

"How are we going to get to the United States of Bolivar from here, Rowan?" Nayla asked as they approached Sequoia. They could see the community in the distance perched high up on the flank of the mountain.

"I'm not sure. I first want to get these helicopters off our tail. If we can make it to the river unseen, it could carry us a long way without passing through any villages. If they can't find any information about our whereabouts, it will be like the country gobbled us up, and they'll be seeking a needle in a haystack. No doubt they realize that, so they'll likely increase their efforts to catch us over the next two days."

Suddenly an impressive golden eagle descended from the skies and came flying just a little distance ahead of them—like it was guiding them on the trail. In the distance then they heard the sound of helicopters. At that very moment, the eagle took to the skies and disappeared in a southerly direction.

"Is that what the shaman meant about omens?" Nayla asked after the magic display of the king of the winged ones.

"That's exactly it."

"So what does it mean? What did the eagle tell us?"

"I've no idea," Rowan replied. "That's the problem with omens; they're difficult to read. My guess is that we should go south. Hopefully we'll get better at reading them over time."

They veered off the main trail and started to climb the mountain flank towards Sequoia.

It was close to noon on this sunny spring day in the mountains. As they got closer to the village, Nayla noticed that some of the men and women she saw were only half dressed. She was glad Rowan had warned her. But like Rowan had indicated, no one else seemed to care or even notice.

The sturdy houses in Sequoia were built from rock. The village was situated on the northern flank of a mountain just where the valley they'd been traveling through was opening up to the west. The mountain provided protection from the cold north, and the stone facades of the houses facing south were perfectly positioned to absorb the warmth of the sun. In addition, their orientation provided a stunning vista over the pastures and river in the valley. A fresh water stream was running to the west of the village, where a large evergreen forest covered the mountain's flank. On the east the villagers had terraced the terrain to allow for the cultivation of their fields.

"It will be more difficult to figure out who we need to talk to and where in the village to find that person," Rowan warned. "As I said, nothing is really structured or organized in pagan communities, or at least not in a pyramidal way. They won't have a market square, nor will the village layout have any structure to it. The streets will curve, run or bend in just about any direction. They won't have a religious building like a mosque or church, since they consider nature to be their spirit house. They usually do have a large community center, since community activity is central to their culture."

Rowan asked an athletic, bare-breasted young blonde woman for directions.

As her guide communicated with the young lady, Nayla was surprised by her sudden feelings of jealousy.

When they rode on, she sarcastically remarked, "And you couldn't have picked anyone else to ask your question?"

"What do you mean?" Rowan asked, confused.

"Like you don't understand what I'm saying?" she asked in disbelief.

"I don't! What do you mean?"

"Oh, just forget it. Men will be men," she snorted.

Before they got to the community center, they ran into what must have been a significant group of the community. Together, they were building a house.

"Hi there!" Rowan greeted them.

"Hi, welcome. Are you visiting anyone?"

The response came from a voluptuous older woman with long grey hair—and of course, bare breasts. Nayla felt less threatened this time—no doubt this woman wouldn't prove competition for her.

"No, we're traveling through. We were wondering if you could help us with some food provisions. We also want to warn you about imminent danger from some American Confederacy guards who have been causing havoc in some of the surrounding villages."

The woman didn't react to the news of the potential threat, but turned to Nayla. "You're not from this country," she said resolutely.

"How do you know?" Nayla asked, startled.

"You're staring at our members who have found it too hot to wear any clothes today."

Rowan threw an "I told you so" look at Nayla.

"Just let her go ahead; we don't care," the woman carried on without interruption—clearly picking up every sign from their body language. "It's part of the shock value when visitors first arrive in a pagan community."

Nayla raised her eyebrow to Rowan, as she wondered if this woman was normal.

Instantly the woman turned to Nayla again and continued, "Yes, I know I'm loud, direct and obnoxious. And if you can't handle that, that's your problem. But we appreciate directness in this community. It keeps us from guessing what people think.

"As you can tell, we're building a house ...yes, mostly naked. So get over it; it has nothing to do with sex. We're proud of how the Goddess has created us. There's no need at all to cover our beautiful bodies unless it's cold—actually, it would be shameful to do so. We're proud of showing off our figures—every part of them, and at every age. It's a celebration of the beauty of the Goddess.

"Just in case you are wondering, no one is paying us for this work today. See that couple there?"

She pointed at two elderly people who were walking down the hill hand in hand and bare naked. They must have been in their seventies, and seemed as in love as teenagers can be. The scene was pure, loving, harmonious and touching. The elders' genuine care and love for each other stirred Nayla's heart.

"Their roof was leaking, and the walls were about to cave in. So a number of us decided to get together and build them a new house today. We couldn't let our elders live in substandard circumstances. They raised us, taught our children and carry invaluable wisdom for our community.

"I think she gets the picture now," she said as she turned to Rowan, talking like Nayla wasn't even there anymore. "You're welcome to stay here for lunch. We're about to take a break. Why don't you entertain us with your story while we eat, and we might find it worthy of some provisions for your journey ...and don't forget to let us know more about the danger we face. Not that it really scares us, you know; we live in the mountains and so we're used to all kinds of dangers."

Then she turned to the workers— a mix of men, women and children. "Let's break for lunch," she hollered. "These travelers are going to share their story with us."

On their way to the terrace overlooking the entire valley, Nayla got surrounded by villagers who wanted to find out where she was from. These people also spontaneously shared details of their village life. She learned that most things in the village were done together with the community. The children here simply learned by helping and observing their parents and elders.

Nayla started to appreciate the directness of the community. It was normal here to act according to the emotions one was feeling. This made the human interactions and relationships very clear, and provided for an absence of underlying, unexpressed emotions that lingered and could be misinterpreted or go unnoticed.

The mother of a few toddlers explained, "We have a strong level of trust—a foundation of community support—which sets the context and provides the understanding that whatever is being said, is being said in support of the person and for the benefit of the community."

Certainly this was the most unstructured, most uninhibited and spontaneously friendly culture Nayla had ever encountered!

During lunch Rowan and Nayla shared their entire story which clearly—without any doubt whatsoever—was well appreciated in this community. People cheered, threw in agreeing 'yeses,' and clapped their hands when they felt like it.

"And you think we could expect a visit from these soldiers who are searching for you?" queried the loud, direct woman, whom quite a few people referred to as 'mother' and who seemed to have some form of authority.

"That's right."

Rowan's words had barely left his lips when the sounds of helicopters announced the arrival of two black dots in the sky over the eastern mountains.

Undeterred, the mother said, "We'll welcome them!"

She started giving out orders to the community members, and minutes later, half-dressed men, women and children were running with rifles, bows and arrows, and spears in seemingly different, uncoordinated directions. But somehow everyone seemed to know exactly where they should be going.

Rowan grabbed his bow, which he preferred over his rifle. He gave Nayla the gun while taking her with him to find a sheltered position.

"This time, shoot!" he commanded Nayla as they ran for shelter. "Kill the General when you have the chance."

Dick's lieutenant directed the pilots as to where they should land. He hated those villages that didn't provide a landing spot, and here they would have to put the choppers down on the banks of the river, after which they would have to hike up the mountain flank to the community. Checking this village out would take hours.

Yesterday they had searched for traces of Nayla and Rowan in a westerly direction, but without any luck. He hadn't held back, however, for Dick had given him free rein. So he'd followed Dick's example of threatening to shoot a child after having shot some of their livestock, only to discover there wasn't any information to uncover. Nayla and Rowan hadn't been seen by anyone.

The lieutenant ordered the pilots to stay with the helicopters while he and the rest of the men started their hike to the village. As they struggled up the mountain, he recalled Dick's last orders.

"Just find Nayla and bring her back," the General had commanded just before leaving for the American Confederacy. "Make sure though you don't harm her—at all," he had emphasized. "But you can do whatever you want with the trapper."

When the lieutenant and his men entered the village, they first thought it had been evacuated, just like Al Saeed. Then to their surprise, they saw some bare-breasted women a little further ahead, on what looked like a large patio overlooking the valley. As they got closer, the women ran into the little alleys crisscrossing the village.

The guards found the place difficult to search or control, due to the absence of any structure in its street pattern. The good news was that they'd seen people, so someone should be able to give them some information. But since on their hike up they hadn't seen any livestock, other than some goats a large distance away, the lieutenant couldn't start with the same ploy he'd used in the other villages.

The lieutenant spread his men out in patrols of two, and directed them to search the streets.

When he reached the large terrace, only one of his men was by his side.

"Hey, honey?" a woman's flirtatious voice floated out from one of the alleys.

The two men entered the small street, eager to get a better glimpse of the attractive female.

Eyes focused on the woman ahead of them, they moved past the first few houses and into the alley, forgetting to observe the proper search protocol. Suddenly strong arms grabbed them from behind, disarming them and clubbing them to the ground.

Within fifteen minutes of entering the village, the lieutenant and his men had all been rounded up, hands bound behind their backs and legs tied together with short pieces of string.

"Don't ever think about entering our village again with these guns of yours," the loud voice of the mother thundered.

As she reprimanded the intruders, the scene simulated a bunch of young boys who'd been caught by their mother and were about to get spanked.

As she saw the embarrassment on the men's faces, she let out a booming laugh that echoed through the valley. "Got distracted, right? See where that gets you!"

The rest of the villagers laughed boisterously.

Nayla was watching the whole spectacle from her hiding place. Rowan had left her earlier, saying he had "an idea." He still hadn't returned. She also hadn't seen Dick yet. What if this was all a trap to round up the villagers? She was concerned.

"So what are you going to do now?" the lieutenant asked defiantly.

"Not sure," the mother grinned.

"Let me tell you what the smart thing would be. You're going to untie us, give our guns back, tell us if you've seen the travelers we're looking for and let us walk back to our helicopters."

The mother stopped laughing, pulled her eyebrows up as high as she could and asked with a mocking curiosity, "And why should we do that?"

"You don't really think I was stupid enough to walk in here without cover, do you?" the lieutenant asked arrogantly.

"Well, you Americans are still unable to live off the land. Since you're not the smartest kind, it wouldn't have surprised me," the mother snarled back.

Nayla started to get a really bad feeling. The lieutenant was up to something, and she knew these men knew no mercy.

"See these helicopters down below at the river?" the lieutenant asked. "If I'm not back there within the next ten minutes, or if I don't check in over the radio, they're ordered to fly off and level this village to the ground—just like we did a few days ago with Davidstown," he boasted.

The mother's face turned serious.

"Well, for now, let's put you boys out here on the terrace. If those helicopters come, we'll try to all hide behind you. If your helicopters are going to roast us, you'll be burning first," she said.

A sudden gunshot broke the silence in the valley. It came from the direction of the helicopters.

A few minutes later Nayla spied a man hiking up the trail towards the village. It was Rowan. He must have snuck up to the helicopters using the forest and terrain as his cover.

When he passed her hiding spot, she accompanied him to join up with the Sequoia villagers.

There, he informed the mother that he'd killed one of the pilots with a well-placed arrow. He had then rushed forward and struggled with the second man. A shot was released during that fight, but no one got hit. Rowan had forced this guard to the ground and tied him up to one of the helicopters.

"Well, that kills the back-up plan," the mother barked loudly.

"You kill us, and our country will declare war," the lieutenant threatened.

Everyone ignored his words but Nayla turned to him and inquired about Dick. The lieutenant told her he had returned to the American Confederacy due to his wounds.

Now that they were all certain the threat was under control Nayla, Rowan and the mother sat down secluded from the rest to converse quietly about the next steps.

Rowan suggested that they let the guards walk back, unarmed, to their base along the railroad track, located south of Huntingville. Then he turned to Nayla and said, "The eagle told us how to get to the United States of Bolivar. We're going to fly there." He pointed to the helicopters. "That's why I only killed one of the pilots; we need the other one."

At his words, a broad smile stretched across Nayla's face. She couldn't wait until Dick found out one of Carsanto's helicopters had aided them!

When their meeting ended the mother took charge.

"Here's what we're going to do," her loud voice boomed out to the villagers and the guards. "We're going to fly around in one of those helicopters. Everyone in the village gets a turn."

She pointed her finger at the lieutenant. "You're going to tell your pilot to fly us around. Meanwhile, since we were building this house and you interrupted our task, you and your men are going to finish our building under the careful supervision of some of our men who might be inclined to use your guns in case you don't work hard enough. Then we're all going to spend the night together, and tomorrow you guys can walk back to your base."

"That's a four day hike," the lieutenant complained.

"Well, alternatively you could decide to settle here; you seem to like our women already," the mother scorned.

She withheld from them any news of Nayla's and Rowan's escape plan.

237

For the rest of the afternoon the villagers took turns flying in the helicopter, seeing the earth for the first time from the air. They all had great fun.

By early evening, Rowan and Nayla were ready to go. They had decided to fly during the night. The United Canadian Communities didn't have any helicopters or airplanes, so when they crossed the border the Confederate guards would know it was an American craft flying in. It would take longer to identify the helicopter and take appropriate action if they were flying under the cover of darkness. Besides, she would enjoy waking Dick from his sleep!

When Nayla and Rowan said goodbye and thanked the pagan villagers for their help, they received heartfelt embraces from pretty much everyone in the community. Nayla gave some of the mutating germinator seeds to the mother.

"I'll never forget you," she smiled. "If you ever hear a story of nude people in the rainforest in Latin America, you'll know what you started."

"Don't kid yourself, honey! Those were the people who taught us to be proud of our bodies in the first place," the mother replied.

Rowan and Nayla then got into the helicopter with the pilot, who received his instructions at gunpoint. Since Rowan had killed his companion earlier in the day, the pilot knew the trapper wouldn't hesitate to use his weapon.

At sunset, they lifted off. By morning they would be in the United States of Bolivar—if all went well.

The huge amount of adrenaline that was racing through Nayla's body wasn't allowing her any sleep—not that she was planning on getting any.

Rowan told her he would keep a close eye on the pilot and the flight course. They planned not to make radio contact but only to listen to the airways.

They had instructed the pilot to first set course for Dallas, assuming both Dick and the border security would think they were either bringing back Nayla or some wounded guards from the United Canadian Communities. Once the pilot was actually approaching that city, they planned to order him to change course and head for the United States of Bolivar.

Dick would likely figure out that something was seriously wrong when they bypassed Dallas. However, Nayla knew they wanted to capture her unharmed and not destroy the seeds. It was therefore unlikely that they would shoot the helicopter down.

To kill time, she read for a while in her grandmother's diary.

February 8, 2022.

Today I took the plunge. In some people's book I'm now a criminal; according to others, I'm a freedom fighter. How I go down in the history books will now depend on who wins the war. Yes, it's a war—a full-fledged war, right here on American soil by American people …for American people.

Things really escalated in late December. The day before Christmas thousands of people in the country disappeared: activists, authors, moviemakers, singers, and university professors—virtually anyone who had at any time in the past been critical of the American government. The arrests were executed by Whitefog. No one knows where the arrested people are today.

On Christmas the media pretended that everything was normal. But many people were not celebrating. The time of prayers and hope had passed. It was time for action.

Over the weeks that followed, dams and electricity lines were blown up on a daily basis right across the country. Minneapolis and Seattle were particularly targeted. Then on December 31, the rebels—unorganized groups of people who all called themselves Sacred Earth—managed to shut off all of the power supply to those two cities. Within weeks the large metropolises turned into ghost cities, controlled by roving bands whose vision was to turn the cities into a collection of organic gardens.

With the success of the Seattle and Minneapolis power cutoffs, the rebels across the country started to focus on the electricity grid—the "nervous system" of society as we know it. They had learned that by taking out the grid neither the authorities, security forces, nor the media could function properly. The economy collapsed, and people went hungry. The rebels promised to turn all land over to the commons so that everyone would get access to it and could feed their families. Freedom of culture and religion was promoted among rebel groups. Lots of people who couldn't find an income anymore in the collapsing economy joined the rebels.

Over the last few weeks San Francisco, Denver, Las Vegas, Washington DC, Boston and New York have been under siege.

When the sustainable farming movement in Canada offered their support, the Canadian government declared the association a "terrorist organization." In turn, within a week, the group had put the country down with a national strike, and they were now demanding a complete overhaul of the way society was designed. They concluded that large scale cities were not sustainable since the surrounding land couldn't support them. They demanded that land be returned to the commons, and that people be given the right to set up small, independently governed farming communities across Canada. When the government called the demands "absurd," riots broke out from coast to coast.

I've a responsibility now. There's a child growing in my womb—a child whose future depends on me. What kind of a world do I want my child to be born in? What kind of society do I want to raise my child in? What kind of world will my child inherit from me? Will my child accept that I did my best with growing organic vegetables when he or she receives a trashed planet ...or will my child question why I didn't fight for a better world and protect the miracles of Creation in cooperation with all mothers in the universe?

I have a responsibility now. I've been granted a miracle of Creation, a miracle sparked by love.

I have a dream, a dream of a better world. A dream sparked by love. So I've decided to throw out my fears and follow my dream, because love is the source of Creation ...and miracles. I love my dream. I love the child that's growing in me. I love my husband, my lover, ...and I'm going to fight for all of it. No more compromises, no more fears. We've been given paradise, and we should never have allowed ourselves to be seduced into giving it up.

Today I said "no" to those who were preventing me from living in paradise. I joined Alejandro and we removed the bolts from seven electricity pylons. The wind will do the rest over the next few days. Amazing that the very foundation of our society can be dislodged and destroyed with a simple wrench.

For too long I sat back and gave my power to create the world to those who were messing it up, to those who did not care. Today, I took my power back! Today, I started to create the world I always dreamed of—a world I will be proud to leave to my child.

Nayla was proud of her grandmother, proud of the world she had created. The diary had formed a bridge through time, connecting their souls during two similar times of great transformation.

She reflected on her past life, and the person she used to be before that night when everything had changed, that night when she took the destiny of the world into her own hands. What world had she been creating for Gaya? And what world did she want to create now?

She had changed since then, and the world was about to change. Her life had changed, her feelings for her grandmother had changed, and she felt reborn. She had become a new woman, a new

241

lover, a new mother—a mother who fights for the germination of Creation, a mother who fights for the future of her children.

"Gaya will be proud of the world I'll help to create," she smiled.

It was the middle of the night when Dick was woken up by the telephone.

"What's up? This had better be good," he barked, knowing this could only be one of his security people.

"One of the helicopters has just entered our airspace on the northern border," the security officer said on the other end of the line.

"You did say one of ours, right?"

"Yes. The United Canadian Communities have no aircraft."

"Exactly my point! Why are you waking me, then?"

"We were unable to establish radio contact," the voice sounded a bit more timid.

"Probably just a broken radio. Where are they heading?" Dick inquired, upset that his much-needed sleep had been interrupted for such a stupid reason.

"Their flight pattern indicates that they're heading for Dallas."

"Let me know when they're closer. They might be bringing me the little cat," he replied more pleasantly, as he began to get inspired by more enjoyable thoughts. Yes, there was just enough time for some sweet dreams of the Latin whore who was soon to be his.

As they were approaching Dallas, Nayla directed the pilot to change course and pass the city to the west on course to the United States of Bolivar. Now that they were heading for their final destination, it had dawned on her that the United States of Bolivar might see the intrusion of their airspace by the American helicopter as a violation of their sovereignty and shoot it down. After discussing the scenario with Rowan, they had decided to put the chopper down just south of the wall that separated the two countries in the wide strip of no-man's land. While the area was heavily guarded from both sides, at least they would not run the risk of getting shot down from the sky.

The phone rang again, and Dick realized he wasn't going to get a lot of sleep this night.

But then again, if he was given the news that his men had captured Nayla, they could steal his sleep for a week!

"How close are they?" he asked as soon as he picked up the receiver.

"They were close, sir, but they're now flying further away from the city."

"Have they turned back?" he asked, confused by the news.

"No, sir. The helicopter is passing Dallas to the west on a southern course."

"What? Have you made radio contact yet?" he asked.

"No, sir. They're not answering."

"I'll be over at our airbase within half an hour. Keep trying their radio, and get another chopper ready. We're going after them. I can already guess what's happening, and it's not good."

After hanging up, he immediately called George.

"George, we have a rogue helicopter flying south."

"It must be one of ours, right? So what does 'rogue' mean, and why are you waking me up for this?" George asked grumpily.

"I can only assume Nayla has hijacked it and is using it to get to the United States of Bolivar. It came in from the United Canadian Communities. Meet me at the airbase within thirty minutes. We are going after it, and I might need you to stop her."

"What do you mean? How are we going to handle this?" George wondered out loud.

"Execute plan B. I am so glad you kept me here or we wouldn't have had this chance," the General crowed.

"What's plan B?"

"You'll see," the General said, a tone of pride and self-satisfaction in his voice.

Nayla was expecting to hear Dick trying to contact them on the radio at any minute. The chopper had passed Dallas, and they were now over the bay of Mexico, well on their way to their final destination.

But the voice that came across the radio didn't belong to Dick.

"Mommy?" Gaya's voice trembled in fear.

Shivers ran up her spine as Nayla realized what this cruel man had done.

"Gaya! My little Gaya! Mommy is coming to get you, sweetie," she comforted her, trying to sound as convincing and upbeat as possible. Inside though, fear, rage and guilt were tearing her apart.

What had she done? She'd endangered the life of her child, the very reason why she wanted to create a better world in the first place.

"So you think you should come home now?" Dick's cruel voice laughed across the radio.

There was nothing she could say. She couldn't even form a response.

"Keep your course!" Rowan ordered the pilot.

Then he took Nayla's hand and his deep blue eyes penetrated into her heart.

"I've lost my family, and know how hard this situation must be for you. But if we fly to Dallas and play into his plans, you're bound to lose your daughter, your life and the seeds. Let's propose a trade, but a trade on our terms somewhere more neutral—somewhere from where you and Gaya can escape."

Nayla was so glad for the collected composure of this brave man. She would have lost her battle right here if it weren't for him.

As they discussed a new strategy, Naya recalled something from her past travels across the southern border. She remembered the skyscraper towers along the wall from which the no-man's zone was observed. The platforms were large enough to land two helicopters on!

When she was in control of her emotions again, she spoke coldly and decisively into the radio.

"You hurt one hair on my daughter's head, and I'll make it my life's mission to torture you to death," she hissed quietly. "I'm not coming home, but if you want your seeds, I'll trade them for my daughter."

Then she gave him the location of where the exchange should occur.

"Done!" Dick cheerfully answered. "You know I only want those seeds. You should have just left them here, and no one would have ever bothered you. We actually wouldn't even have missed you. Oh, of course, yes, George might have for a few days, but trust me; he would have gotten over you as well. You're not the first bimbo he has lost.

"See you in a few hours. I'll take good care of your package. Make sure you do the same with mine."

When George arrived at the airport Dick was waiting for him at the helipad. George's initial confusion when he saw Dick holding the hand of a little child changed into rage when he recognized Gaya from the pictures at Nayla's penthouse.

"You heartless bastard," he screamed furiously. "Have you lost your mind?"

"Ah, George, you used to like me for this very reason until this stupid woman made you all weak! You really think I was going to give up world control that easily? Here's my insurance policy, our insurance policy! *This* is how you are going to get your seeds back, George. In fact, Nayla has already agreed to a trade. So you see, maybe it wasn't such a bad idea," he scoffed.

"We're going to return Nayla's daughter, and then you can crawl back under the same godforsaken stone you surfaced from. I don't want anything to do with you anymore, and certainly not with this," George raved, his emotions getting the best of him.

"Well, that's too bad, George, as you are right in the middle of it. After all, you still rule this country and this company. I did all this on your behalf, let me remind you. Now, are you going to keep mother and daughter waiting longer while you're evaluating my ethics? Or should we go and get our seeds back?"

As they stepped into the helicopter, George inquired quietly about how the girl had been taken hostage. He didn't want Gaya to hear the ensuing discussion.

"It was a quick and focused paramilitary action, George," the General said crisply. "The important thing is, the men succeeded. Our insurance policy is right here. The child's father and grandparents are unfortunate casualties of war. Nayla started this, George! Remember?"

"You killed her husband and her parents?" George asked in disbelief.

"Ex-husband! And no, I didn't personally do it. I stayed here, and followed your advice from the hospital: I got a different perspective on the matter, and that led me to make sure we had the daughter under our control.

"Yeah, the kid's dad and Nayla's parents got in the way. But my men had strict orders to bring the girl in, no matter what. George, these germinator seeds that Nayla has will break our stranglehold on the world. If she succeeds, she will single-handedly collapse our economy and everything we've worked towards for decades! Toughen up. I wouldn't have cared if my men had to kill a whole city to get this girl! We're on our way to securing our position of control once again."

George was fuming, but decided to stay quiet. Dick had lost his mind, or was it his heart? Maybe he already had a long time ago; hadn't he always known Dick didn't have a heart? How could he have liked him for that? How was it that this could benefit his country, the country George was leading?

George's heart wept for the first time in his life. It wept for the loss of Nayla, the only woman he had ever truly loved. She was the woman who had opened his heart, who had accepted him for who he was rather than what he was. The woman who had pushed him outside of his comfort zone, who had stretched him to explore new perspectives. The woman who had brought color back to his empty life of numbers. How could she ever forgive him for this? Through his inaction he had lost her forever.

His heart also wept for the pain and suffering he'd caused by never taking any action that could negatively impact his numbers. But what was the meaning of all that money, and of world control, if love and happiness eluded him?

Caringly George reached over and stroked Gaya's hair in an attempt to comfort the terrified girl.

owan and Nayla were waiting on top of the most eastern tower at the wall. Rowan had tied the pilot to his seat so that he couldn't escape or do anything stupid.

The sun was rising from the ocean to the east. Today was the day of reckoning. Would the world stay the same with Carsanto and the likes of Dick in power—exploiting the rest of the planet? Or would Nayla and Rowan find a way to rescue Gaya and still save the seeds?

In the distant northern sky a black dot announced itself by its monotonous thundering sound. As the helicopter got closer, Nayla's anxiety rose. They'd agreed that Rowan would stay in the helicopter and keep his rifle aimed at Dick at all times. She didn't trust the General. Trading wasn't in his nature. Dick just took things. He didn't ask or trade.

The helicopter slowly descended. Only when it had landed, the engines had shut off and the rotor had come to a complete stop, did the doors open so she could hear Gaya's scream.

"Mommy! Mommy!" the little girl screamed. Heavy tears were falling from her eyes.

"Shut up!" Dick barked while he shook the girl by the arm.

"Leave her alone, Dick!" Nayla shouted. "Let her go! How could you involve an innocent young child in this?"

While she was yelling at Dick, her eyes sent comforting messages to Gaya and pleas for mercy to George, whom she hadn't expected to be here.

"Let the girl go, Dick!" George ordered.

But Dick ignored both Nayla's question and George's order.

"First, the seeds! Show me the seeds, Nayla!"

Nayla showed him the package. "Trust me, they're in here. I'm sure you don't want me to unwrap them in this wind."

Reluctantly Dick agreed. "I'll bring you the kid; you bring me the package. We trade in the middle and walk back to our helicopters."

Nayla's eyes sought approval from Rowan. When he seemed comfortable with it, she agreed.

Both Rowan and one of Dick's guards had their guns aimed on the traders as they started to move towards each other.

Nayla and Dick walked cautiously towards one another until they stopped, face to face in the middle of the platform.

Both sets of eyes were hard, fearless and determined—two souls driven by a different dream. Neither showed any signs of doubt or remorse.

Nayla coldly gave Dick the seeds while he handed her Gaya's hand. Not a word was spoken.

While Dick checked the contents of the package, Nayla passionately embraced Gaya. The embrace carried all the love she should have given her daughter in person over the past years.

"I love you, Gaya."

"I love you too, Mommy."

Mother and daughter looked each other in the eyes, connecting their hearts and souls and exchanging their love—the light of life's miracles and of Creation itself.

Then Nayla said determinedly, "See that man?" and she pointed at Rowan. "I want you to run to him and stay with him."

As Gaya obeyed and ran towards Rowan, Nayla turned around. George was sitting defeated in the helicopter. Dick was about halfway back to the chopper. Right then, she decided she wasn't going to let her little girl and all other children on this planet grow up in a world where seeds terminated their offspring—a world where dreams are terminated every day, a world where Creation was controlled by this heartless man. She sprinted after Dick.

A shot rang through the air, but the guard's bullet missed Nayla. Another shot, and the guard collapsed, bleeding from his chest from Rowan's well-marked shot. Dick spun around, and Nayla threw herself onto him in an attempt to wrestle the seed package from his hands. He almost lost his balance, but regained his footing close to the edge of the tower platform.

"I was hoping you would do something stupid like this," he said contemptuously.

He grabbed her in a chokehold while trying to smother her with the seed bag.

"Mommy!" Gaya screamed again. She started to run towards Nayla, but Rowan put his rifle down and grabbed the little girl.

"I've other plans for you," Dick whispered lustfully in Nayla's ear.

"Dream on," she snapped back, and at that moment she kicked her foot as hard as she could in the back of his knee.

As Dick lost his balance and fell backward, she felt his arm tightening around her neck while jerking her head upward. The following moment they were free-falling towards the bottom of the tower.

"Nayla!" both Rowan and George yelled as they ran towards the edge of the tower.

"Mommy, Mommy!" Gaya screamed out hysterically from Rowan's arms.

At the foot of a tower, on the Bolivar side of the wall, lay two dead bodies.

One was of a man who'd fought for a vision of world control. Control through the termination of life.

251

One was of a woman who held, wrapped in her arms, a package of seeds—seeds of germination, seeds that give life and celebrate creation.

The seeds of dreams.

*A*ugust 4*th*, 2084

I'm writing this while looking out over the magnificence of Creation from the Incan ruins of Machu Picchu. I'm writing in a diary that is not mine. A diary that was started by a woman who loved life and lived her life in an effort to create a better world. She put her life at risk to create a world she could proudly leave for her children. A woman who gave birth to a girl. A girl who became a woman and in turn gave birth to a girl. A girl who became a woman, a brave woman, a woman I loved but never made love to. A woman who left me a child, a child that teaches me daily the essence of love, passion, friendship and Creation. Her name is Gaya.

She has been playing, discovering the hidden treasures on this magnificent mountain while I have been writing the story of her mother Nayla, who in the footsteps of her grandmother shaped the world we live in. A woman who believed in life, who searched for herself until she realized she only had to create herself. She was passionate about a vision and yet made mistakes, fell down but got back up, and eventually she found her way, her purpose, her dream—a dream for a world that celebrates Creation. She was a woman who fought to protect the germinating, miraculous power of Creation. A woman whose love of life transformed nations and the world we live in. A woman who secured the germination of Creation and was prepared to make the ultimate sacrifice for it. A woman who gave life. A woman who gave her life to give us ours.

In loving memory,
Rowan.

Somewhere in the United States of Bolivar
July 4th, 2101

A young woman with fine Mayan facial features but who is taller than most of the people in the village smiles as she climbs towards one of the cornfields on top of the hills surrounding the community. The sun sparkles in her eyes, and reveals the loving strength and determination of her spirit.

As she gains altitude she can see in the distance the ruins of what was once a thriving civilization. She always marvels at this sight, and at the speed with which the jungle has reclaimed its ground and restored it to health. The transformation represents the power of paradise. Nature is heaven on earth, if we can just leave it alone and allow ourselves to be nurtured in its loving embrace.

Today, though, she doesn't even see the distant ruin. Her eyes are focused on the little wonder of life in her arms. Love pours out of her heart, and her spirit dances with joy while she keeps on climbing. Through the warm fragile baby skin against her arms and body, she feels the beauty of the spirit of her newborn daughter. She feels the love, and the unbreakable bond that exists between mother and child. It's the ultimate testimony of love, Creation and survival on this planet.

She reaches the top of the hill and walks through the cornfield, which is beaming with kernels soon to be harvested. As she arrives in the center of the field, the corn gives way to an open circle. She stops and turns to the east.

"My name is Gaya," she starts. Lifting the baby up to the sky, she continues, "Today I'm here to introduce to you Nayla. My mother's spirit lives on!"

She takes the baby back in her arms and walks over to the corn. With admiration for the life that grows, the food that sustains her people, she gently touches the corn with the back of her hand while she turns to her baby. "This is the food that sustains us. It is part of us, it is us, it carries the seed of life. We're here, this seed is here, and each year it still germinates thanks to your grandmother, my mother, after whom I named you. We women are the protectors of life, and the protectors of this seed. We love it, and we do whatever it takes to allow it to germinate."

She walks back to the center of the field, where she sits down on her knees and puts Nayla on the blanket she has taken from her shoulder bag. She grabs some dirt and lets it gently slide out of her hand.

"This earth and the sun are wonders from which all life grows. They nurture every seed so it can germinate and grow strong. When the seed matures it will perform the same loving, life-giving interaction with the opposite sex to celebrate this sacred relation. And so new life is created! We women, life givers on this planet, will always protect this cycle."

She reaches in her bag and pulls out a worn book with a leather cover.

"As has been the custom now for years, I will read to you from your great-great-grandmother's diary and share your grandmother's story."

She opens the book and as she reads the first line, her voice echoes through the gates of time.

"A dream is a seed. What we do with that seed is a choice—a choice of germination or termination—a choice we make that is reflected in our every action, every second, every breath."

re your dreams germinating or terminating?

Augo Bonjean

"*Modern man likes to pretend that his thinking is wide-awake. But this wide-awake thinking has led us into the mazes of a nightmare in which the torture chambers are endlessly repeated in the mirrors of reason. When we emerge, perhaps we will realize that we have been dreaming with our eyes open, and that the dreams of reason are intolerable. And then, perhaps, we will begin to dream once more with our eyes closed.*"

–Octavio Paz

"*Cowardice asks the question, "Is it safe?" Expedience asks the question, "Is it politic?" And Vanity comes along and asks the question, "Is it popular?" But Conscience asks the question, "Is it right?" And there comes a time when one must take a position that is neither safe, nor politic, nor popular, but he must do it because Conscience tells him it is right.*"

–Martin Luther King, Jr.

"*Peace: It does not mean to be in a place where there is no noise, trouble or hard work. It means to be in the midst of those things and still be calm in your heart.*"

–Catherine Marshall

Augo Bonjean

About the book

Two years ago, I read *Stolen Harvest: The Hijacking of the Global Food Supply* by Vandana Shiva and learned about terminator seed technology. It was then that a seed for this story was planted in my heart. I was shocked and appalled by man's audacity to terminate the germinating wonders of nature in his strive for money, power and control.

And what on earth are we thinking when we put dioxin into the very seeds from which a harvest will grow, a harvest—food—that will nourish us? Isn't it bad enough that mothers' milk today already contains such toxins? When do we learn, and what happened to the precautionary principle? This moral and political guideline should protect the public and environmental health against serious and irreversible damage from actions not proven completely safe by science. It seems this principle, which should protect our citizens and our country, now only gets brought up when certain economic powers are being threatened.

The term "terminator seed" sounds diabolic to me. A seed should be producing new life. It is the essence of creation, and it contains all the germinating power of life on earth. How can we even consider terminating that power? How can we consider poisoning the miracles of creation? And for what do we do so: money, power and control? While the mutating variations of the terminator seeds as I described them in the book don't exist (just yet), the terminator seed technology does exist and has already threatened the environment in field trials, just like corporate ownership of seeds through patenting has already impacted poor farming communities around the world.

I first made the link between the metaphor of seeds and people's dreams through my involvement in youth leadership programs—something which I have enjoyed over the last ten years. What has always struck me is that the dreams adolescents have are no different from the dreams I had when I was sixteen, seventeen and eighteen. As a matter of fact, from my presentations I've learned that most people hold the same kind of dreams in their hearts. But if we all have had the same dreams for decades, as so elegantly described in William McDonough's example (see quote on the first pages of this book), why have we not created a reality that mirrors those dreams? This question made me realize that we allow our dreams to germinate or terminate by the choices we make and the actions we take.

The idea of setting the story in the future came when I read *Endgame* by Derrick Jensen last year. It was a book that shook me to the core and made me question aspects of our society that I hadn't considered before. *Endgame* inspired the character of Nayla's grandmother and the organic rising up of people in search of a sustainable way of life.

Many of the insights in *Seeds* I developed by spending lots of time in nature and contemplating design based on the unfolding universe in front of us. When I say design, that doesn't only include the tangible necessities of our current culture like energy and buildings but also the intangibles like the structures of our organizations and society itself. It's not my intention to sell my ideas, but to make people think and at least consider nature to be our teacher.

In the end, I wrote *Seeds* with four goals in mind: First, to create awareness of the existence of terminator seed technology; second, to make you think about the values, motives, results and sustainability of the society we've created; third, to provoke debate around possible solutions; and lastly, to invite you to listen to the voice of your soul, grab hold of your dreams and allow those dreams to germinate.

In wonder and with gratitude,

Hugo Bonjean, June 19, 2008

Related websites

Large parts of the story find their roots in real life events, new technologies and innovative streams of thought. Below you'll find lots of useful websites with information about the many subjects touched on in *Seeds*.

For information about terminator seeds—the campaigns against that technology, up-to-date news on the subject and the dangers of the science, visit the following websites:

www.banterminator.org (news and campaigns)
www.econexus.info (the science)
www.precautionaryprinciple.ca
www.etcgroup.org/en

For information about the air car, visit:
www.theaircar.com

For information about the savage deforestation (using napalm bombing) of the Tasmanian rainforest, visit:
www.tasmedia.org/node/1085
www.nativeforest.net

For information about the Las Vegas water project, visit:
www.npr.org/templates/story/story.php?storyId=10953190

To find out how organic farming not only produces tastier, more nutritious food, but also helps to combat global warming and store carbon in the soil, visit:
www.rodaleinstitute.org

If the quality and sustainability of our food production is important to you, visit:

www.slowfood.com

www.terramadre.info

www.100milediet.org

A good book that makes us think about mindful eating is *Harvest of Hope* by Jane Goodall.

If you're interested in learning more about how you can participate in building a new sustainable economy, visit:

www.livingeconomies.org

To learn more about 'decentralism' as a sustainable model for our society, visit:

www.smallisbeautiful.org/about/decentralism.html

I also strongly recommend Schumacher's book, *Small is Beautiful: Economics as if People Mattered.*

More information on cooperatives and the social economy can be found at:

www.ncba.coop

www2.ulg.ac.be/ciriec

www.usaskstudies.coop

If you want to significantly reduce your footprint on the planet, check out:

www.simpleliving.net

To sponsor an organization that reduces both global warming and poverty through sustainable farming education, visit:

www.sustainableharvest.org

For Book Clubs

Book clubs enjoy Hugo's stories because they provoke thought and are excellent material for dynamic discussions. From time to time when his schedule permits, Hugo meets with book clubs either in person or, for those clubs with a wide angle webcam and a quality speaker, over Skype.

To request a book club visit, write an e-mail to bookclub@hugobonjean.com and mark clearly in the subject line: "book club visit," and add the date and location to it.

Below are some questions to spark your book discussion.

1. What's the meaning of the title?
2. Is terminator seed technology ethical? Why or why not?
3. Is it our birthright to have access to healthy food? Why or why not?
4. What have we learned as a society from our experience with DDT and the dioxin that's currently fed to babies via mothers' milk? What could or should we learn from this?
5. How high are healthy food, water and air on our society's priority list? How high is it on your list? Can we live without it?
6. What comforts are we prepared to give up to secure healthy food, water and air?
7. What dreams did you have when you were sixteen, seventeen, or eighteen years old? Which of those dreams did you allow to germinate, and which did you terminate? Do any of the dreams that didn't germinate still linger in your heart? What can you do to allow them to germinate?

8. Watch "The Story of Stuff" (www.storyofstuff.com) and discuss the ethics of our consumption society. How will this knowledge affect your day-to-day life?

9. What are the political, cultural, economical, environmental and spiritual advantages and disadvantages of a decentralized society?

10. Why do we have intellectual property rights? How do these laws benefit humanity and the planet? Why do we have these laws? Are there other ways to secure a fair living wage for people who currently depend on those laws for their income?

11. Do we have the right to destroy nature—our soil, air and water—to obtain the resources that provide us with the comforts in our consumption society? Why do we give corporations those rights? Are those resources limited or unlimited? What are we doing with the income from those resources to secure the future of our society?

12. What's the meaning of democracy—for the people, by the people? How do you feel about the French people who shut their country down when they feel their government doesn't make the right decisions? Why are people in North America less vigilant and more complacent about their rights?

13. Do we have the right to break the law, if the law isn't just? What is just? Who has the authority to decide what's just? Why? Where would we be without people like Rosa Parks, Martin Luther King, Nelson Mandela, Thomas Jefferson, George Washington, Mahatma Gandhi and many others who broke the law driven by a vision of a better world?

14. What's the meaning of equality (on a global scale)? How do land ownership and inheritance rights affect equality? Is it possible to protect a commons and have free entrepreneurship?

15. How does technology allow us to reduce our footprint on the planet? Which technologies are promising and should get attention and funding? Are they getting such attention and funding? Why or why not?

About the Author

Hugo Bonjean was born in Antwerp, Belgium. As a critical thinker with a strong sense for humanitarian issues and justice, he decided to study Social and Political Sciences at the University of Louvain. However, when he realized that a world revolving around money could only become sustainable through understanding and adjusting its driving economics, he changed direction and graduated in Antwerp with a B.S. in Accounting, thereafter completing his M.B.A. at the European University. After a few accounting jobs in the manufacturing industry, he joined Holiday Inn in a strategic development role. This was the beginning of a fast-paced twelve-year career that took Hugo all over the world.

When Marriott International appointed Hugo to the position of Vice President of Operations & Development for one of their divisions in Latin America, his firsthand experiences with poverty there rekindled the humanitarian values of his teens. After two years in this role he decided to dedicate the rest of his life to help shift the world towards sustainable models of living—economical, political, social, environmental and spiritual.

When his first book, *In the Eyes of Anahita*, made a life-changing impact on many readers, he became aware of the power of storytelling and he is now using that vehicle to engage people in social and environmental action.

Hugo is the chair of Sustainable Harvest International – Canada, a charity that educates farmers in Central America about sustainable farming practices in order to restore the rainforest and improve their lifestyles. Hugo lives with his family in the Rocky Mountain foothills near Calgary, Canada. He recharges his batteries while riding his horse in the backcountry.

Are Human Beings Being Human?

Paul, a successful business executive, gets confronted by his seven-year-old son with the question: "Dad, why do people have to pay for food?" When he realizes his son questions why, in our civilized society, we allow hunger to exist, he fails to produce an answer. During Paul's next business trip to South America, where he deals with some of the richest people on the continent, the question haunts him as he opens his eyes, heart and mind to the poverty around him. When he intends to help a begging grandmother in Argentina, he is dragged into a mysterious sequence of events during which he has to solve the riddle, "Are human beings being human?"

It is the start of a spiritual adventure to a poor farming village in Chile, across the "corner of dead" in the Peruvian Andes and into the slums of Salvador, Brazil. Bit by bit Paul's comfortable world disintegrates as he becomes more aware of the flipside of global trade and the role he has been playing in the world. Will he be able to integrate the extremes he is dealing with, find his purpose and rediscover his happiness? Will he solve the riddle? Will he finally be able to answer his son?

Praise for "In the Eyes of Anahita"

"*In the Eyes of Anahita* is a captivating read that presents profound truth in the entertaining guise of fiction. Hugo Bonjean shares the story of a vision quest in the tradition of James Redfield's *Celestine Prophecy* and Daniel Quinn's *Ishmael,* but with deeper practical and spiritual insights. Highly recommended."

– Dr. David C. Korten, international bestselling author of *When Corporations Rule the World.*

"A spellbinding journey of discovery! Magically woven, suspenseful and evocative, it takes us from the world we know into the heart of what it means to be human."

– Diane Dreher, author of *The Tao of Personal Leadership*

"...a book you will want to read again and again!"
– *Synchronicity Magazine*

"If your goal is to change the world one person at a time, you have succeeded with me. I have read many books on similar subject matter, but none have moved me like yours. Thank you for your gift."
– David Britton

This inspiring bestseller by Hugo Bonjean is based on events in the author's own life. Thought-provoking yet open-minded, *In the Eyes of Anahita* will most certainly challenge your perspectives and put you on a path of conscious decision-making in both your business and private life. This is a wake-up call to use your personal power to co-create a better world, and find true happiness in the process. Question the meaning of life to discover a life of meaning!

Contact Information

You can send your comments to Hugo at:

info@hugobonjean.com

Take Action! Get further inspired, choose a cause, find volunteer positions and learn about Hugo's other involvements, his events, recommended reading list and speaking services at:

www.hugobonjean.com

Spread the word about *Seeds* by directing others to:

www.seedsofgerminationortermination.com

Check out Hugo's first book, *In the Eyes of Anahita*, at:

www.intheeyesofanahita.com

Join Hugo's network at:

www.facebook.com